CHRISTOPH

THE PERFECT M

CHRISTOPHER BUSH was born Charlie Christmas Bush in Norfolk in 1885. His father was a farm labourer and his mother a milliner. In the early years of his childhood he lived with his aunt and uncle in London before returning to Norfolk aged seven, later winning a scholarship to Thetford Grammar School.

As an adult, Bush worked as a schoolmaster for 27 years, pausing only to fight in World War One, until retiring aged 46 in 1931 to be a full-time novelist. His first novel featuring the eccentric Ludovic Travers was published in 1926, and was followed by 62 additional Travers mysteries. These are all to be republished by Dean Street Press.

Christopher Bush fought again in World War Two, and was elected a member of the prestigious Detection Club. He died in 1973.

By Christopher Bush

The Plumley Inheritance
The Perfect Murder Case
Dead Man Twice
Murder at Fenwold
Dancing Death
Dead Man's Music
Cut Throat
The Case of the Unfortunate Village
The Case of the April Fools
The Case of the Three Strange Faces

CHRISTOPHER BUSH

THE PERFECT MURDER CASE

With an introduction
by Curtis Evans

DEAN STREET PRESS

Published by Dean Street Press 2017

First published in 1929 by William Heinemann

Cover by DSP

ISBN 978 1 911579 67 0

www.deanstreetpress.co.uk

To
Marjorie

All the characters in this story have never lived, are certainly not living, and will almost as certainly never be born. They are, in short, wholly fictitious.

INTRODUCTION

THAT ONCE vast and mighty legion of bright young (and youngish) British crime writers who began publishing their ingenious tales of mystery and imagination during what is known as the Golden Age of detective fiction (traditionally dated from 1920 to 1939) had greatly diminished by the iconoclastic decade of the Sixties, many of these writers having become casualties of time. Of the 38 authors who during the Golden Age had belonged to the Detection Club, a London-based group which included within its ranks many of the finest writers of detective fiction then plying the craft in the United Kingdom, just over a third remained among the living by the second half of the 1960s, while merely seven—Agatha Christie, Anthony Gilbert, Gladys Mitchell, Margery Allingham, John Dickson Carr, Nicholas Blake and Christopher Bush—were still penning crime fiction.

In 1966--a year that saw the sad demise, at the too young age of 62, of Margery Allingham--an executive with the English book publishing firm Macdonald reflected on the continued popularity of the author who today is the least well known among this tiny but accomplished crime writing cohort: Christopher Bush (1885-1973), whose first of his three score and three series detective novels, *The Plumley Inheritance*, had appeared fully four decades earlier, in 1926. "He has a considerable public, a 'steady Bush public,' a public that has endured through many years," the executive boasted of Bush. "He never presents any problem to his publisher, who knows exactly how many copies of a title may be safely printed for the loyal Bush fans; the number is a healthy one too." Yet in 1968, just a couple of years after the Macdonald editor's affirmation of Bush's notable popular duration as a crime writer, the author, now in his 83rd year, bade farewell to mystery fiction with a final detective novel, *The Case of the Prodigal Daughter*, in which, like in Agatha Christie's *Third Girl* (1966), copious references are made, none too favorably, to youthful sex, drugs and rock and roll. Afterwards, outside of the reprinting in the UK in the early 1970s of a scattering of classic Bush titles from the Golden Age, Bush's books, in contrast with those of Christie, Carr, Allingham and Blake, disappeared from mass circulation in both the UK and the US, becoming fervently sought (and ever more unobtainable) treasures by collectors and connoisseurs of classic crime fiction. Now, in one of the signal developments in vintage mystery publishing, Dean Street Press is reprinting all 63 Christopher Bush detective novels. These will be published over a period of months, beginning with the release of books 1 to 10 in the series.

Few Golden Age British mystery writers had backgrounds as humble yet simultaneously mysterious, dotted with omissions and evasions, as Christopher Bush, who was born Charlie Christmas Bush on the day of the Nativity in 1885 in the Norfolk village of Great Hockham, to Charles Walter Bush and his second wife, Eva Margaret Long. While the father of Christopher Bush's Detection Club colleague and near exact contemporary Henry Wade (the pseudonym of Henry Lancelot Aubrey-Fletcher) was a baronet who lived in an elegant Georgian mansion and claimed extensive ownership of fertile English fields, Christopher's father resided in a cramped cottage and toiled in fields as a farm laborer, a term that in the late Victorian and Edwardian era, his son lamented many years afterward, "had in it something of contempt....There was something almost of serfdom about it."

Charles Walter Bush was a canny though mercurial individual, his only learning, his son recalled, having been "acquired at the Sunday school." A man of parts, Charles was a tenant farmer of three acres, a thatcher, bricklayer and carpenter (fittingly for the father of a detective novelist, coffins were his specialty), a village radical and a most adept poacher. After a flight from Great Hockham, possibly on account of his poaching activities, Charles, a widower with a baby son whom he had left in the care of his mother, resided in London, where he worked for a firm of spice importers. At a dance in the city, Charles met Christopher's mother, Eva Long, a lovely and sweet-natured young milliner and bonnet maker, sweeping her off her feet with a combination of "good looks and a certain plausibility." After their marriage the couple left London to live in a tiny rented cottage in Great Hockham, where Eva over the next eighteen years gave birth to three sons and five daughters and perforce learned the challenging ways of rural domestic economy.

Decades later an octogenarian Christopher Bush, in his memoir *Winter Harvest: A Norfolk Boyhood* (1967), characterized Great Hockham as a rustic rural redoubt where many of the words that fell from the tongues of the native inhabitants "were those of Shakespeare, Milton and the Authorised Version....Still in general use were words that were standard in Chaucer's time, but had since lost a certain respectability." Christopher amusingly recalled as a young boy telling his mother that a respectable neighbor woman had used profanity, explaining that in his hearing she had told her husband, "George, wipe you that shit off that pig's arse, do you'll datty your trousers," to which his mother had responded that although that particular usage of a four-letter word had not really been *swearing*, he was not to give vent to such language himself.

Great Hockham, which in Christopher Bush's youth had a population of about four hundred souls, was composed of a score or so of cottages, three public houses, a post-office, five shops, a couple of forges and a pair of churches, All Saint's and the Primitive Methodist Chapel, where the Bush family rather vocally worshipped. "The village lived by farming, and most of its men were labourers," Christopher recollected. "Most of the children left school as soon as the law permitted: boys to be absorbed somehow into the land and the girls to go into domestic service." There were three large farms and four smaller ones, and, in something of an anomaly, not one but two squires--the original squire, dubbed "Finch" by Christopher, having let the shooting rights at Little Hockham Hall to one "Green," a wealthy international banker, making the latter man a squire by courtesy. Finch owned most of the local houses and farms, in traditional form receiving rents for them personally on Michaelmas; and when Christopher's father fell out with Green, "a red-faced, pompous, blustering man," over a political election, he lost all of the banker's business, much to his mother's distress. Yet against all odds and adversities, Christopher's life greatly diverged from settled norms in Great Hockham, incidentally producing one of the most distinguished detective novelists from the Golden Age of detective fiction.

Although Christopher Bush was born in Great Hockham, he spent his earliest years in London living with his mother's much older sister, Elizabeth, and her husband, a fur dealer by the name of James Streeter, the couple having no children of their own. Almost certainly of illegitimate birth, Eva had been raised by the Long family from her infancy. She once told her youngest daughter how she recalled the Longs being visited, when she was a child, by a "fine lady in a carriage," whom she believed was her birth mother. Or is it possible that the "fine lady in a carriage" was simply an imaginary figment, like the aristocratic fantasies of Philippa Palfrey in P.D. James's *Innocent Blood* (1980), and that Eva's "sister" Elizabeth was in fact her mother?

The Streeters were a comfortably circumstanced couple at the time they took custody of Christopher. Their household included two maids and a governess for the young boy, whose doting but dutiful "Aunt Lizzie" devoted much of her time to the performance of "good works among the East End poor." When Christopher was seven years old, however, drastically straightened financial circumstances compelled the Streeters to return the boy to his birth parents in Great Hockham.

Fortunately the cause of the education of Christopher, who was not only a capable village cricketer but a precocious reader and scholar, was taken up both by his determined and devoted mother and an idealistic local elementary school headmaster. In his teens Christopher secured a scholarship to Norfolk's Thetford Grammar School, one of England's oldest educational institutions, where Thomas Paine had studied a century-and-a-half earlier. He left Thetford in 1904 to take a position as a junior schoolmaster, missing a chance to go to Cambridge University on yet another scholarship. (Later he proclaimed himself thankful for this turn of events, sardonically speculating that had he received a Cambridge degree he "might have become an exceedingly minor don or something as staid and static and respectable as a publisher.") Christopher would teach English in schools for the next twenty-seven years, retiring at the age of 46 in 1931, after he had established a successful career as a detective novelist.

Christopher's romantic relationships proved far rockier than his career path, not to mention every bit as murky as his mother's familial antecedents. In 1911, when Christopher was teaching in Wood Green School, a co-educational institution in Oxfordshire, he wed county council schoolteacher Ella Maria Pinner, a daughter of a baker neighbor of the Bushes in Great Hockham. The two appear never actually to have lived together, however, and in 1914, when Christopher at the age of 29 headed to war in the 16th (Public Schools) Battalion of the Middlesex Regiment, he falsely claimed in his attestation papers, under penalty of two years' imprisonment with hard labor, to be unmarried.

After four years of service in the Great War, including a year-long stint in Egypt, Christopher returned in 1919 to his position at Wood Green School, where he became involved in another romantic relationship, from which he soon desired to extricate himself. (A photo of the future author, taken at this time in Egypt, shows a rather dashing, thin-mustached man in uniform and is signed "Chris," suggesting that he had dispensed with "Charlie" and taken in its place a diminutive drawn from his middle name.) The next year Winifred Chart, a mathematics teacher at Wood Green, gave birth to a son, whom she named Geoffrey Bush. Christopher was the father of Geoffrey, who later in life became a noted English composer, though for reasons best known to himself Christopher never acknowledged his son. (A letter Geoffrey once sent him was returned unopened.) Winifred claimed that she and Christopher had married but separated, but she refused to speak of her purported spouse forever after and she destroyed all of his letters and other mementos, with the exception of a book of poetry that he had written for her during what she termed their engagement.

Christopher's true mate in life, though with her he had no children, was Florence Marjorie Barclay, the daughter of a draper from Ballymena, Northern Ireland, and, like Ella Pinner and Winifred Chart, a schoolteacher. Christopher and Marjorie likely had become romantically involved by 1929, when Christopher dedicated to her his second detective novel, *The Perfect Murder Case*; and they lived together as man and wife from the 1930s until her death in 1968 (after which, probably not coincidentally, Christopher stopped publishing novels). Christopher returned with Marjorie to the vicinity of Great Hockham when his writing career took flight, purchasing two adjoining cottages and commissioning his father and a stepbrother to build an extension consisting of a kitchen, two bedrooms and a new staircase. (The now sprawling structure, which Christopher called "Home Cottage," is now a bed and breakfast grandiloquently dubbed "Home Hall.") After a falling-out with his father, presumably over the conduct of Christopher's personal life, he and Marjorie in 1932 moved to Beckley, Sussex, where they purchased Horsepen, a lovely Tudor plaster and timber-framed house. In 1953 the couple settled at their final home, The Great House, a centuries-old structure (now a boutique hotel) in Lavenham, Suffolk.

From these three houses Christopher maintained a lucrative and critically esteemed career as a novelist, publishing both detective novels as Christopher Bush and, commencing in 1933 with the acclaimed book *Return* (in the UK, *God and the Rabbit*, 1934), regional novels purposefully drawing on his own life experience, under the pen name Michael Home. (During the 1940s he also published espionage novels under the Michael Home pseudonym.) Although his first detective novel, *The Plumley Inheritance*, made a limited impact, with his second, *The Perfect Murder Case*, Christopher struck gold. The latter novel, a big seller in both the UK and the US, was published in the former country by the prestigious Heinemann, soon to become the publisher of the detective novels of Margery Allingham and Carter Dickson (John Dickson Carr), and in the latter country by the Crime Club imprint of Doubleday, Doran, one of the most important publishers of mystery fiction in the United States.

Over the decade of the 1930s Christopher Bush published, in both the UK and the US as well as other countries around the world, some of the finest detective fiction of the Golden Age, prompting the brilliant Thirties crime fiction reviewer, author and Oxford University Press editor Charles Williams to avow: "Mr. Bush writes of as thoroughly enjoyable murders as any I know." (More recently, mystery genre authority B.A. Pike dubbed these novels by Bush, whom he praised as "one of the most reliable and resourceful of true detective writers", "Golden Age baroque, rendered remarkable by some extraordinary flights of fancy.") In 1937 Christopher Bush became, along with Nicholas Blake, E.C.R. Lorac and Newton Gayle (the writing team of Muna Lee and Maurice West Guinness), one of the final authors initiated into the Detection Club before the outbreak of the Second World War and with it the demise of the Golden Age. Afterward he continued publishing a detective novel or more a year, with his final book in 1968 reaching a total of 63, all of them detailing the investigative adventures of lanky and bespectacled gentleman amateur detective Ludovic Travers. Concurring as I do with the encomia of Charles Williams and B.A. Pike, I will end this introduction by thanking Avril MacArthur for providing invaluable biographical information on her great uncle, and simply wishing fans of classic crime fiction good times as they discover (or rediscover), with this latest splendid series of Dean Street Press classic crime fiction reissues, Christopher Bush's Ludovic Travers detective novels. May a new "Bush public" yet arise!

Curtis Evans

The Perfect Murder Case (1929)

Dear Sir.

I am going to commit a murder. I offer no apology for the curtness of the statement. Had I not attracted your attention, however, the prolix defence which now follows would never have been read....

--first of the "Marius" letters in *The Perfect Murder Case*

During the latter months of 1888, when a series of horrific murders of women appalled and absorbed all of London, Christopher Bush, then a mere toddler, had just been brought to live in the City with his aunt and uncle. On 27 September the Central News Agency of London received a most disturbing epistle concerning the killings, which two days later it forwarded to Scotland Yard. The letter began: "Dear Boss, I keep on hearing the police have caught me but they wont fix me just yet. I have laughed when they look so clever and talk about being on the right track. The joke about Leather Apron gave me real fits. I am down on whores and will keep ripping them till I do get buckled." It was signed, "Yours truly, Jack the Ripper."

To this day Ripperologists have disputed whether or not the "Dear Boss" letter (and those that followed it) was actually written by the bestial slayer of five prostitutes in and around the Whitechapel district between 31 August and 9 November 1888. Whatever the truth of the matter, however, the letters transfixed the British public at the time; and, four decades later, they likely inspired Christopher Bush when he was writing his impressive second detective novel, *The Perfect Murder Case* (1929). In the novel, an individual taking the name "Marius" boasts that he will commit "The Perfect Murder," daring Scotland Yard detectives to catch him if they can. For those who fear this material portends a Ripperish tale of blood and terror, rest assured that "Marius"—the name evidently is derived from the harsh, pre-Christian era Roman general Gaius Marius—with rather more chivalry than Jack, continues: "The murder is necessary; of that I am more than ever convinced. I should, however, never cease to reproach myself if I gave a moment's further uneasiness to any member of the public. Women and children particularly need not be frightened because the matter in no way will concern them." Writing at the height of the Golden Age, Christopher Bush, like his future colleagues in the Detection Club, in his cunning tale made intellectual reasoning, rather than emotional repulsion, the goal of the game.

The Perfect Murder Case has been called a serial killer novel, but in truth it is not. (Truer examples of this mystery subgenre from the Golden Age include Anthony Berkeley's *The Silk Stocking Murders*, 1928, John Rhode's *The Murders in Praed Street*, 1928, S.S. Van Dine's *The Bishop Murder Case*, 1929, A.G. Macdonell's *The Silent Murders*, 1929, Francis Beeding's *Death Walks in Eastrepps*, 1931, Philip Macdonald's *Murder Gone Mad*, 1931, and *X v. Rex*, 1933, Ethel Lina White's *Some Must Watch*, 1933, Q. Patrick's *The Grindle Nightmare*, 1935, Agatha Christie's *The ABC Murders*, 1936, and Christopher Bush's own *The Case of the Monday Murders*, 1936.) When the commission of the so-called "perfect murder"—the slaying of the highly disagreeable Thomas Richleigh—takes place, there are four likely suspects to be found in the form of Richleigh's nephews, each of whom possesses a rational, economic motive for having committed the heinous crime. Attempting to break down the alibis of the nephews is an abundance of detectives, including the fatherly but fatally efficient, where the hunting of murderers is concerned, Superintendent George "the General" Wharton (he gives a slippery suspect "the kind of smile that might have been given by a lion who had missed a particularly plump but evasive Christian"); ex-CID man John Franklin, lately recovered from a nervous breakdown; and lanky and boyishly bespectacled Ludovic "Ludo" Travers, Cambridge educated author of "that perfectly amazing *Economics of a Spendthrift*, a work not only stupendous in its erudition but from the charm of its style a delight in itself," and, not altogether incidentally, the nephew of Sir George Coburn, Chief Commissioner of Police.

Both Franklin and Travers are affiliated with Durangos Limited, "expert consulting and publicity agents for the world in general." Travers, who has additionally authored *World Markets* ("Now a textbook in the schools") and *The Stockbroker's Breviary* ("a return to the whimsical style of his best known work'), is the firm's financial authority and Franklin is head of its Enquiry Agency. In detective novels to come, devoted Bush readers would see more of these three individuals, as well as Sir Francis Weston, fabulously wealthy head of Durangos, and the dutiful and phlegmatic Palmer, Travers' impeccable manservant. ("In some previous incarnation, according to Ludovic Travers, he had probably been a raven, black-coated and not unmindful of his young.") In Ludo Travers and Palmer readers may detect a certain similarity to Dorothy L. Sayers' Lord Peter Wimsey and Mervyn Bunter, yet Ludo is less flippant and more fallible, not to mention altogether more modest. ("Good Lord!" he exclaims at one point in the novel. "You don't suspect me of being one of those amateur people who come along and settle everything?")

"All the points of the good detective story are here," declared the London *Observer* in its laudatory notice of *The Perfect Murder Case*, "excitement, ingenuity, suspense, crescendo, and a satisfactory conclusion." Certainly fans of classic detection will find within the pages of *The Perfect Murder Case* a most intricately plotted murder problem. The opening chapter (entitled "By Way of a Prologue")--in which Christopher Bush, like a grand master of the shell game, deftly and daringly waves "the solution of the mystery or at least its main ingredients" before readers' eyes--is particularly impressive in this regard. (It is as well a bravura performance that the author was able to repeat in later novels.) There are also well-conveyed characters, particularly a housekeeper of doubtful virtue, a pretty maid on the make, a fulsome cleric ("His smile was dental, conventional, vicarial, and somehow condescending.") and a schoolmaster who happens to bear considerable resemblance to the author himself. In the novel John Franklin passingly refers to schoolmastering as "the most unappreciated, unromantic, and unremunerative profession there is," foreshadowing Bush's own early retirement from this very profession two year later, as his alternative career as a detective novelist burgeoned. Vintage mystery addicts are fortunate indeed that in his mid-life Christopher Bush so successfully pulled off this spectacular career quick change.

CHAPTER I
BY WAY OF PROLOGUE

A PROLOGUE is often an annoying thing, since it may tell too much or too little. Those, however, that are worth having may be regarded as the cocktail that precedes the really sound meal; those that are not, as the long-winded conversation with strangers that is often the prelude to an indifferent one.

As for this chapter the reader will have to judge for himself. The fact that it has to be apologised for should either make him suspicious of it at the outset or else fairly confident that it would never have been perpetrated had it been avoidable. There are, for instance, one or two things that may be said in defence of its appearance, if not for the manner of its presentation. For one thing you will be spared the trouble, if you get so far, of harking back to the past. You will be able to take the meal in your stride and swallow it in the order of its courses. Moreover, if you are an amateur detective you are forthwith assured that it contains the solution of the mystery or at least its main ingredients are there put before you.

The short episodes which directly preceded the actual murder and which form this prologue are not however necessarily in chronological order. One of them is moreover hypothetical. Nevertheless the facts as described in it must have been so nearly true as makes no difference, and even if the individual actions which compose it are wrong, yet the scene as a whole is not falsely presented.

(A)

Mrs. Wilford must have been a sensible sort of soul. As she kissed her daughter and saw the tear-stains and the redness of the eyes which betokened a miserable three hours in the train she showed no signs of the perturbation she must have been feeling. Indeed she took charge of the situation like a wary and competent nurse. She first possessed herself of the small case and the wicker basket.

"Well, how are you, my dear?" and without waiting for an answer, "Is this all the luggage you've got?"

"There's only one trunk in the van," began Milly forlornly, and forthwith a porter was hailed. The trunk was on a barrow and before the daughter was hardly aware that she had arrived at Thetford she was in a taxi and moving homewards. But there was a brief expostulation at the expense.

"Mother, you shouldn't really! We could have waited for the bus."

"Now, dear; you let me have my own way for once," replied her mother. "We'll be home in two ticks and the kettle's all ready." Then feeling the urgency for conversation, however inconsequent, "And what sort of weather have you been having, dear?"

But it was when they got inside the small living-room of the tiny villa that Milly broke down. Familiar things and the inevitable rush of memories were too much. Both women had a good cry, and when the daughter finally wiped her eyes it could be seen that she had summoned from somewhere a new fortitude.

"Crying won't do any good, mother. And there's plenty of time to see what we're going to do."

But over the tea there was no talking of generalities. To the older woman it was still a thing incredible and irreligious that a wife should leave her husband. The situation was cutting clean across a comfortable morality and yet, much as she would have liked to argue on divine injunctions, she realised that the position required some circumspection and must be approached by devious ways.

"What have you done with the flat, dear?"

"Given it up, mother, and sold every stick we had except what I brought with me. If Fred wants to do any explaining he ought to know where to find me."

The mother thought about that for a moment. "You're right, dear. A girl's place is with her mother when all's said and done."

"Oh, you might as well know everything," burst out Milly passionately. "I don't want to upset you, mother, and that's why I said Fred and I couldn't hit it off and were going to separate and I was coming home for a bit." She flew to her handbag on the dresser and returned as quickly with a letter which she fairly thrust into her mother's hands. "You read that, mother, and you'll see for yourself."

Suppose that you as a detective had examined that letter with scrupulous exactitude, realising that your inferences might mean the difference between life and death. This is what you would have noticed.

The envelope matched the paper which had probably been torn from a block, and hastily if the ragged top were a guide. Both were of poor quality and the pinkish shade indicated lack of taste, expediency or purchase by artificial light. The former was belied by the writing which seemed to have a certain character about it. The place of posting was Holloway and the time stamped showed 7.30 p.m. So jagged was the tear of the envelope that the opener must have been in haste or completely indifferent. The letter must have been pored over many times since one of its creases had become a slit. It had no date and no address. The envelope had however two addresses; the original to Thetford in a man's hand and a second for re-posting to a London address, this latter in the quavering hand of an elderly woman.

> DEAR AGGIE:
>
> I was very glad to get your letter but sorry to hear about your rheumatism. If you take my advice you will on no account do as you suggest; go and stay with Tom's wife. Stuck down in the mud as it is, Great Oxley is no good for rheumatism and nobody could ever think otherwise if he had any sense. Change of air doesn't cure all rheumatic cases and so surely one needn't expect it to be a certainty in yours.
>
> You are not to trouble about me either. I am absolutely all right and doing fine and may have to go abroad on business if I hold the job I'm on. At present I'm only on trial, but when I do see you again the news ought to make a real record if everything doesn't go wrong in the meanwhile.

> The money is to help you out until I see you again. I may be able to send an address some time soon but in any case don't worry.
>
> In great haste,
>
> With love as ever,
>
> FRED.
>
> P.S. —I expect I shall roll up like a bad penny one of these days when you least expect it.

The perplexity on the mother's face grew as she read, and when she gave back the letter she could find no words. But her face seemed one unspoken doubt. Then she felt that something had to be said, and in a less tragic situation the naivety of the remark would have been droll.

"But, dear, your name isn't Aggie!"

"I know it isn't, mother. And I've never had rheumatism or written a letter. Keeping two homes going; that's what he's been doing, and put the letters in the wrong envelopes. Just a bit too clever this time." There was no sign of tears now; nothing but a cold intensity.

The mother laid her hand on her daughter's knee. "Tell me, dear. When did you see Fred last?"

"You know, mother, when I told you he was looking for a job. He went off that morning and didn't say where he was going, and then a week after that I got a letter with ten pounds in it and he said he thought he'd got a job but he had to keep quiet about it and there was an address I could write to. Then I thought I'd go to his address instead, and when I went they said they didn't know anything about him. Then I got another a few days later full of all sorts of rubbish and I couldn't make head nor tail of it—you know, mother, the first one you sent on from here—and I was so angry I threw it in the fire. That had ten pounds in it too. Then the next was this letter and that had twenty pounds in it. But *she* didn't get it!" This last venomous and triumphant.

• • • • • • •

(B)

In the front sitting-room of a villa within a few hundred yards of Finsbury Park Tube Station and on a September evening, two men were engaged in what might have been a serious business conference. Whether it was that the gas mantle had designedly been turned down or that it was faulty could not be said, but whatever it was, the light was uncertain and the drab furnishing of the room could with difficulty be distinguished in the remoter corners.

Of the two men, one had resorted to the most threadbare artifice in the interviewer's repertory—he had his back to the light. He wore glasses and his moustache was dark and heavy. From what could be seen of him he was an incongruity in that particular setting; his clothes, for instance, were well cut and he wore them with a difference. There was a kind of incisive air about him, and you might almost have persuaded yourself that here was the product of a public school. But then again you might have hesitated. There was something wrong somewhere, though hardly to be placed; a false gesture perhaps or an intonation.

The other man might have been a senior clerk or a shop-assistant of the best type. His grey suit was neat and the black tie gave an air of restraint. His age was probably about thirty, his height slightly under the average, and his figure slim but athletic. At this moment his face was the most arresting thing in the room, not so much because the little light caught it fully as from its deadly seriousness. His eyes were fixed upon the other with such intent that they scarcely flickered. It seemed as if he would catch not only every word but as if the missing of the last syllable might mean everything that mattered. It is to the end of their conversation that we are listening.

The first sentence showed which of the two men was in command, if the placing of the chairs had not already told it.

"As far as you yourself are concerned, Wilkinson, you are perfectly satisfied?" The voice was almost intoned, so monotonous was its level.

The other showed a certain nervousness or maybe eagerness or a desire to please. "Yes, sir; I'm perfectly satisfied, if you are."

"That's all right then. I might as well tell you, by the way, that my superior to whom I have to report is particularly pleased with the way you're shaping. The Secret Service—and always remember this—rarely praises and it never forgives mistakes."

The other began half-stammeringly to express his thanks, but the voice cut in with a finality that was chilling.

"As you were told, everything is up to you. Now for your new instructions. This is Thursday. You will catch the 9.00 p. m. from King's Cross for Peterboro, where a room has been engaged for you at the George. Just before ten to-morrow morning you will go to Flanders Road and watch as unobtrusively as you can No. 35. If there leaves it or visits it a tall, thin man of foreign appearance, you will follow him and note his actions. If, however, there is no sign of him by 2.00 p. m. it will be certain that he is not coming. In that case, as soon as it is dusk, you will go to a spot opposite the police station and keep your eyes fixed on the door. Keep both hands in the pocket of your overcoat and act as if you were waiting for a friend. If during the two hours you are there a man or woman asks you for a match and remarks, 'The matches they sell nowadays are getting worse and worse,' you will follow that person until you are given an envelope. With it you will return here at the earliest possible moment. If not, you will repeat the procedure the next two days and if still unsuccessful will return by the 7.25 p. m. on Monday. Repeat, please."

The instructions were repeated, and from the amazing correctness of the repetition one could have been certain it was not the first time such a performance had been gone through.

"In the room are the bag and the suit you will wear. Retain gloves as last time. Repack the bag and leave it locked." From a pocketbook he took a thin wad of notes and told out five. "These are for expenses." He replaced the balance, and from the bulging contents of the book produced a slip of paper. "The usual receipt, please."

The other scanned the slip carefully and then signed his name—"Arthur Wilkinson."

"Anything else before I change, sir?"

"Nothing else, Wilkinson, thank you."

Ten minutes later there was a further curious ritual.

"Everything in order, Wilkinson?"

"Yes, sir."

"The disc then, please."

From his hip pocket the other took what looked like a button and passed it over for inspection. On receiving it again he examined it carefully.

"This is not the one I gave you, sir!"

"Good work, Wilkinson!" The button was handed back and the original given in exchange for it was placed in the hip pocket with special care. Then he picked up a small case he had brought from the inner room and moved to the side door.

"Good night, sir."

"Good night, Wilkinson, and good luck." Then came an addition that showed the speaker was really human. "I expect I shall be a good while yet. It's a good thing you're not married. Nobody to grumble at *your* being late for meals!"

The door closed quietly. From his pocket the man with the glasses took a bundle of slips fastened with a rubber band and with them he placed the last receipt. Save for the amounts all were alike in their wording, but the signatures were all different. Yet strangely enough there was about them all something curiously alike.

• • • • • • •

(C)

When they reached the end of the platform Geoffrey Wrentham looked around for Ludo's car and, not seeing it, for a taxi.

"Oh, I forgot to tell you," said Ludovic Travers, "but I've got a job of work I want to do. Do you mind if we walk?"

"Not a bit," said Wrentham, and then added hastily, "That is if it isn't a marathon."

When they were in the straight for Southampton Row, Ludovic explained: "I knew I should be meeting you here and I rather thought you might be interested." He fumbled in his waistcoat pocket and produced a newspaper cutting; then passed it over without comment.

> Leading British Film Company requires actor to take Gene Allen parts in forthcoming productions. Big salary to right man. Apply personally 9.00 a. m. to 4.00 p. m. to-day and to-morrow at 75 Maryford Sq., Holborn.

Wrentham's joke was rather laboured. "You're not counting on me for a testimonial?"

Ludo smiled. He had known Geoffrey Wrentham far too long to be ignorant of the implied request for information. And the other knew too that a busy fellow like Ludo had no time to waste over unnecessaries at eleven in the morning. Weird sort of bird, Ludo! You never knew what the devil he was driving at.

"I take it you've seen Gene Allen?" said Ludo.

"On the screen you mean? Can't say I have. Name seems familiar though."

"Well, you can take it from me that in less than a year you'll know him well enough," said Ludo oracularly.

"What's the idea, Ludo? You getting a movie fan?"

"In a way, I suppose. Still, perhaps I was a bit premature. But I do think this chap will get the mantle of Chaplin. He's mobile and not too effervescent. He's refreshingly original and not too much at the mercy of his scenario."

"What's he like, this chap? Allen did you say?"

"Gene Allen. It's rather difficult to put into words. You see he isn't a set type with a fixed make-up. I've seen him as the henpecked father of a flapper family, as an insurance agent, and as ... oh, yes, he was the doctor in that delightful screen version of 'Make-shifts.'"

"Yes; but why is he funny?"

Ludo took off his glasses and polished them; a sign that the question required thought.

"That's frightfully difficult," he began diffidently. "After all, humour of the better sort is incapable of analysis. The man's a genius, of course, and of a particularly sympathetic type.

Everything he does seems so intimate and personal. He makes just the kind of fool of himself that we all do. When you see him dropping bricks you feel you want to say, 'There but for the grace of God goes myself.'"

"Yes; but what sort of a face has he got?"

"That's what I'm bringing you along for. Actually, I suppose, his face is unique. I couldn't describe it, but I could recognise it anywhere under certain conditions. You see," he went on, "what is really fascinating about this advertisement is what it's going to show us. Fancy, for instance, an advertisement for a Charlie Chaplin; the monotony of a queue of hundreds of moustaches, bowler hats, splay feet, and baggy breeks. Now you see what I'm getting at. If there's a queue for this job, and I expect there will be, just what will the applicants be like? What will be their conception of the face, figure, and even personality of Gene Allen? That's what's intriguing me. Oh, this rather looks as if we were there."

There certainly was a queue. It extended two-deep along the south and east sides of the square. By Fishwick's antique shop a policeman was falling-in the stragglers, and at the head a kind of commissionaire in mufti was admitting the first-comers into what looked like the side door of a shop. The usual crowd of sightseers had collected, and under their scrutiny it must have been hard to maintain a pose of serene indifference.

The two stood there for a good ten minutes, one peering intently through his hornrims and the other bored to extinction. To him the crowd was a collection of fairly uniform but decidedly seedy individuals. The uniformity was due, had he known it, to the screwed-up eyes and look of puzzled wonder wherewith the queue sought to imitate the face of the original; a look Allen-esque enough and reasonably obvious.

As a matter of fact the chief thought that ran through Wrentham's mind was one of fervent prayer that nobody whose opinion he valued should see him doing something so blatant and beyond the pale. All very well for Ludo with a reputation for eccentricity and his don't-give-a-damn attitude. It was with difficulty therefore that he refrained from a petulant comment at his companion's, "Well, shall we move on now?"

What he did say was, "Spotted the winner, Ludo?"

"Hardly that," was the reply. "Still, there were one or two extraordinary types. Do you know, Geoffrey," he went on, perfectly unaware of the other's indifference, "I really am convinced that these new film corporations are making a very definite mistake in retaining American types. I don't mean importing ready-made artists from Hollywood; that of course is unpardonable. Don't you agree?"

"Don't give two hoots," replied Wrentham sardonically. Ludo looked pained. Then he agreed tentatively. "Perhaps you're right. Still, it's an awful pity. If you'd seen those early pictures made..."

CHAPTER II
THE MARIUS LETTERS

(A)

HAD THE NOW famous letter of the 7th of October, 193—, arrived at the editorial offices of the *Daily Record* at so late an hour as 9.30 p. m., it could have assisted in a much more exciting chapter than this is likely to be. We could have seen the Night Editor on the telephone in a desperate attempt to summon a special conference; the attenuated gathering; the waiting for the verdict of Scotland Yard; the holding up of the printer; and finally, on the very last dot of the very last minute, the copy let loose and the presses humming. It might have been quite a movie story with its fight against time and the Editress of the Children's Corner dragged in as heroine.

As a matter of fact the letter caused no perturbation and its arrival was positively prosaic. The morning's mail arrived as usual and some hundreds of letters found their way to the News Editor. Before the arrival of the Managing Editor they had been sorted out. Of the hundred and thirty-five communications, for instance, intended by their writers for the "From Our Readers" column, he retained exactly a dozen for final selection and the rest were very definitely W. P. B.

Among these dozen was the "Marius" letter, retained not as a valuable or chatty contribution from a reader but because of its possible news value. Indeed it had been obvious from the first to so trained an observer that here was matter for the General News Page and not for the Correspondence Column. It was moreover so entertaining that he read it twice and carefully at that.

October 7th, 193—.

DEAR SIR:

I am going to commit a murder.

I offer no apology for the curtness of the statement. Had I not attracted your attention, however, the prolix defence which now follows would never have been read.

Firstly, the murder has to be committed, and I assure you there is no other way out of the peculiar and difficult situation in which I find myself. Why then am I announcing my intentions?

The reasons briefly are these. I have stated that the murder is inevitable. By announcing it therefore I give the law due warning and a fair chance. If I am caught the law will demand my neck; nevertheless by giving the law its sporting chance I raise the affair from the brutal to the human. At the same time I shall be satisfying to some extent my own conscience.

You may say that the law needs no such sporting chance, and there I think you are wrong. Because I am driven to commit a murder, that is no reason why I should not save my neck. I venture for instance to call the murder I am about to commit "The Perfect Murder" since, though I say I am about to commit it, that involves no admission that I have the least apprehension of being caught.

Speaking recently at a dinner on the occasion of the visit to England of the Commissioner of the New York Police the Home Secretary remarked—somewhat gratuitously I thought at the time—that the chance of a murderer's escaping was a very small one. He forgot very conveniently that in the last seven years there have been twenty murder mysteries. By this time next year there will be twenty-one.

Now as to actual facts. As near as I can at present judge the murder will take place on the night of the 11th inst. and in a district of London north of the Thames. It will be no cowardly cut-and-run business or furtive blow in the dark but reasonably open and above board. Before the event itself I will give you fuller particulars.

A copy of this letter has been sent to all the principal London dailies and to New Scotland Yard.

May I add that I am utterly and most boringly sane.

I have the honour to be,

Yours etc.,

MARIUS.

When the Managing Editor came in he passed it over. "Something rather unusual, don't you think?"

Briggs had a look at it, scowled at the first line, and then settled down to read it in earnest. "Rather like a hoax," was his comment. "Have you got it on the statement?"

"No. I wanted you to have a look at it."

"That's three I can remember in the last two years," said Briggs reminiscently. "The others were fearful bilge. This chap's a bit talkative and writes like a dutch uncle." He had another look at it. "Be rather interesting to hear what everybody else is doing about it."

"Mac will probably have all the news there is," suggested Holloway.

Briggs turned to the secretary. "George; ring up the N. P. A. and ask for McKay urgent." Then while the call was coming he set about yet another reading.

His end of the telephone conversation was something like this: "Hallo! That you, Mac? ... Yes, Briggs speaking. Do you know anything about a letter signed 'Marius' in which the writer ... Oh, you have! Yes ... Very good. In half an hour? Good-bye!"

He passed the letter over. "Four copies, George; absolutely confidential." Then to Holloway, "Mac seems to have got hold of something from various quarters. He says he'll pass on the dope in half an hour. You might see to Peters, will you?"

When McKay did ring up, however, his unofficial news was that the letter was being published but would on no account get into the evening papers. If, however, there was no further communication they might take it that publication was not against the public interest. "Useful chap, Mac!" remarked Briggs. "Still, we should have published in any case unless Scotland Yard stepped in."

Forthwith the letter was put on the midday conference statement. Peters, the crime expert of the *Record,* had already got to work. The postal district and time of collection he had obtained from the envelope. Then he got an enlarged facsimile of both it and the letter. Between the two conferences it was up to him to find if possible the postman who collected the letter and the box into which it had been put. He also consulted Godovski of Harvard St. and ascertained that the typewriter was a Rolland Portable. He was given also its probable service in terms of hard wear and the minutest peculiarities of its type. Another reporter had in the meantime been sent to Scotland Yard to receive any statement and make a preliminary write-up.

When in the conference room at midday the "Marius" letter came up in due course there was no discussion. The Editor had decided to publish and no injunction had arrived. The Picture Editor was instructed to prepare a full-sized facsimile for the back page. On the general news page would be envelope and splash headlines. The Circulation Manager arranged to bill Hampstead, the district where the letter was posted, and the contents of these splash bills was decided on. The Leader Page Editor was also sounded as to a literary write-up.

Much about the same kind of thing was of course being done as a matter of pure routine in the offices of those other London dailies which had received the "Marius" letter. If the *Daily Record* be instanced particularly it is only because it is a sort of medium between the austere white of the aristocratic and the proverbially yellow of the sensational press; a kind of champagne or biscuit as it were.

By five o'clock, the hour of the Chief's conference, Peters had most of the information he needed. Lawrie had produced a chatty article on the sensational letters of fiction. The Scotland Yard write-up was also ready. As to the letter itself, the policy was to be noncommittal with a bias on the hoax side.

And so at 8.50, perfectly normal and may I say normally perfect, the wheels went round. One by one the presses started until the hum became a deafening roar and speech a thing of signs. The operatives snatching papers from the waterfall were not concerned however with the "Marius" letter; they were merely watching ink. The long line of tenders left the garages and drew up at the chutes. And so on and on and on. The outside noises rose, ebbed, and, except for an occasional horn, died away into the early hours of morning. The lights went out one by one and the last operatives left.

But in another hour or two the public would awake to find a new sensation and Gossip, whether of clubs, suburban trains, or backyard fences, have considerable cause for thankfulness.

(B)

When, following as usual the day's routine, the secretary of the Chief Commissioner of Police went through the correspondence and arrived in due course at the "Marius" letter, he was mildly speculative and the least bit intrigued, but no more. He could remember roughly the contents of half a dozen similar letters addressed to the Commissioner during the last year or so, though none so verbose and dramatic, and none with so direct a challenge. Before he had got halfway through it he had concluded that he held in his hand the beginnings of yet another public and hilarious hoax. Still, there had better be a copy.

He dictated the letter to a typist. Ten minutes later the original, in company with all other correspondence relating to the Criminal Investigation Department, was on the desk of Chief-Constable Scott. And five minutes later, when McKay of the Newspaper Proprietors' Association rang up, the secretary was decidedly pleased he had treated the letter with sufficient seriousness as to take a copy.

When Sir George Coburn came across this copy he was rather annoyed. Anonymous letters received at New Scotland Yard are a kind of auriferous seam; liable to peter out at any moment after much trouble, liable to show flagrant signs of salting, and liable yet again to give results of first-class importance. Then the telephone bell rang and he took up the receiver. A minute later he rang up Chief-Constable Scott.

"Of course you've seen this, Scott?" he said, passing over the copy. "Would you mind telling me what you make of it? I'll be back in a minute, by the way."

But when he returned it was twenty minutes later, and one might have guessed that it was business relating to the letter and matters not unconnected with the Home Office that had kept him.

"I'm awfully sorry, Scott, keeping you like this. Now then, what do you make of it?"

Scott, notorious for speaking his mind without fear or favour once he had determined on a course of action, was inclined to be ironical. "Well, Sir George; I don't see it matters who wrote it. As far as we're concerned it's got to be as genuine as holy writ."

"As a matter of fact," and Sir George made the statement somewhat in the manner of Sir Oracle, "I thought perhaps you'd like to know that everybody seems to think there's something in it. The press will probably publish—for to-morrow—and I should imagine without committing themselves very far. And talking of that, you've heard the story of the chap who holed the putt?"

Scott had—many times—but he knew he would hear it again; and he did.

"I forget which of the professionals it was; missed a putt no longer than this. Chap who was watching knocked one the same length into the hole with the handle of an umbrella. 'All very well for you, sir,' says the pro., 'but I can't afford to miss 'em. I have to get my living at it.'"

"That's true enough, sir," said Scott, who knew from experience the story's application. "The papers can print any cock-and-bull story they like and even make fools of themselves into the bargain, but it's our living and we can't afford to make mistakes. But between ourselves, Sir George," and his voice instinctively became confidential, "I think the whole thing's a hoax."

The other also knew the value of being noncommittal. "Perhaps you are right. Would you mind telling me, by the way, what you've done with it?"

"We've gone over it for prints, though that doesn't help much. Also a man's gone to Hampstead to pick up details of posting and collecting, and Marshall's doing the typewriter investigation. I don't know if there's anything else you've thought of, Sir George?"

"I don't think there is. Of course you're sending a confidential circular to all divisions concerned." He made a gesture of irritation. "These letters are the very devil. As you say, it's got to be treated as if it were genuine and neither hoax nor bluff. But what guarantee is there that a single word in it is reliable enough to justify the enormous amount of work entailed?"

Scott ran his eye over the letter. "I think I shall gamble on whether the other letters which this one mentions do really arrive."

"You mean that if a further letter distinctly limits the area to say, Hampstead or Highbury, and mentions anything like a definite time, then you can make more detailed arrangements?"

"That's it. Meanwhile all divisions can be warned and Hampstead in particular. I thought I'd see Gowing myself."

And after all, what else could be done? The inhabitants of North London could not very well be segregated, nor could each citizen be provided with a custodian for whose bona fides the police could vouch. As far as the press were concerned, therefore, Scotland Yard had received the letter but had no statement to make. Nevertheless within a very few hours all the divisions concerned possessed a copy of the letter with an enlarged record of the peculiarities of type, spacing, and alignment. Thanks to a lucky hit and the dropping of a letter face downwards on the damp of the pavement, the authorities knew the postman who had collected the series and the box into which they had been put. That pillar-box had since been under observation as had every other box and office in the Hampstead district.

So much then for the first letter and its reception.

(C)

That this letter was England's principal topic of conversation during the two days that followed is a fairly obvious thing to say. Five only of the big dailies gave facsimiles of the letter and two only accompanied it by more than the barest necessary explanation. But you can imagine what happened. What one's paper did not dare to suggest was supplied by the demands which conversation made. Wherever people were gathered together the utterer of the most plausible theory was listened to with the most respect. Those who had no theories resorted to hint and innuendo until they could, in a securer place among a new audience, repeat as their own the theory of the other fellow.

If one judges from the innumerable letters received by the press from its readers and from the trend of that gossip with which one came into immediate contact, it was clear that three schools of theory survived the mass of surmise and circumlocution. The most popular was that the whole business was a hoax; grisly, in bad taste, what you will, but a hoax for all that. It was admitted that it might go on even to the last second. An ostensible murder might be committed but still as part of an elaborate and carefully planned spoof. Only when the victim was found to be very much alive would the public realise that it had been sold a particularly mangy pup.

Then came the "madman" party. How could the letter, so they argued, be the work of a normal person? Clearly it was the result of homicidal tendencies and a superiority complex that had run wild. As a hoax it would be only too apparent and the writer was clearly too much in earnest for that. Here was another Nero and some Rome or other had to burn as a background. Another variation of this theory was expressed in a letter sent by a famous sportsman to the press. "Take," said he, "a cricketer of world reputation and put him in a domestic or financial hole from which there is no escape save by a necessary murder. This then is the kind of letter he would write with its sporting chance for the law and easing the pangs of conscience."

Then there were those who took the letter strictly at its face value, as the work of a man who intended to do a terrible deed and escape its consequences. Its adherents were to be found among the lowest of the lowbrows and the highest of the high. The former took the affair to heart and made it, as they always do with the world's scandal, a thing personal and provocative. Those of the latter who decided that to mention it was a thing which might be done deplored the letter's extravagance and looked up Freud.

Then came the morning of the 10th of October and the arrival of the second letter. This time eight papers printed it in facsimile. The same typewriter had been used and the postal district was Holborn.

Oct. 9th, 193—.

Dear Sir:

I much regret the bother my letter has caused. To be perfectly candid I hardly expected publication for an epistle so flamboyant. It has, however, had one effect, if only a humorous one, to make notoriety no longer the peculiar perquisite of Park Lane.

Certain plans have now been completed, and the Perfect Murder will take place on the night of the 11th and in the district known as the "O" Division of Police. I think I owe it to the general public to make these disclosures. One cannot stop morbid curiosity, but the legitimate nervousness of the innocent is a different matter.

Within a minute or two of the murder Scotland Yard will be informed. In order that there may be no opportunity for the practical joker to cause trouble I am sending to-morrow morning to those concerned a special communication giving the method of telephoning. Further, the public will then be aware that the Perfect Murder has been committed.

Now if you will pardon me one last word. The murder is necessary; of that I am more than ever convinced. I should, however, never cease to reproach myself if I gave a moment's further uneasiness to any member of the public. Women and children particularly need not be frightened because the matter will in no way concern them.

Finally, if after the event I feel that I have given the law its chance and have eased in any way the reproaches of my own conscience, these letters will not have been written in vain.

I have the honour to be,
Yours etc.,

MARIUS.

This added to the excitement with a vengeance. England suffered from an orgy of speculation. Maintainers of theories almost came to blows. Jokes were made at the shows and music halls. Flapperdom arranged murder parties at the hotels. The Ragamuffin Club had a special dance gala, and a gallows scene was painted for it by Rubenson. Hawkers sold maps of the "O" Division. The medical students organised a gigantic rag. An enormous fortune must have been laid in bets. Though the cinemas prepared for enormous crowds it seemed as if the general public had made up its mind that the affair was merely a glorious hoax and, therefore, an excuse for a little temporary excitement. It seemed, in fact, that what Marius had intended to be the sublime was likely to become the gorblimey.

The morning of the 11th brought, as far as the public was concerned, no further announcements. Scotland Yard still had nothing to report, or at least it reported nothing. Nevertheless the final "Marius" letter had arrived as promised.

"In accordance with my last letter herewith information. First, to test the genuineness of this communication compare the word 'thesis' for peculiarities of type.

"The murder will be committed in the 'O' Division of Police and in the Postal District known as N. 22, this night of October the 11th. As soon as is reasonably safe Scotland Yard or an Exchange will be rung up and the formula used will be, 'A murder has been committed.' At the same time information will be given as to the address of the murdered person, unless that person should happen to be a subscriber, when it will be unnecessary.

"Yours, etc.,

"MARIUS."

This time the place of posting was Charing Cross. Immediately on its receipt the following precautions were taken.

The superintendent of "O" Division and Detective-Inspector Eaton had a long conference with Chief-Constable Scott and Superintendent Wharton at the Yard. A fast motor tender of the Flying-Squad was to be in readiness at Woodmore Hill Police Station. Details of liaison by telephone from the Yard were worked out. Given reasonable luck and provided always that the exact place of the murder were mentioned in the promised telephone message, the actual scene should have a cordon round it in a very few minutes. And though the chances of catching the murderer within such a net would be infinitely remote, yet the authorities would at least be on the scene far sooner than the public could imagine possible and the scent, what there was of it, be hot.

Such in barest outline was the situation on the afternoon of the 11th as far as it affected Scotland Yard and the public in general. There remains to mention, and very briefly, Durangos Limited.

CHAPTER III
DURANGOS DECIDE TO SIT IN

THOSE WHO CALLED Sir Francis Weston a lucky man were in little danger of being contradicted. It is true that when he founded Durangos Limited he had behind him an immense private fortune, but after all that may be an aid to success and yet no guarantee of it. Nevertheless in only ten years and from the smallest of beginnings the firm of which he was the head had become expert consulting and publicity agents for the world in general, with Durango House, its colossal skyscraper of a headquarters in London and its branches in every city of note.

He had been lucky too in the heads he had obtained for the great departments, since you may offer what salary you will and find no man good enough for it. Take for instance Ludovic Travers, his financial expert; head if you like, of the Durango Exchequer. After an exceptionally brilliant career at Cambridge he had written that perfectly amazing *Economics of a Spendthrift,* a work not only stupendous in its erudition but from the charm of its style a delight in itself. Then had come *World Markets,* now a textbook in the schools, and finally with *The Stockbroker's Breviary* a return to the whimsical style of his best known work. The luck of Durangos consisted in the acquisition, since Travers, supposed generally to be a dilettante with economics as a passionate and private hobby, had no need to put his nose to the grindstone; his fortune being a considerable one and his royalties a large additional income.

But in nothing was the luck of Francis Weston more exemplified than in the case of the Perfect Murder. The situation was like this. The Cinderella of the Durango departments was undoubtedly that known as the Enquiry Agency, a bureau which undertook genealogical research, finding of missing relatives, and much the same kind of work that is done by the better class detective agencies. For some time Sir Francis had had in mind a complete overhaul of this department and the forming from it as nucleus of a wholly new section of Durangos Limited which, while in no way comparable with Scotland Yard, should yet be able to take up any kind of investigation for private clients.

But two things were necessary. For this new department there would have to be found a head who was not only competent but so known to the general public that his name would give an immediate cachet. Once that was settled all that was needed would be some measure of success in a case in which the country as a whole was interested. Such success would be an advertisement uniquely direct and place the department definitely on the map. The trouble was, where were both to come from? Then, at the exact moment, chance took a hand. There came to his ears certain information that led him to believe that at least one difficulty could be solved.

John Franklin, after some really distinguished service in the Intelligence Department during the war, found himself at a loose end. Having experienced a few months of unemployment and then of uncongenial work he decided to do what he should have done before, enter the Police Force; a service which at that time offered exceptional prospects to men of character and undoubted ability.

These he certainly possessed. Add the influence that he had behind him, and a likeable and level-headed personality wherewith to counter the jealousy this might create among his colleagues, and you will admit that his rapid rise in seniority was not unmerited. Five years after his period of routine work he was a detective sergeant. Then came his chance with the Murder in the Waiting Room, a classic that now ranks with the Mahon and Crippen Cases. He would be the first to acknowledge the luck that came his way; the cards, as he said, fell for him as if they had been stacked. Be that as it may he was thereafter regarded as one of the coming men in the service.

Some twelve months before this October of 193—however, Detective-Inspector Franklin was recognised one night by a plain clothes officer behaving in such a way that something had to be wrong. When the pair of them got to the nearest police station Franklin did not know even his own name. That nervous breakdown cost him twelve months' sick leave and he was just due for medical examination when Sir Francis Western became aware of the facts. The offer he made—complete control of the new department—and the salary proposed demanded consideration. Then Franklin decided as Weston hoped he would. His resignation was sent in and already he had been at work some days on the affairs of the new department and its reorganisation.

Then the gods tossed another favour into Durangos' lap—the "Marius" letter. Immediately upon its publication Weston had felt a hunch that there was something in it. The preliminary steps he had taken, however, were somewhat unusual. He had called a special conference and after explanation and apology had asked, on the plea that each was representative of a different aspect of public life, for the considered opinion of each of the departmental heads present as to the genuineness of the letter.

The discussion, human and indeed rather acrimonious, that took place does not matter, but when the voting came two only—Franklin himself and Ludovic Travers—were found to have taken the letter at its face value. Sir Francis expressed no opinion. As a matter of fact, however, he left the conference room more than ever of the mind that the writer of the letter was a most unpleasant individual who was perfectly serious in the garish attitude he had chosen to adopt.

The morning of the publication of the second letter found him two hours early at the office where Franklin was hurriedly summoned. Sir Francis had been in fact decidedly uneasy. Like so many of us who put our trust in hunches, whether for Derby winners or five spades, he was beginning to wonder if the other fellow's hunch ought not to be taken into account. If the letters were genuine the world would be waiting to see what happened. If Durangos could prove that the murder was far from being a perfect one, the world was thenceforth their oyster. But was it genuine, all this palaver about committing murder? That was the question that had occupied the best part of an hour and by now had been more or less settled.

He swivelled the chair round and with a twinkle in his eye surveyed the clock. “Well, we may be a couple of fools, Franklin, but we’ll have an awful lot of fools on our side. And what’s your opinion of our chances?”

“We’ve a good sporting one, sir; we can’t hope for more.”

“Hum!” grunted the other, and rubbed his chin. “That’s true enough. Now let’s leave all the theories and keep to the supposition that the murder has actually been committed. What about that Scotland Yard monopoly I was mentioning just now?”

As Franklin looked down at the notes he had been making preparatory to stating a case, you could not fail to be struck by the quiet earnestness, the keenness of the man. He at any rate had no fears about diving into an unknown pool. There was about him, too, much that was attractive; the dark, almost foreign-looking face with its deep brown eyes, the trim set of the grey suit and the note of colour lent by the regimental tie, the absence of professional mannerisms; everything made one think of anything but a detective, and of Scotland Yard at that.

“I think, Sir Francis,”—the voice was an extraordinarily pleasant one—“we might consider that their monopoly lies only in such things as finger-prints, photographs, and the right to enter or interview. I know that seems a lot but if either Chief-Constable Scott or Superintendent Wharton has the handling of the case I think I might be able to get facilities, at any rate, for knowing what the Yard were doing.”

There was about the statement, however, a hesitancy which the other could not fail to notice. He decided to open some of his reserve artillery.

“I expect you will imagine I am not without some influence there. I think we can guarantee that part of the problem—I mean the granting of facilities—if it’s going to be of any help.”

Franklin looked up suddenly at that. “What you’ve just said, Sir Francis, is rather curious, because I was just going to add that if this letter is absolutely genuine in every line, that isn’t going to be the usual kind of Scotland Yard case. What I mean exactly is this. If this fellow—call him Marius for convenience—is definitely out for a perfect murder, there should be no clues in the generally accepted sense of the term; no traces of him or clues of the finger-print nature, and no possibility of witnesses. The only real clue should be the one of motive; the fact that Marius says he's *got* to commit the murder, and even there everybody is at the mercy of the letter. After all, even that may be merely a deliberate bluff."

"You mean that Scotland Yard may be as much in the dark as we are?"

"Perhaps even more so. I know it sounds unnecessarily quixotic to say so because in a way it leaves no excuse for failure, but as far as this case is concerned the Yard and ourselves start level. Our chances may even be better than theirs because we shan't run any risk of trying to work out an unusual case along stereotyped lines."

"I quite agree with you there. But just one other point. I admit that the understanding was a verbal and implied one that your name should not appear publicly with Durangos until we were in a position to regard the new department as ready to operate. Now tell me frankly. Are your former colleagues aware of your new association or do they simply imagine you resigned purely for reasons of health?"

There was the suggestion of a smile on the detective's face. "Where the Yard is concerned, Sir Francis, it's hard to say what is known and what isn't. As far as I'm concerned, of course, I've told nobody."

"Well, now; what I'm driving at is this. Supposing arrangements could be made for you to be on the spot soon after the murder is committed. Would you feel uncomfortable—under false pretences—so to speak—if your former colleagues gave you a welcome, imagining, of course, that you were a freelance? In other words, am I to keep what influence I've got as a last reserve or could you achieve practically the same results off your own bat?"

Franklin's reply came with unexpected rapidity. "I take it you want me to speak frankly, Sir Francis?"

"Most decidedly!"

"I'd rather not, sir. I should feel more than uncomfortable all the time, and once I had to own up the results might be very serious as far as concerned any chance of future help."

The other nodded. "Well, I oughtn't to say so, but I'm rather glad you feel like that about it. But tell me. On what lines would you propose to work, supposing we did take a hand?"

"I hardly know," was the reply. "There ought to be lines of inquiry that become more or less public property through the press; I mean names of relatives, if there are any, or friends of the murdered person. Not only that, but if I should happen to have a stroke of luck and pick up something the Yard doesn't know, there might be the chance of exchanging what they want for something *I* want."

"True enough. Exchange is no robbery." Then he fired the question point blank. "Well, it's up to you. Shall we sit in or shall we not? Mind you, I know you'll put up a real good show, but all the same I'd rather we left it alone than fail; that is, if it becomes generally known that we're interested."

Franklin's face coloured slightly. "I think we ought to sit in, Sir Francis."

He was about to add something, but the other rose and stretched his arms. "Splendid! I'm glad that's settled. Now come along and have some breakfast." He paused to make an entry in the big engagement book. "We'll arrange the rest at 3.00 this afternoon. I shall probably have all sort of news by then."

There, however, the matter was left and all that Franklin had to do, in the company of some millions of his interested fellow-countrymen, was to wait and see if the "Marius" letters would, as the minority expected, prove to be absolutely genuine.

CHAPTER IV
THE NIGHT OF THE 11TH OF OCTOBER

(A)

WHEN DETECTIVE-INSPECTOR Eaton of the "O" Division arrived at the Police Station, Woodmore Hill, that evening he was accompanied, not by Superintendent Gowing but by that officer's next in seniority, Inspector Veer. The Superintendent, it appeared, had had one of his sudden attacks of malaria just after the earlier visit of the afternoon, and at short notice Veer had been put in possession of the facts.

There had also drawn into the station yard a fast motor tender of the Flying-Squad, ready to move off again at a second's notice. Before the station itself the car which had brought the divisional officers remained standing; its driver had, however, been changed for a man who knew every detail of the district. The night was a mournful one, cold and with drizzly rain which occasionally freshened to showers.

In the office of Inspector Orwell was a cheerful fire. On the table was spread a large-scale map of the district, and with the local inspector as mentor the two others got a grip of their bearings from the position they then occupied.

"You know the district pretty well, I suppose," said Eaton.

"Fairly, considering I've only been here three months," replied Orwell.

"Any roads up?"

"Not now. The Council were starting to-day on Wilson Avenue," and he indicated the spot, "but I got them to put it off till to-morrow."

"Doctor all right?"

"Yes. He'll be warned automatically as soon as we go, if anything happens."

They drew their chairs up to the fire. After all there was nothing to do except wait, and even if there were a call it might not come before midnight. Somewhere about ten was the time Orwell hazarded as a guess.

"What about Northern Exchange?" he asked. "Any chance of a direct call here? It might make all the difference."

"Nothing's been done that I know of," replied Veer. "For one thing," and he took out a sheaf of papers, "here's the last information received by the Yard," and he held out a copy of the third "Marius" letter. Orwell read it carefully and passed it back.

"As far as we know," said Veer, "this chap may have a confederate. All he's got to do is give a message, apparently harmless, but which contains a key word and the confederate then gives the message of the letter to the Yard or the Exchange. That's why, or I imagine one of the reasons why, the Yard will call us direct."

"'Reasonably safe' might mean anything," observed Eaton. "The murderer's only to hop on a bus or tram or take a train and be miles away in very few minutes. I'm open to lay threes against the local exchange having anything to do with it."

"Not only that," said Veer, "but there's no definite statement that the murdered person is a subscriber. In any case it's my opinion, gentlemen, that theorising before the event isn't going to get us very far."

"There is one good thing," said Eaton, "and that's that nobody knows a word about the area being limited to the postal district. We shan't be troubled by reporters and a crowd. It's a filthy night, too; that'll make the roads clear."

But all the same, in spite of Veer's remark about theorising, the conversation went on, about it and about. The case was discussed from all angles and even its improbabilities were not overlooked. But when each had given his personal opinion they retreated collectively behind the rampart of duty; in fact, there they were and there they had to be, ready for eventualities. If nobody were murdered after all, so much the better for at least one person.

Yet all this time there was a strangeness in the air; something in the conversation itself that made for restraint. They were like men who only partly sleep because they must hear a vital alarum. It was the waiting for the telephone, the sudden call, that made speech unreal and disjointed. Still, a blue haze from the pipes settled over the room, and from outside the voices must have sounded one long, steady murmur. Then at 7.37 by the round-dialled clock the telephone shrilled sudden and urgent.

. . . .

The hour was, and it was most carefully noted, 7.33 p. m. One of the few operators on late duty at Northern Exchange, Miss Bennett, sat with her chair at the required angle of ninety degrees to the switch-board, covering with the least visional effort the steady field of view from side to side. In spite of the fact that she had three positions to look after and that the tiny electric lamps were winking all too frequently, she was finding time to ruminate on a certain bit of bad luck concerning meal reliefs, when—Board!

"Number, please!"

A man's voice spoke; sharp, authoritative, clear. "That you, Exchange? ... Listen carefully, please. Ring New Scotland Yard immediately! A murder has been committed!"

As if to assure him that the message had been received, "New Scotland Yard!" then she connected at once. "You're through!"

At the other end Scotland Yard took off the receiver. "Hallo!... Hallo!!... Hallo!!!..." this last very imperative. But no reply. He flashed Exchange. The operator, knowing automatically that a satisfactory connection had to be made, entered circuit and listened.

"Hallo! Scotland Yard speaking. Are you wanting us, miss?"

"One moment, please. There *is* someone wanting you."

By ringing on the line she tried to recall the original subscriber. At the same time she reported the matter to the supervisor, repeating his message and adding the number of the line—Northern 30003. Then, while the supervisor traced the name and address of the subscriber from that number, the operator spoke back to Scotland Yard.

"Are you there? ... You are wanted by Northern 30003, who said a murder had been committed. I have been unable to ring them as they have left the receiver off. Just a moment, please. I'll connect you with the supervisor who is tracing the subscriber's address."

Officially she plugged in on C. P. and rang, and at the answer of the supervisor, "You are through to Scotland Yard," she connected on the same pair of cords. Then unofficially she found time to whisper to the operator on her left, "Murder! Scotland Yard!" Meanwhile Scotland Yard was listening with every second of importance. "Are you there? ... The subscriber's name and address are—Richleigh, T. T., 122 The Grove, Woodmore Hill. I'll repeat that," and she did so.

What happened thereafter at Northern Exchange does not concern this story. But no sooner had that name and address been repeated than Scotland Yard rang up Northern 011. The time then, however long the interval has seemed in its relating, was 7.37 p. m.

(B)

Before the bell had rung for two seconds Inspector Veer had the receiver at his ear.

"Veer speaking." There was a pause. The others scarcely breathed and their eyes never left the inspector's face. Then, "Yes, sir. Very good, sir. Goodbye."

He snapped the receiver on the hook and spoke the one phrase, "122 The Grove."

Orwell gave a lightning glance at the map and with his finger marked the spot. Then already the plan which had had its dress-rehearsal earlier that day was in operation. Eaton moved like a streak through the side door to the police tender. He repeated the address to the local officer who acted as driver. The tender passed out of the yard and followed the closed car, which was already in motion.

There was not overmuch room for three, but between Veer and the driver sat Orwell. The speed of the car was a good fifty in the straight, and the corners were taken with gurgling of horns and the scrape of braked wheels. And between the intervals of this Veer had to get somehow into his head from Orwell's rapid description the situation of the house and plan the immediate disposition of his forces. As far as he could gather, the house was a detached one with a large garden backing to the gardens of Maple Terrace with a private alleyway between.

The road itself lay deserted, a residential backwater where even the distant roar of the traffic was unheard. The trees that bordered the pavement masked the light of the lamps, but in the wet of the surface the reflections ran streakily. In the quiet and the chill of the drizzle everything seemed moribund, autumnal, almost eerie. There was not even the footfall of a wayfarer to break the silence; only from the smooth twigs of the plane trees the streams trickled to the road. Then there was a hurried whispering as the tender drew up. The ten men became three groups. Two moved up the blackness of the alleyway, the other passed along the road. In a moment or two, save for the cars and the dimmed lights, the street appeared as untenanted as before. And just at that minute there was a larger drop or two and the drizzle became a shower.

In the private way at the back of the gardens two men were posted, one to the east of No. 122, the other to the west. Four others entered the garden by the gate, which was latched but unlocked. Keeping in touch with each other and with torchlights moving steadily they passed through the shrubbery and along the scantily stocked border. At the house they split apart, two to each side, and awaited the arrival of two men who had similarly searched the front and side shrubberies. All this was the matter of a minute or two, and, nothing being reported, Orwell placed two men at each south corner of the house, two inside the carriage way and two out of sight by the pavement. The last man, Sergeant Harrison, was in general charge and maintained liaison.

Inspector Veer and Detective-Inspector Eaton had, however, made straight at the start for the front door of No. 122. Veer rapped smartly on the brass knocker. Above the door a faint light could be seen coming through the semi-circular fanlight, but elsewhere the house appeared dark as doom. There was no sound; the inspector rapped again. For half a minute he studied the brass knocker while both of them listened for a movement. It came. Almost before they were aware of it the door opened and the figure of a maid showed plainly. But her actions were extraordinary. Her eyes opened staringly, her mouth went agape, and if ever there were terror depicted on a woman's face, there it was. She raised a hand nervously, spoke a word that was unintelligible but which might have been, "Don't!" with vowel long and shuddering, and then collapsed at their feet in a dead faint.

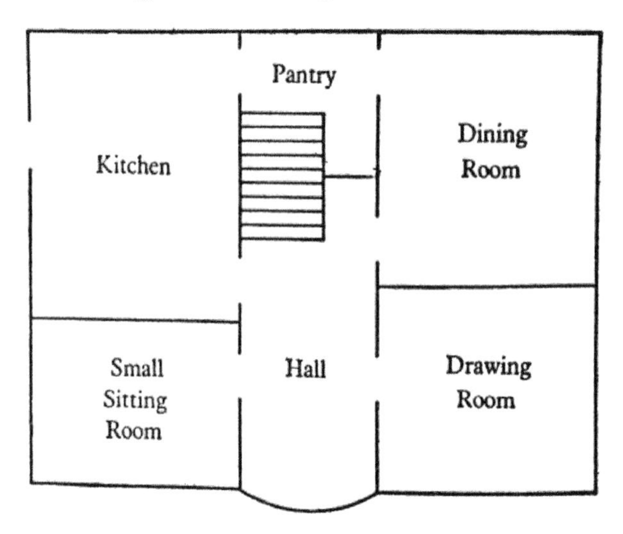

The inspector stooped and picked her up—a burden light enough. "Put the door to, Eaton, but don't let the catch work." He moved forward to where on the left a half-opened door showed itself. He entered with his burden and, hard on his heels, Eaton felt for the switch and snapped on the light.

Veer grunted. "Some sort of a sitting-room. Find Orwell if you can." By the time the unconscious maid was lying on the sofa and he had had a good look around the room the two entered. "Stop here a moment, Orwell, will you. You, Eaton, come with me and fetch some water. I'll be trying all the rooms. Keep an eye on the hall, Orwell."

They went out quickly to the hall, rectangular, spacious, and with the red of the pendant giving an effect at once obscure and diffused. Three doors were plainly to be seen.

"Probably the kitchen," said Veer, making for the far left, and his guess was correct. And while Eaton got the cup of water and returned to the sitting-room he made a survey. To what must have been the outside was a door with key in lock. Almost opposite was another door. "To the dining-room for a fiver," was his conclusion as he tried the knob. But the door was fastened, and from the far side at that.

He doubled for the hall, almost colliding with Eaton.

"Stand fast there, Eaton!" and he indicated the foot of the stairs which ran back to a top landing. While the detective watched, wondering what the scheme really was, he tried the first door to the right of the entrance. It opened, and the light revealed a drawing-room; knickknacks, greenery, chairs in loose covers, yellow piano and burr walnut table. But the room smelt musty, and there was no sign of murder.

There remained the fourth door leading apparently to the room which he had supposed to be the dining-room. He turned the handle but again the door was locked on the inside. At that moment, too, Orwell came out of the sitting-room. "She's coming round!"

"Stay at the doors and watch the stairs!" snapped Veer. "Lend me a hand, Jack!" and he put his shoulder to the door. It was immovable. Eaton drew back a couple of feet and launched thirteen stone of weight, but it still held. "Try the kitchen—that door—for a lever!" ordered Veer and in second or two Eaton was back with a hammer and an ironing board.

A minute of desperate smashing and the room was visible. Veer stepped first through the ruined door, fumbled for the light, and switched it on. From the sitting-room came the sound of moaning and a voice. At the same time steps were heard outside; the front door opened and a doctor entered.

"Just got your message," he began breezily to the back of two heads. There was no answer. The room came first.

It had one occupant—a man grey haired and bearded. He lay sprawled back in a leather-covered easy chair, mouth open, arms flopping, eyes staring. On the waistcoat of the suit was a stain, circular in shape and no bigger than a half crown, but from its centre protruded the handle of a knife. Of signs of disorder there were none. A cheerful fire burned in the grate before which the chair was drawn. On a pedestal table at its left were a half-filled glass, a decanter, and a syphon.

Veer turned round then to the doctor. "Doctor Greenlaw, isn't it?" and without waiting for an answer, "See if he's dead, will you?" Then while the doctor got to work he went quickly to the sideboard by the smashed door where a telephone receiver stood on the mahogany. Using the wire he hung it on the hook. "Ask Orwell to cover you to the top landing, Eaton, and go through the upper rooms. What's the verdict, doctor?"

"Oh, he's dead all right," replied Greenlaw. "Matter of a few minutes, I should judge."

"Hm! Well, sorry to trouble you, but this can wait. In the sitting-room there—the light's on—you'll find a girl lying on a sofa. Pull her round as fast as you can. There'll be the devil of a lot depending on what she can tell us."

He took off the receiver, holding it by the cord with finger and thumb, and while waiting to be put through to Scotland Yard let his eyes wander round the room. In the far left corner was a door leading to the kitchen. Back of the dead man were two windows and a French window, the former surmounted by mahogany rods from which the curtains hung and the latter covered by a blind. In the lock of the splintered door was no key.

Just as he finished his brief report to the Yard Eaton re-entered. "Two women's bedrooms, one unused spare, and one man's. Two others unfurnished. No sign of a soul."

"Good! I'll go and see what I can get out of the maid. You have a look round."

In the hall he motioned Orwell to follow him. Outside the front door stood the sergeant, almost invisible in the darkness.

"Looks as if there ought to be a light here," said Veer. He slipped inside again and found the switch which controlled an outside light above the steps. "Better leave it on. It won't be too conspicuous. Now, Orwell, have the house watched from the outside while you go over the inner rooms. The bird's probably miles away by this time, but it won't do to take any chances." And leaving the inspector to carry on he made for the left-hand gate of the front drive.

The hour was then 8.00 P. M., and the rain was falling heavily.

(C)

Had you seen the three of them in mufti and in places not connected with their daily bread, this is how you might have placed them. VEER: Tall, wiry, high cheek bones, waxed moustache, alert eyes and the least touch of the supercilious in his manner. "Regimental-Sergeant-Major." ORWELL: Thickset and therefore looking shorter than his height, clean-shaven, high colour, outstanding ears and manner bluffly jovial. "Butcher or Bookmaker." EATON: Of precise regulation height, well-built, friendly eyed, well-cut mouth, and quiet bearing. "Probably a bank cashier."

There was in short something about the detective that was certainly not official. What you would not have known was that he was extraordinarily well read and that his hobby was an unusual one—Borroviana. From Eaton therefore one could expect at least an originality of outlook.

As soon as Veer had left the room he got to work. On hands and knees he examined the worn blue carpet as far as the sideboard on which the receiver had stood. He squinted along the furniture and let the light from his torch play on it. He peered beneath the dead man's chair and then stood erect before the body. The fingers held nothing. He bent quickly and sniffed at the lips. For half a minute he watched the grey, bloodless face, the drooping, sensual lower lip, and the vulpine features which death made even more repulsive. Then he turned to the windows. Across them were drawn repp curtains hanging from massive mahogany poles. Beneath were roller blinds. The windows themselves, of the sash type, were fast and immovable, and behind the glass the heavy hasp of the wooden shutters could be seen. The key of the French window was in the lock, and at top and bottom bolts were firmly home. Facing you as you entered the room were two more windows, overlooking the side shrubbery, and these had the same curtains and shutters and were equally secure. The door which led to the kitchen was bolted top and bottom. And while he was in the act of trying the stiffness of the bolts Inspector Veer entered the room with a stranger.

"Can't get a word out of that maid yet. The doctor's still pulling her round. This is Mr. Wrench of No. 124."

He caught the detective's signal of direction. "Now, Mr. Wrench, if you'll be so good as to come this way, Would you mind telling us if this is Mr. Richleigh: Mr. T. T. Richleigh?"

Wrench, a man of about fifty and plainly very nervous, passed behind the table somewhat awkwardly. One look was enough for him.

"Yes. That's Mr. Richleigh."

"You known him long? Sit down, Mr. Wrench, and make yourself comfortable."

The invitation was rather ironical since Wrench was mopping his forehead with his handkerchief. The inspector repeated his question.

"Yes, er—about seven years."

"Anybody else kept in the house beside the maid?"

"Yes; there should be the housekeeper; Mrs. Carton or Carlton or some name like that."

"Nobody else? The deceased was unmarried?"

"Oh, no! I mean I've always been given to understand he was a widower. I believe his wife died a good many years ago."

"Any relatives or family, do you know?"

Wrench mopped his head again. "I really don't know. I understood he had some nephews, and I've occasionally seen a car outside, but I really don't know."

"You didn't hear anything unusual to-night?"

"I'm afraid I didn't," replied the other, very apologetically. "As a matter of fact I was listening-in from tea till just now when you saw me."

"Everything gone wrong!" exploded Veer when Wrench had been shepherded home by the back way. "What do you make of it?"

"More or less what we expected," replied Eaton. "He left apparently by the front door and took the key with him. I can find nothing and I've been over the place with a small-tooth comb."

Veer grunted, then, "Let's try the pockets."

The body could hardly have been placed more conveniently. The arms were so apart as they hung loosely over the narrowish chair that with no disturbance of its position one could with finger and thumb or a couple of fingers remove the contents of the pockets. The yield was a mixed one—a handkerchief, two shillings, sixpence, two pennies, a bunch of small keys and one Yale, a pencil, a penknife, a white metal watch marked "Chronomètre" on face, a thin packet of papers, a note case containing fourteen pound notes irregularly numbered, and lastly an envelope.

It was the latter that was first examined. Typed in the centre were the words

Thesis
THE PERFECT MURDER

The eyes of the two met and fell again. "Helpful sort of chap!" remarked Veer bitterly, then, "Try those keys on that secretaire bookcase. Probably where he keeps his papers. I'll look over these," and he set to work on the papers from the breast pocket of the dead man.

With one exception they were unimportant, consisting as they did of odd scraps of scribbling paper, two receipts for oddments of clothing, an estimate from a local plumber, and a series of clippings, questionable pornographic innuendoes from some discursive, sporting rag that was accustomed to sail very near the wind. The exception was a typewritten letter, folded in four. From its condition it had been carried about for days and read frequently. In two places the paper had actually cracked, and the whole was soiled and finger-stained. The paper was probably that of the hotel mentioned.

Constable Hotel,
Oct. 1st, 193—.

My Dear Uncle:

If you think you can get away with it you are welcome to try. If, however, you think I have come all the way from South Africa to be made a fool of, you are in for the shock of your life. You have two choices and ten days to choose. Either disgorge and look pleasant or keep your money and take the consequences.

Yours,

T. W. R.

"Anything there?" asked Veer, turning the letter face downwards and going over to where the other was rummaging in drawers and pigeonholes.

"Address of solicitor, addresses of two nephews, and partly used check book on local bank," replied Eaton, indicating the small pile he had placed on one side. But at that moment there was a double interruption.

The doctor popped in with, "Excuse me, inspector, but I think she's all right now," and voices were heard in the hall. The police tender had arrived from Scotland Yard. In five minutes the fingerprint experts were at work; photographs and detailed measurements of the room were being taken; the doctor was making out his preliminary report after a conference with the newly arrived Divisional Surgeon, and Chief-Constable Scott, having received a rapid précis of all there was to tell, took up his position with his back to the sitting-room. Behind him he could catch the low voice of Eaton, and from time to time he spoke a quiet word or two to a tall figure in thick travelling coat and bowler hat who stood by his side, hands deep in the coat pockets and eyes peering through hornrimmed spectacles.

The hour was then 8.45. The first tender was about to return to Camden Town, and duty reliefs had already arrived from the local station. A second car had been dispatched to The Ridgway, Enfield, to fetch, if possible, Ernest James Richleigh, who appeared to be not only the dead man's legal adviser but also his nephew and the eldest one at that.

CHAPTER V
THE NIGHT OF THE 11TH OF OCTOBER (*contd.*)

(A)

AS THE DOCTOR left the room he met Eaton at the door and whispered in his ear, "She's all right now, but I'd go a bit easy. She's badly scared about something."

That was reasonably clear to the detective as soon as he entered. The girl, her face whiter against the conventional black of her dress, sat bolt upright on the sofa, handkerchief in hand, with a look that was both furtive and defiant. One could have assumed that normally she was fluffily pretty and knew it, but her features were just a bit too sharp, her mouth too thin and calculating. But the detective's manner was perfect bedside; his smile as friendly and reassuring as he could make it.

"Well, young lady; feeling better now?"

The reply was unexpected. "Am I going to be taken away?"

Whatever the effect of the revelation the other showed no signs of having heard anything unusual. "I don't think we want to take you away. All we want you to do is to get better and tell us all about it. Take your own time."

Then there was another unexpected development. The words came with a rush. "I really didn't mean to do it. I've never done anything wrong before." She put out her hand in appeal, then started to cry, and finally blubbered through her tears, "If I own up and tell you everything, you won't take me to prison? I didn't mean to do anything wrong when I saw the parcel. ..."

Eaton was getting out of his depth. "I don't think you need worry about going to prison." He patted her on the shoulder. "There, now. Don't worry about anything. There's nothing to cry about."

The sobbing died away into spasmodic hiccoughing, and she dabbed her eyes. The answers she gave were not too distinct, and the voice was that of a martyr.

"What's your name?"

"Mary. Mary Adams."

"How long have you been here, Mary—I mean in your present post?"

"Only three weeks—sir." This last maybe a tribute to the bedside manner.

"Housemaid?"

"House-parlourmaid sir. Mrs. Cardon does the cooking and she's housekeeper."

"Where is she now?"

The voice became more certain. There was even a hardness in it. "It's one of her nights out, and she won't be in before ten."

"Now, then, Mary; tell me everything that happened tonight. Start at the very beginning and don't leave anything out"

She turned her eyes with sudden suspicion on the other's face. Then she looked down. Then she dabbed her eyes. Apparently she was finding difficulty in starting.

"I took in Mr. Richleigh's tea at five and cleared away at half past. Mrs. Cardon, she'd gone out before that, and I was all alone in the kitchen because she don't like you having a fire in the sitting-room, where we are, when she ain't there. So I sat in the kitchen where there was a fire, and then there was a knock at the door, and I saw the parcel—"

"Just a minute," interrupted the other. "What time was this knock?"

"About half-past seven, because I'd just looked at the clock and I thought I'd soon have to be laying his supper. There wasn't any cooking to do, because he was having cold ham and cheese. So I went to the door—"

"The kitchen door?"

"The kitchen door, and when I opened it there wasn't nobody there and then on the ground in front of the door I saw the parcel."

Again the look of pathetic innocence and a hint of more tears. "Yes, go on!" urged Eaton. "Tell me everything that happened."

"Well, I picked up the parcel and read it and it said, 'Mrs. Malone, 129 The Grove,' so I thought there'd been some mistake, but I couldn't see or hear nobody, so I took the parcel into the kitchen and—and—" and here the tears came in earnest.

"And you thought you'd like to see what was inside it. Well, I might have done the same thing myself."

And so, bit by bit, the story came out. The parcel had been taken up into the bedroom for better examination and had turned out to be two pairs of silk stockings. Then, according to her story, she flew downstairs intending to lay the supper and take the parcel round after. Also while in the bedroom she heard the master cough as if he were moving about. When she got back in the kitchen she was just about to put out the supper things when there came the knock at the front door, and when she finally decided to answer it the shock of seeing the men and the police moving in the background was enough to send her off into a faint.

Now, however unsatisfactory the story, Eaton accepted its outlines as true. The first discrepancy was seen when the parcel was asked for. Amid more tears the stockings were produced from under an ironing blanket in the dresser drawer. The brown paper and the partially intact label thereon were recovered from the ash pan of the kitchen grate, perforated by dropping cinders but sufficiently whole to prove at least the story of their arrival. Had the fire been clear at the time of their depositing they would have undoubtedly gone into the flames and not where they did.

The next job was a flying visit to Mrs. Malone. She had ordered no stockings and expected none. As a widow of over seventy she would in any case have had no use for the flesh-coloured gaieties of the parcel. So much for that then. Chief-Constable Scott received at once an account of his preliminary cross-examination.

"Bring her into the kitchen," said Scott. He made a remark to the man in the travelling coat, and the two of them moved off to the kitchen where in a second or two Eaton and the girl joined them.

Mary Adams speedily realised that the truth and nothing else, unadorned by tears and protestations, was the only safe line. The real reason for the visit of the police was moreover news that left her in precious little mood for further prevarication. By the time Scott had finished with her the following facts seemed definitely established.

(1) Taking into account all her actions from the time she picked up the parcel to the time when she heard the noise which she described as coughing, not less than four minutes elapsed.
(2) After hearing this noise she was actually in the kitchen within half a minute.
(3) From start to finish she heard no other noise.

The verbal dressing-down which was administered to the witness was a stiff one. If she got one thing into her fluffy peroxide head at the end of it it was that the prison gates were yawning and martyrdom at a discount. But there was no point in pushing things too far. With a last and tactful injunction to get ready a big pot of tea—Scott and his cups of tea were proverbial and to be not only thankful for favours received but ready for further examination at any minute, she was left to think things over.

Nor was there time for anything else. Orwell arrived with Mr. Ernest Richleigh, who, as the former whispered to his chief at a convenient moment, had undoubtedly spent the evening at a local cinema with his wife and daughter. Eaton returned to the dining-room; Orwell kept an eye on Adams and things in general. The newcomer, with the two officers and the stranger, adjourned after further identification of the body to the drawing-room, where the gas fire was lit. The time was then 9.30.

(B)

Ernest Richleigh, senior partner in the legal firm of James, Richleigh and James, was far from being a conventional type. He was short, sturdy, fiery hued, and, in spite of a certain ability to freeze up at a second's notice, naturally breezy and cheerful. That night, however, he was unnatural in the sense that he could hardly enliven the proceedings with his usual stock-in-trade of humour. One felt that in keeping so lugubrious a countenance he was undergoing an unwonted strain. He did unloose one flippancy which had stood him well on many a sad occasion, but it fell flat on the cold, official air.

"This is a sad business for you, Mr. Richleigh," Scott had said.

"Well, we've all got to die; even you and I," returned Richleigh.

Scott waved his hand to a chair. "Sit down, Mr. Richleigh, and let's see what we can make of this terrible affair." He held up to the light the card of the visitor and read it again. "I take it you want to help us all you can?"

"Oh, certainly! Most certainly!"

"When did you last see your uncle alive?"

Richleigh frowned as in thought. "A week ago tonight."

"Business visit, courtesy, or pleasure? What would you say?"

"Oh, business. Strictly business. As a matter of fact, my uncle hinted at the possibility of his marriage and wished to discuss the drawing up of a will."

"A new will?"

"Oh, no! As far as I am aware my uncle made no will. I had advised him from time to time that it was his duty to indicate his wishes as to the disposal of his estate and that it was my duty so to advise him."

"You are prepared to tell us who the heirs are—I mean if the deceased actually died intestate, as you suggest?"

Richleigh met this with a circumlocution. "The only surviving relatives are my three brothers and myself, nephews of the deceased."

"Would you mind giving me the names and addresses of those nephews?" asked Scott, and Veer prepared to write down the statements.

"Hm! Let me see," and he took from his pocket what one felt to be a wholly unnecessary pair of pincenez and, having adjusted them, consulted a packet of miscellaneous papers and a small diary book which he placed on the table.

"Mr. H. Richleigh, c/o Rupert Pyne Theatrical 75 Georgia St., W. C. I."

"Your brother is an actor on tour?" suggested Scott.

"That is so. Poor fellow, he—er—still, that's neither here nor there. 'The Rev. C. Richleigh, Little Martens, Suffolk.'" He waited till that was down, then passed across a paper. "This letter is from my brother, Frank, the youngest of us, at present on tour in France."

Oct. 9th, 193—.

DEAR ERNEST:

So sorry to be a nuisance to you already, but I left behind me two new brushes. You'll find them in the unlocked bag I left in the spare room. Can't get the same kind here, so will send them on to me Poste Restante, Quillan, Aude, France.

Weather pretty decent. Many thanks. In great haste,

FRANK.

"What is he, this brother?" asked Scott as Veer passed the letter back. "An artist or another actor?"

"Neither. He's a schoolmaster; on special leave of absence. A grace term, I believe they call it."

"Did your brothers know about this proposed will?"

"I may have mentioned it to them. I probably did. There was no reason why I should not."

"None whatever. Now, Mr. Richleigh, you have no other cousins? In other words, your uncle had no other nephews?"

"None whatever."

"Quite certain? No connection with South Africa, for instance?"

The lawyer cast a sharp look over the top of his glasses.

"Most of the estate of the deceased came to him at the death of his brother, my uncle, Mr. Peter Richleigh of Cape Town. The deceased, Mr. Peter Richleigh, and my father were the only three children of my grandfather. Mr. Peter Richleigh actually died in this house and was unmarried."

"Deceased was comfortably off?"

"Very! Between ourselves, his income was over £2,000 a year."

Scott showed polite but inwardly very real surprise. "One wouldn't have guessed it. But with regard to the question of heirs and also entirely between ourselves, what do you make of this?" And he handed over the Constable Hotel letter.

The question was a poser; at least the lawyer could make nothing of it. But he made one admission. "Of course Mr. Peter Richleigh may have been married secretly. It's most improbable, and further than that I'm not prepared to go. I do take it, however, that this supposed nephew can be got hold of at the address he gives?"

"Don't worry about that," retorted Scott grimly. "There's a chap sitting in the manager's office at this moment. But one other thing, Mr. Richleigh. Do you know the lady your uncle was proposing to marry?"

The reply came with peculiar emphasis. "A Mrs. Cardon; his housekeeper!"

"Hm! By the way, we're expecting her at any minute. You any objection to seeing her?"

"I'd rather not," was the hasty reply. And though the lawyer must have had some exquisite reason for the objection he did not even trouble to give reason good enough.

"Just one other thing. Is there anybody who, to your knowledge, might have done this deplorable deed? Any enemies of the deceased?"

"I might name a good few," replied the other with obvious satisfaction, "but unless you're prepared for an hour's conference it's not much use beginning."

"You mean the deceased was not exactly popular?"

The lawyer closed up as suddenly as he had opened. "Perhaps I've hinted at more than I care at present to substantiate. But you can take it that the deceased was a hard man: in many ways a much hated man. More I would rather not say."

"You realise the importance of the question?" said Scott soberly, looking at his man with an expression of singular earnestness. But the other held his ground.

"I most certainly do. He quarrelled with everybody. If there was a trick to be won or an advantage to be gained, he won it at any cost. A Mr. Steward who used to come here and play cribbage refused to enter the house again because he wouldn't put up with cheating at tuppence an end. He couldn't keep servants, the tradesmen detested him, and he hadn't a genuine friend in the world. That's a plain statement except in so far as it errs on the side of sympathy. After all," he added with an irony that masked a growing anger, "we're enjoined to speak well of the dead."

"A final afterthought," said Scott. "Nothing unusual about the deceased last week? No signs of panic? No expressed or hinted wish for confession?"

"None whatever," was the instant reply.

There was a tap on the door, and Orwell entered. "Mrs. Cardon is here, sir. She's in the sitting-room at the moment."

"Very good," said Scott. "We'll be there in a moment. Now, Mr. Richleigh, we're most grateful to you for what you've done. There's nothing else you can think of at the moment? Nothing you want to ask?"

The lawyer shook his head. He removed the glasses and put them slowly and carefully back into his pocket. "I'm sorry for the notoriety. I'm sorry for everything but I've felt for some time that things couldn't go on." He rose from the chair and shook his head again. "A bad business! Of course, if there's anything I can do ..."

"We know where to find you," completed Scott as the two passed out into the hall.

Inspector Veer cast a glance at the stranger who in a seat by the window had watched the scene so quietly that his presence had been forgotten. The two caught each other's eyes.

"A pretty shrewd customer that!" remarked the inspector with a jerk of his head to indicate the departed lawyer.

Ludovic Travers gave a look that was meant to be inscrutable and ventured an assentient, "Very! Very!" After all, when among the detectives it is as well for the inexperienced to be mysterious.

(C)

When the four of them arrived in the sitting-room they found Detective-Inspector Eaton and the housekeeper already there. The former had been explaining the situation, but if he had expected tears he found none. One might have looked for an expression of regret, of sorrow at the untimely end of a fellow being, whatever had been the frailties or vices that were part of his humanity.

The housekeeper was a massive woman, well above the average height; of ample bust and blowzy; a typical barmaid without the good humour of the type. She looked coarse, defiant, sullen; a woman with a grievance. Eaton's courtesy had passed her by as the idle wind and as she sat there one might have imagined a cat, steady eyed, tail a-swish and claws that could scar.

In front of her Scott took the limelight. The others faded into the background.

"Now, Mrs. Cardon. It is Mrs. Cardon, isn't it?"

"That's my name."

"We're very glad you've come so opportunely to help us. This must have been a great shock to you?"

There was no reply. She just watched steadily. Whoever made the first slip it would not be Rose Cardon.

Scott moralised a bit. "Death, at any rate by violence, is always a shock. You're a widow, Mrs. Cardon?"

"Why are you questioning me? What are these men doing here?"

"These men are here as I am—in the interests of justice. I am questioning you because at this moment you are the head of this house. From what you can tell us we may discover who killed Thomas Richleigh. You are here to help the law and us. Don't you want to do that?"

"Very well."

"You are a widow?"

"My husband died fourteen years ago."

Scott tried a little finesse. "Then if you'll excuse my saying so, you must have married very young." But not a muscle of her face moved.

"How long have you been with Mr. Richleigh as his housekeeper?"

"Eight years come Easter."

"You found him a good master?"

"I did."

"He confided in you, perhaps. Told you things he would not have told anybody else?"

"Perhaps he did."

"Then did you notice anything in his conduct recently or did he tell you anything which might lead you to suspect that he was in fear of being murdered?"

"He didn't say anything to me."

"There was nothing peculiar about the conduct of the deceased when you left him this afternoon?"

"Not that I noticed."

"Have you heard him speak of a nephew in South Africa?"

She shook her head.

"No such visitor has ever come to the door and asked to see Mr. Richleigh?"

"Not that I know of."

"Now think carefully, Mrs. Cardon. Is there anybody who in your opinion bore such a grudge or enmity against your late employer as to threaten murder or vengeance at any time?"

"Not openly. He ordered a Mr. Steward out of the house once when they had a few words, but that was nothing."

"Why did you say 'not openly'? Do you mean there might be secret enemies?"

Now things began to show themselves. The amount of concentrated venom in the answer was a revelation.

"Only those who lost his money."

"You mean, for example ..."

"His nephews. They'd been after him for years, but he did them in the end."

"You mean," and he leaned forward on the table until his face almost touched his hands, "that by your marriage you would have had control of his money?"

"And I have now!" This with triumph.

"Exactly how, may I ask?"

"Mr. Richleigh told me he'd made a will and everything he had would be mine."

"Well, that may be so and it may not. But don't be disappointed, Mrs. Cardon, if it turns out that Mr. Richleigh died without making a will."

That flustered her somewhat, and Scott went on: "He told you the name of the solicitor who drew up this will? Or did he draw it up himself?"

She shook her head.

"Now, Mrs. Cardon; purely as a matter of form and please don't take offence at the question. You spent the evening out?"

"I did."

"With whom?"

"With Mrs. Clarke, Mr. Steward's housekeeper. We went to the pictures and had some supper afterwards."

"Thank you, Mrs. Cardon. Mr. Steward lives at what number?"

"No. 124."

"Excuse me a second." He made a signal to Veer who left the room; then he whispered to Eaton. Finally he turned to the housekeeper. "I hope to have a cup of tea now, Mrs. Cardon. Will you have one with me?"

"No, thank you."

Eaton left the room and after a second or two Scott continued his questioning. "Mr. Richleigh, or should I say yourself, had some trouble in keeping maids."

"That's not uncommon."

"You had bad luck, I take it. They were treated well enough?"

"Too well, in my opinion."

"How, may I ask?"

Over her face came an expression half sneering, half impudent. "If you kept one you'd soon find out." here was a tap on the door, and the maid, Mary Adams, came in with a small brass tray on which were a cup of tea and a sugar basin. Eaton slipped in behind her. From the moment she entered, the eyes of the other woman never left her face, and the look was not a pleasant one. And when the maid's eyes caught that of her mistress there was in return a look of absolute contempt, a kind of bravado that said, "Your reign's over!"

"Thank you, Mary," said Scott, dropping two lumps into the cup. "You sure you won't have one, Mrs. Cardon? What about you, Mr. Travers? Well, you don't know what's good for you. Now, then, Mary; you're not afraid to sleep in the house to-night? Two of us will be here all the time."

"Not if I can shift my bed, sir. I don't want to sleep next to her."

Then there was a scene. "You common slut! So you're the one who's been telling tales ..."

"You keep your tongue to yourself, Mrs. Cardon. If I were to open my mouth ..."

"You pack your box and get out of the house!"

"Not even respectable, you aren't. I've seen your goings on, you dirty ..."

Then having heard the lie of things Scott asserted himself. "That will do, Adams! You keep your tongue under control or I'll put you where you'll have time to get cool." Then to the other woman, whose bosom was heaving and whose face was flushed almost to purple, "Mrs. Cardon, I may want you again in the morning. If you take my advice you'll go straight to bed."

He got up and held open the door, and after a tantalising delay the housekeeper went out, head in air, and with a pose that poorly simulated indifference.

Scott turned to the girl. "The key of the dining-room—where was it kept?"

"In the lock, sir."

"Inside or out?"

"Sometimes in and sometimes out, sir."

"Hm! Well, tell me all about it."

"When Mrs. Cardon was out late, sir, the master used to go to bed early, and he always used to lock the door on the outside so that if burglars got into the dining-room they couldn't get out. Then when I got up in the morning I used to unlock it so as to get in, and then I always had to put the key inside, so if he didn't want to be disturbed he could lock himself in—and her, too."

"What exactly do you mean by that?"

"They used to be in there together in—"

"I don't want to hear that, thank you. Keep to what I'm asking. The pantry—was that locked tonight?"

"Not that I know of, sir."

"And the key of the front door—who had that?"

"Mrs. Cardon had one, sir, because she used to let herself in."

"And did you ever have the key in your hands?"

"Oh, no, sir!"

"How did you unlock the door, then?"

"It went with a chain, sir, and bolts, and you could undo it from the inside."

"Hm! You answer all bells?"

"Yes, sir, except when I'm dressing or Mrs. Cardon happened to be handy."

"Has a stranger called to see Mr. Richleigh during the last week or two saying he was a nephew from South Africa?"

"A man did call, sir. On the Wednesday night, a week ago, it was."

"What happened?"

"He asked to see Mr. Richleigh, and I said he was out, and he said where was he? So I said he was out on business, and as

I didn't know when he would be in, would he leave a message? Then he said, very nasty, he'd give him a message he wouldn't forget in a hurry. Then he went off and didn't leave no message."

"And where *was* Mr. Richleigh?"

"Gone out to get his money in, sir; least, that's what I've always understood. He's got two hairdresser's shops in Tottenham, and it's early closing day, and he always goes there then."

"What time did he get in?"

"I don't know, sir. I had a headache, and Mrs. Cardon she sent me off to bed about nine."

"Of course you told her what happened?"

A pause, then, "She'd just popped out for a minute."

"But you could have told her when she came in?"

A sullen look came into the girl's face. "I don't hold with telling *her* everything. I did mean to tell the master in the morning, but I forgot all about it."

"What was he like, this man? Could you describe him?"

"Well, I thought first of all he was Mr. Harold—Harold Richleigh—and I couldn't see him very well in the dark, and then as soon as he spoke I knew it wasn't him."

Scott seemed on the point of going further into that question, but he changed his mind and made an entry in his notebook. "Now, just one other thing. You're quite sure the noise you heard was Mr. Richleigh coughing?"

"Oh, yes, sir! It was just like Mr. Richleigh was clearing his throat of something. It's a long way from where I was, but that's what it sounded like."

"And afterwards you didn't hear the front door click? No further noise of any kind?"

"No, sir—least, not till the front door was knocked."

Scott finished the cup of tea, which must have been tepid by this time, and remained silent for a good minute. Then he got up. "Now, my girl, you go to bed and let's hear no more about wanting to change your room. Tap on Mrs. Cardon's door and say I say she's to put the key of her room outside the door, and you do the same with yours."

As she passed out he turned to Travers, whose presence one might reasonably have supposed he had forgotten. "Women are the very devil!"

Travers found no comment but nodded sympathetically. Out in the hall Scott's first duty was to post a constable on the landing upon which the bedrooms opened. The keys which were brought to him he pocketed.

The hour was then 10.40 p. m. and the rain was coming down in torrents.

CHAPTER VI

THE NIGHT OF THE 11TH OF OCTOBER (*concl.*)

(A)

SIR GEORGE COBURN arrived a few minutes later and in a purely unofficial capacity. Chief-Constable Scott, who had spent the interval in telephoning, then had with him a short interview. Then Veer, who had returned from a visit to No. 124, was with them for some time. Eaton seemed to be here and everywhere. He also had a conference or two and found time, moreover, to examine the outside of the shutters, the lock of the broken door, and even the contents of the ash bin.

The rest had gone their several ways: Orwell back to the station, the photographer to the Yard, the finger-print experts to their homes after spending a couple of hours in looking for what wasn't there, and most of the constables to their normal duties. The divisional-surgeon had gone long since, but in the morning would come the post-mortem when his preliminary report would be supplemented by more exact observations as to the extent of the injury.

Ludovic Travers, having had a word with his uncle on his arrival, found himself thereafter at a loose end and spent the time in making a circuit of the empty rooms on the ground floor. Whether his wanderings were aimless or with an object is hard to say, but it rather looked as if he were trying to absorb the atmosphere, to get into the milieu as it were, of what was for him an extraordinary house.

The furniture, smug and massive, the marble mantelpiece with clock and bronze figures, the table with macramé covering and woollen flowers beneath a glass dome, the engravings after Martin, Greuze, and Landseer; all that dining-room, for instance, was a sort of queer anomaly, with the telephone a curious anachronism and the thought of murder a discord incredible and blatant. In the air there still seemed to hover the smoke from the flashlight, but the general atmosphere was not sinister; it was merely unreal, theatrical, and somehow hard to accept.

The house itself was deathly still. From outside came the splash of rain, but even from the drawing-room there was no sound. In the air was a chill, and the ash of the grate gave to the room a forlornness that was almost drab. He hunched his shoulders in the big coat and wished he could hear again Scott's offer for a cup of tea. And when the sound of voices in the hall announced that the powwows were over he was by no means sorry to be rid of his own company.

Sir George was looking rather worried. Normally a man of considerable shrewdness, he was feeling at the moment full of information, hurriedly absorbed and badly digested. He could see little daylight; lines of action and perhaps methods of approach, but little that was of immediate promise. It was Scott's pigeon, it was true, but for all that he would have been relieved to hear less of the abstract and more of definite and tangible results.

"A deplorable business!" was his trite but feeling comment.

"It certainly seems to have its unusual features," said his nephew, who felt that under the circumstances he had better say something. Then he turned to Scott. "It was awfully decent of you to let me come along. I hope I haven't been too much of a nuisance."

Scott smiled. "To tell you the truth, Mr. Travers, I don't think you've said three words beyond 'yes' and 'no' since we got here.

I'd rather like to know, as a matter of pure curiosity, just what you've been *thinking.*"

Ludo was horrified. "Good Lord! You don't suspect me of being one of those amateur people who come along and settle everything?"

"I don't know; you might be a dark horse."

"Dark! I'm as black as Egypt's night."

Sir George was regarding his nephew with a slightly puzzled air. Why he and Scott always got on so well he didn't know. When Ludo had remarked casually earlier in the evening that he supposed he couldn't come along he had noted with vague disapproval that Scott had made no objection. He would have been the last to deny pride or affection, but the fact remains that he had no use for the literary temperament. There was perhaps one saving grace; Ludo took after the Coburns in looks, even if he did find the pen more profitable than the sword.

When the five of them reassembled in the drawing room they found the exhibits placed on the table, and round these they grouped themselves. The fire made a note of comfort, and Scott stoked his pipe as soon as he sat down. The amateur retired discreetly to a corner.

The details of that conference would be too long to give in their entirety. The main arguments and high lights were, however, as follows.

"We will put our ideas into a common pool," said Scott, "and examine them with as little discussion as possible. Then we can discard and see what's left. The only two things I would say, however, are that firstly the writer of the letters has apparently lived up to his promises, and that secondly this case, as Sir George agrees, throws us more into the public eye than any of us can remember. As the murder is in the nature of a challenge, the public will expect quick and definite results. I do not admit for a moment that the peculiar circumstances will alter either our methods or our attitude but I do suggest it as an additional stimulus. As far as the press is concerned, for to-night, at least, a six-line smudge has been issued from the Yard. Inspector Veer has recognised, as we expected, that already the case is one that will make demands with which his division will be wholly unable to cope, at least unaided."

From his notes Veer gave his first, and as he was careful to insist, tentative reconstruction of the crime.

"The murder was committed by somebody who was perfectly familiar with the household. He knew the housekeeper was always out on Thursday nights, and he had a perfect knowledge of the lie of the house. He knocked at the back door, and while the maid was looking at the parcel he had prepared, entered the front door with a Yale key—a duplicate, or one stolen or even lent him for the purpose—and went very quickly to the dining-room. He was wearing rubber soles and had probably drawn over them a pair of socks, since the carpet shows no trace of mud.

"He was known to the dead man, otherwise there would have been a struggle and a cry. With the knife there, one of a common type used by most cooks and from its sharp point particularly murderous, he struck the deceased as he rose from the chair, using a gloved right hand. The blow was dead straight to the heart. Then the murdered man was thrust back in the chair. The murderer entered the pantry and came out after fastening the door. He then bolted the outside pantry door and locked the dining-room door. In the waistcoat pocket of the dead man he put the prepared paper so as to show us that the murder was the one announced. Then he rang up Exchange, using as few words and speaking as quietly as possible, and then left the receiver off. Then he let himself out of the dining-room, re-locked it, and left the house. The times taken can be tested by trial.

"With regard to possible suspects I discard Adams and Cardon, unless either employed a confederate, since neither could have written the 'Marius' letters. The man Steward I discard for the moment. He was alone in the house all the evening, it is true. His supper was laid in another room, and he claims to have spent the time reading a book, which I saw. Before their quarrel he used to play cribbage every Thursday night while the two housekeepers went out. He is well over seventy and far from active.

"The most promising line seems the writer of the letter from the 'Constable Hotel,' but then he's never been inside the house.

Also he'd not have been such a fool as to leave behind him such an obvious clue as his letter. Then there are the four nephews who inherit in all probability. Their alibis will have to be inquired into, and all the while there is to keep in mind the fact that the murderer is the writer of the 'Marius' letters."

Next came Eaton, and he seemed far less certain.

"If you don't mind, gentlemen, I'd like to go over some things that puzzle me. The first is the parcel. It was labelled for No. 129, and the name and address could have been got from a local directory. Now 129 is just across the road. Why then should the murderer entice the maid across the road and then leave by the *front* door, where he'd be bound to run into her? Why didn't he address the parcel to a corresponding number at Maple Terrace? The maid would then have gone out by the back and returned by the back."

"I suggest," said Scott, "that as the distance would have been greater, there was the risk that she would have asked permission before going out so far. Also the back way is unlighted, and she might have been too nervous to have ventured at all."

"That satisfies me, sir," said Eaton. "The next point is, why did that nephew from South Africa have the bad luck to call on his uncle the only evening he was ever out?"

"I ought to say here," said Scott, "that a man answering to the description and signing himself T. W. Richards—obviously an alias for Richleigh—was at the Constable Hotel from the first to the third inclusive. He left on the morning of the fourth with a heavy suitcase, bound for Liverpool Street, and that's the last heard of him. Superintendent Wharton is handling that now."

"All the same, sir," insisted Eaton, "I don't see why T. W. R. should have been so ignorant as to have called to see his uncle when he was bound to be out, and so lucky as to have come and murdered him on the only night when the housekeeper wasn't in."

"He might have learnt about the housekeeper later," remarked Veer.

"That is so," agreed Eaton. "Still, I thought it worth mentioning. Now about the maid. We all recognise that the murderer must have summed her up uncommonly well. But there's something curious arising out of that. We know he must have planned out his times to a second, *but,* he didn't know it was going to rain. Suppose the maid had stopped in the house waiting till the end of the shower. What would have happened to his scheme?"

"Perhaps he had two: one for fine weather and one for wet," suggested Scott.

"Well, sir, to-night was both," retorted Eaton. "However, one or two smaller matters, and then I've done. Was there any discussion of the 'Marius' letters in this house? If the deceased had so many enemies as we're told, why didn't he shut himself in? And the last thing I'd like to point out arises out of Inspector Veer's statement. If a man so vindictive as the deceased is represented to be permitted his housekeeper to keep friendly, after the quarrel he had with Steward, with the Steward household, it shows she must have had him absolutely under her thumb."

"I think your remarks most provocative and important," said Sir George. "I might suggest, however, that Richleigh was hardly so much under her thumb as it appears. He certainly deceived her over the will."

"There *might* have been a will, sir," said Scott. "If there were, then the whole case is clearer. Possibly the murderer took it and then we have a motive to work on. Still, leaving that for a moment, Eaton's questions brought one at least to my mind. Why should the murderer not have opened the dining-room door and dashed out into the street? There was only a helpless woman in the house, and he must have known her temperament pretty well, as Eaton remarked. Even if she'd screamed, he could have got away with absolute ease."

"The 'Marius' letters tend to show that he preferred any line of conduct that was spectacular or sensational," suggested Sir George.

"I agree, sir," added Veer. "Also perhaps it was desperately important that he should not be seen, even from the back. Suppose he were lame or a hunchback, or slow on his pins, like Steward?"

Travers was just smiling to himself at the thought that while everybody seemed to be right somebody had to be wrong, when he caught his own name. "Anything strike you, Mr. Travers?" Scott was saying.

"Er—may I have another look at the hotel letter?"

"By all means," replied Scott, and passed it over.

"Am I supposed to handle it with gloves?"

Scott smiled tolerantly, "It's been examined. Richleigh probably handled it to-night. You'll see the prints on it."

They were indeed perfectly clear where the expert had exposed them; on one side a thumb and on the other two fingers. The letter appeared to interest him, but when he passed it back the remark he made was decidedly disappointing. "I suppose this is really the hotel paper?"

"We shall know some time to-night," replied Scott with a perfectly serious face. "About those tests. Shall we try them out? You like to see them, Sir George?"

"Very much!" was the reply, and the party made their way into the hall.

(B)

The first test was a simple one, intended primarily to see the amount of time on which the murderer might have counted had the parcel been duly taken to the occupant of No. 129. The test was necessarily an incomplete one, since Mrs. Malone could not very well be disturbed again, but all the same Eaton twice went through all the actions which the maid could reasonably have been supposed to perform. Four minutes was the average and, as Scott remarked, that was the minimum basis upon which they had to work since the murderer dared not expect more.

Next came the test of the sounds as heard by Adams. This was tried by all in turn. The listener stood in the bedroom next to that in which the maid had been. In the closed dining-room was made the last sound presumably uttered by the murderer—the speaking to Exchange. The consensus of opinion was that the sound was quite audible to a listener on the alert, as the maid must have been, and that it could reasonably be said to resemble a protracted cough.

There was next a short discussion on the feasibility of checking up the times as spent by the maid. To do so in her absence was, however, felt to be a hopeless business. The two important things were—

> (1) The interval that elapsed between the first opening of the back door and the hearing of the "cough."
> (2) The time that elapsed after the "cough" and the whereabouts of the maid.

The first had been assessed at four minutes, and there seemed no reason to alter it. As for the latter, upstairs in the bedroom she heard what was supposed to be the telephone message. According to her statement, however improbable the action might appear, she was at once in a panic. She had on a pair of silk stockings and her shoes, since she intended surveying the effect in the glass. In this panic she seized her lisle thread stockings, the unfolded pair of silk ones, and the paper, and flew downstairs. On the top of the landing she halted for a second or two and, hearing no further sound, went into the kitchen as quietly as she could. The panic possibly persisted, but she had sense enough to open the door leading to the hall. Facing this she replaced the stockings, put the new ones in the dresser drawer, and the paper in the ash pan.

From that time until she heard the knock on the front door she neither saw nor heard anything in the hall, though its linoleum would not have deadened sound as a carpet would, and though her ears must have been supersensitive. The time between "cough" and arrival in the kitchen could not have been more than half a minute. Those times were regarded as definite and put aside for comparison with the next test.

This final one was the reconstruction of the crime, and here Veer took the part of the murdered and Eaton that of the murderer. The action was that described in Veer's statement, and ample allowance was made for listening pauses. And, in spite of that, everything that the murderer did in the room could have been done in well under two minutes!

Now that was rather peculiar. The murderer had four minutes at his disposal, and his best time for entering the house was when the maid was examining the parcel. Her attention would then be attracted away from hall and dining-room for an absolute certainty. But if he spent only one minute in the room where he did the murder then he must have waited three minutes before entering the house; surely a dangerous proceeding and one that cut very short his four-minute allowance! Again, if only half a minute elapsed from the time when the maid heard the "cough" to her arrival in the kitchen, he must have made such a quick get-away that he could scarcely have done it noiselessly. Surely the maid must have heard some noise as she flew down the stairs.

Well, that was argued this way and that and no satisfactory answer found. As fast as a reason was given, just so speedily was it proved perfectly unsound.

"What about that theory I put forward, gentlemen?" asked Eaton. "If he didn't leave by the front door a good many things would be explained: why the parcel was addressed to No. 129, for example. Not only that, but it would account for all the time he spent in the room. Before he could leave it and before he telephoned he had to make his arrangements for getting out."

"I admit it sounds all right," said Scott, "but will it work? At any rate we'll soon see."

But there wasn't much seeing to be done. Every window was right and tight. Each one was opened, and it and its shutters were found in perfect order. Each door had been fastened, and as ceiling and floor were both normal and the chimney was out of the question, Eaton's theory hardly seemed workable.

"I'd rather like to ask a question," said Travers. "This type of shutter is, I believe, not uncommon abroad, but I don't recall having run across it in England before. Surely it would be more sensible for the shutters to be operated from the inside and to act as blinds? You see the inconvenience. Before they can be shut at night you have to go outside, whatever the weather, to release the hooks that hold them against the wall."

"That's true enough," replied Scott. "But then, this is an oldish house. It's often easier to put up with things than have the inconvenience of alteration."

"And," remarked Sir George, "the inconvenience would not be brought much to the notice of the owner. It would be more the concern of the one whose duty it was to shut them."

"And if I might point it out," said Eaton, "they have their uses. Rain can't cut in between exposed sashes as it often does with uncovered windows. Also, if they were inside, they'd surely be a bit of a disfigurement."

"I'm sorry," said Travers. "It just occurred to me, that's all."

"There's nothing to be sorry about, sir," said Scott with absolute sincerity. "It was an excellent suggestion, and we can do at the moment with every idea we can get hold of. Still, here are the shutters and here are we. If he got out other than by the door, where he went we can go, too."

"And of course," observed Sir George, "the same problems apply to any confederate who might have been employed by Adams or Cardon."

"Quite so. The only thing is that Adams might have told a lie and really did see the murderer leave. But we've got *her* where we want her."

They stood irresolute for a moment; then Scott pulled out his watch. "Hm! Well past one. I don't know what you think about it, gentlemen, but I'm proposing to sleep on it."

"I don't think you can do better," said Sir George. "In the very rare chance of your wanting me I shall be at St. James's Square."

Veer went with them as far as Kentish Town. But while Eaton was making a temporary bed in the sitting-room, Scott was making a fresh start. Over a breakfast cup of tea and a pipe he was getting ready for the moves that must come next. From the bookcase in the dining-room he fetched a handy Bradshaw, and this he consulted frequently. What he achieved in an hour seemed a poor return.

5.30 Eaton. Breakfast.
6.00 Adams.
7.00 Cardon. All details of year.
8.00 Eaton Little Martens and Norwich.
9.00 Yard. Wharton. Enfield.
N. B. Boat train? Dossiers of Adams, Cardon and T. T. R. See Orwell.

When Scott, in his improvised bed of easy chairs, had finally curled his borrowed eiderdown around him, it was getting on for 3.00 p. m. Outside the wind had risen, and the rain lashed steadily against the front, unshuttered panes.

CHAPTER VII
THE BABES IN THE WOOD

(A)

UP IN THE main restaurant of Durango House Ludovic Travers had just finished his soufflé and was sitting, hands on chin, thinking about shutters and letters, when the waitress brought him a note.

"Can you spare a minute?
"F. W."

Sir Francis was as usual at his round table in the north corner, with a waitress standing by.

"Morning, Travers. Hope you don't mind. Have a coffee? Two black coffees, then!" And when the waitress had gone, "I was right about the black?"

"Quite right, Sir Francis. You don't mind my pipe?"

"Not at all. I was just going to have one myself. What I wanted to ask you was this. I know you're extremely busy at the moment, but a couple of minutes will tell me what I want. I was looking this morning at the prospectus of Britannia Films Ltd. What's your opinion?"

The other confirmed the one lump in his coffee and in the moment's respite collected his thoughts.

"The position is rather complex, in my opinion, Sir Francis. After all, everything depends on what they do and how they do it. Their programme as announced seems conservative and reasonably popular. The 20 per cent, proportion of British film lengths will soon be in operation and both Australia and Canada have preferential tariffs. The managing directors are shrewd men—you know what they made of Paliceums—but, then, on the other hand, their production manager and supervisor is American in experience and background."

"You mean exactly?"

"Perhaps I'm not sufficiently clear. What I mean, Sir Francis, is that if their productions are genuinely British in atmosphere and setting and—er—feeling, then the colonial market should more than absorb their output. The Company is under good auspices and seems to have excellent possibilities. Speculatively it would rather attract me."

"Well, that's clear enough. Between ourselves and the department we've been sounded about taking over their publicity work."

The other expressed polite surprise and gratification.

Sir Francis finished his coffee. "By the way, I saw your uncle this morning on a matter of business. He was not—what shall I call it?—very avuncular. He didn't ask after your well-being."

Travers made a grimace. "For a very good reason. I didn't leave him till two this morning!"

The smile on the other's face faded into surprise. "You were with him all last night?"

"Of course, it was all pure luck. I was rather interested in that 'Marius' case and happened to be in the right place at the right time. Scott—Chief-Constable Scott—and I are fairly old friends, and he helped to work the oracle."

"That's really most interesting!" He looked down and nodded abstractedly. Then he looked up quickly. "I wonder if, without divulging any secrets, you would like to lend somebody a helping hand?"

Travers was a bit taken aback. "Well—er—I think perhaps I would. I haven't done my good deed for the day."

"Between ourselves, it will do me a good turn at the same time. As Chief Commissioner, Sir George has arranged permission for Franklin—you remember, he was at the 'Marius' conference—to go over the scene of last night's murder. Now, I wonder, if I sent him along, whether you'd mind having a word with him before he went?"

"Not at all," replied the other, "but I'm afraid I shall be rather out of my depth."

But Sir Francis knew his listener. Like many others, he had once been inclined to regard Travers as a bit of an original, an eccentric; brilliant in his particular line, but after that—! Then at all sorts of odd times he had noticed other things: unconventionality that was no pose, a catholicity and sympathy of ideas, a shrewdness of observation that nearly always hit the nail on the head, and a strain of boyishness that was unaffected and appealing.

As for Franklin, making his way towards the financial department, he too was disposed to regard the private room of Ludovic Travers as an investigatory *cul de sac*. He knew the famous *Economics of a Spendthrift* and had considerable admiration for its author, but in the bespectacled intellectual who had been on his side in that somewhat humorous "Marius" conference he had precious little interest and still less hope.

Travers welcomed him with that engaging smile of his. He could see that his visitor was not quite at ease and groping, as it were, for a conversational opening.

"And how's the new department going?"

"It's rather hard to say," replied Franklin, somewhat stiffly; "we've scarcely had time to settle down."

"I suppose that is so," said Travers and tried another tack.

"Sir Francis suggested you'd be interested in that deplorable affair of last night. I assured him I shouldn't be much use to you, but all the same I'll do my best. Of course, there'll have to be the one proviso that I can give only my own impressions."

"How did the work of the Yard strike you, Mr. Travers?" asked the other, point-blank.

"Er—well—I take it you've seen the midday papers. If you have I should say they underestimate the work Scotland Yard did and underestimate it pretty badly."

"I'm glad to hear you say that," said Franklin. "The Yard rarely gets the credit it deserves."

It was delightfully droll to see the pair of them, both being suavely courteous and punctiliously stilted. Then Travers sensed that things had better be livened up.

"Tell me," he said, "did you ever know a *published* Scotland Yard case of the detective novel type; solved, shall we say, from anything except a material clue?"

Franklin looked puzzled. "I don't know that I remember one on the spur of the moment."

"Well, it looks then as if this one is going to create a precedent. It has every appearance of becoming a case for Lecoq. What's your opinion of Lecoq, Mr. Franklin?"

"Lecoq? Well, he always appeals to me as the most human and credible of the storybook detectives."

"I haven't your judgment, but I'm perfectly in agreement. Still, I'll tell you all I dare about it," and he ran rapidly through the evening and its problems. "What time were you thinking of getting there?" he asked when the quick recital was finished.

Franklin consulted his watch. "I'm in no great hurry. Somewhere about half-past two, I thought."

The other drew himself up from his reclining position and sat with pipe in hand, arms resting on his knees. There was a whimsical look on his face.

"You mustn't mind me in the least, but I'm going to say something curious and I'd rather like you to understand my point of view. Also, if you think I'm a fool, I'd like you to say so without any reservations." He paused to let that sink in while he relighted his pipe. Franklin hardly knew how to take him. He shot a look at the speaker, smiled, and said nothing.

"Now I've told you a lot of what happened last night but I couldn't tell you what other people thought. If I told you what *I* thought you'd probably wonder what qualifications I had to think at all—that is to say about murder problems. But for all that, are you prepared to throw in an extra minute or two on the chance of a gamble?"

Franklin was intrigued. He was beginning to find a strange charm about this "bespectacled intellectual," and in any case the conversation was vastly different from anything he could possibly have imagined.

"I shall be only too pleased, Mr. Travers."

"Do you know, I'm chattering an awful lot. It's really unpardonable of me."

"Not at all. Please go on, Mr. Travers."

"Well, we'll be a pair of fools together. This case has interested me ever since that conference we had the other day, and I intended by hook or crook to be at the show if there were one. I can see no other reason why but because, perhaps, of my civilian simplicity of outlook I saw one or two things in a different way from other people. What I'm anxious to know is whether my intuitions were correct. Could you come round to my flat—14c St. Martin's Chambers—say at about 7.30 to-night? Ring up my man if you can't manage it after all."

"I'll be there," said Franklin.

"Good! I won't go into details now, but if you don't mind I'll write down a couple of problems for you."

And this is what they were—

(a) You are Sherlock Holmes. In a dead man's pocket you find a letter (no envelope) which has been in that pocket and read frequently for ten days. Calculate the wear marks, assuming the paper to be good quality, hotel parchment.

(b) Take three yards of fine cord and get out of a shuttered, fastened window, and then fasten everything from the outside.

"In a bracket I've written 'Mrs. Cardon'," said Travers. "If you can get from her a list of visitors to the house during the last few months you'll have done some good work, in my opinion."

He rose to his feet. "Do you know, I feel perfectly ashamed of myself. But do you ever have intuitions? Cross-word puzzle ones?"

Franklin smiled. "Sometimes."

"Then you know what intuitions are. I've an aunt who'd never believe it if some scandalmonger told her I could do long tots, but if she said to me, 'What's a theological treatise in nine letters?' and I replied, 'Upanishad,' she'd tell everybody how clever I was. Well, it's the way of the world. At 7.30, then. 14c St. Martin's Chambers. Good-bye."

And he showed a rather bewildered Franklin out of the room. But as soon as the door was shut the first thing he did was to give a whistle, rather a dolorous affair that sounded like a reproach. Then he contemplated his pipe for a second or two and slowly relighted it.

(B)

As the lift decanted Franklin on the Axminster carpet before the door of No. 14c, he felt by no means happy about the lounge suit he was wearing. As Palmer, Travers's man, ushered him into the dining-room and he took a hasty view he was decidedly nervous. But it lasted no longer than a sight of his host. If suede slippers, a flannel cricket shirt, a blue blazer, and grey trousers are not a sufficiently reassuring garb, one would be hard to please.

"I thought we'd stay here, if you don't mind," explained Travers. "I've got a job of work later. We're having the service dinner; neat but not gaudy."

After the meal they adjourned to the library, where in the middle of a veritable lining of books and filing cabinets they settled down before a glowing fire.

"You've got a wonderful place here," commented Franklin. "It takes my breath away."

"Easy enough when you happen to own the lot," said Travers. "Thanks to a fortunate choice of ancestors I didn't have to toil or spin. Now, then; you were going to tell me all about Mrs. Cardon. How did you get on with her?"

Franklin's gesture expressed his opinion of that lady. "A tough proposition, if you like! And she'd had a drink or two."

"The maid had gone?"

"Oh, yes; she'd gone right enough. Scott is doubtless keeping a fatherly eye on her, and she'll have to be at the inquest to-morrow, in any case. Of course, I saw the papers, and I also got a good deal of information at the Yard this morning about that couple."

"An interesting pair!"

"Yes, and it was rather funny you should have mentioned the maid, because that started me off right. There were a couple of men on guard when I got there. Mrs. Cardon let me in with a supercilious air and kept on trying to be what she imagined was high-toned; supposed I'd come from the police and wouldn't believe me when I said I'd nothing to do with them. Then I said I wouldn't dream of troubling her but could I look round, and the maid could keep an eye on me. Then she started cussing maids in general, and I chipped in and cussed some more, and before I hardly knew it I was facing the good lady in the parlour, as she called it; both of us in easy chairs and full of gin and geniality. Then she supposed I'd come about the will, and I said I thought there was something fishy about that business. Then you ought to have heard her! Phew! This time it was the nephews."

"You got what might be called the real dope?"

"I reckon I did. I think that woman told me every detail of the last few months; a lot of lies, of course, but the devil of a lot of truth. By the way, before I forget it. I don't know if you realised—I didn't from the press accounts—but Richleigh was remarkably bad on his feet. That's why he never went out. When he went to Tottenham he always had a closed car from door to door."

"That's news to me. I imagined him as fairly hale and hearty!"

"Well, I don't know what difference it will make, but it's correct. However, to go on. I got all the visitors from her. There was no need to cross-examine. She talked, and all I had to do was direct the traffic. The times are approximate, and I also got their addresses or how to find them.

"HAROLD RICHLEIGH. He's an actor. Called third week in September at supper time, Thursday night, as Mrs. C. was out. Wanted to borrow some money, had some high words and cleared off in a rage without waiting to be shown out. Mrs. C. got her information from Adams and Richleigh.

"FRANK RICHLEIGH. That's the schoolmaster. Called following week early; Tuesday probably. Brought a bottle of old port. Very sociable and played three-handed cribbage. 'Too much of the lah-di-dah for me,' was Mrs. C.'s opinion of him.

"REV. CHARLES RICHLEIGH. That's the parson at Little Martens. Called about three on the following Thursday, just as Mrs. C. was dressing. Only a courtesy visit, as he happened to be calling on an old colleague nearby. Had some tea, however. All 'Our heavenly Father' and 'My good woman,' according to Mrs. C., who hasn't any use for him at all.

"ERNEST RICHLEIGH. That's the lawyer, and him you've heard about."

"And that's all the visitors?"

"Absolutely all. Except the maids and the housekeeper, not a soul has been inside that house for months."

"It's too easy," said Travers. "And what about the problems?"

Franklin smiled. "I think one's all right; the other I'm not so sure about. With regard to the letter, if the paper were stiffish parchment, and even if it were read every few hours, it still ought to be reasonably clean. A bit grubby at the edges, perhaps, but a lot would depend on the state of the pocket, the other contents, and the occupations and habits of the reader."

"Let me butt in," said Travers. "The letter in question was in Richleigh's pocket with other papers, all fairly clean and one at least more than a month old. I should say he was a man of fastidious personal cleanliness, and for another thing, he was in a species of love. This letter, supposed to be from a nephew—the one mentioned in the press and with whom the police are anxious to get into contact—was not grubby; it was filthy. Where it was folded it had cracked. And something else."

He took a sheet of paper from the Queen Anne bureau. "I wonder if you'd mind putting this in my pocket; the breast pocket. First of all, however, smear your finger tips with some of this charcoal."

When the operation was finished he took another sheet and folded it. "Now smear your fingers again, and this time put it in your own pocket and without thinking what you are doing. Good! Now let's have a look at the two sheets."

The difference was plainly to be seen. In the first case the paper had been held stiffly and the prints were clear. In the second, the fingers had shifted and the prints were blurred.

"You can try it over by yourself," said Travers, "and you'll find it comes right every time. Palmer and I tried it out several times before you arrived. Now, if you take the facts about the letter found in Richleigh's pocket, its dirty condition and the clear marks, you may possibly think, as I do, that the letter was purposely carried in the murderer's pocket and made artificially dirty. Then, after the murder, Richleigh's finger and thumb were made to grip it and place it in his own pocket where the police would find it."

"By Jove!" exclaimed Franklin. "Also that would account for the length of time the murderer spent in the room."

"Partly. There remains the window. How did you get on with that?"

"Oh, that was easy!" said Franklin.

"Well, here's a lump of string. Let's go down and try it. In George the porter's pantry there's a capital double-hung sash window of the very type, and it's only a foot from the ground."

So down the lift they went. George grinned and touched his hat as by evident prearrangement he showed them into his cubbyhole, fuggy as a dug-out and chock-a-block with the weirdest collection of impedimenta.

"We've got a bet on, George," explained Travers. "This young lad has got an idea he can get out of your window and leave it shut after him. What's your idea?"

"And fasten the catch, sir?"

"Oh, rather! You see, George, safety catches were first invented to stop people getting *into* rooms, that's why the majority of us, excepting Mr. Franklin here, lose sight of the question of getting *out*. However, out he's going to get, and in such a way that you'd never guess he'd been in."

"Well, good luck to him, sir," said George, and, "Half a mo', sir, before you start," and he cleared the sill of its miscellaneous litter.

Franklin certainly made a good job of it. He folded the six foot of string and put it round the catch, ends outwards. These he put behind the slot and then through it to face the audience. Next he raised the sash and pushed the loose ends between the sashes so that they hung down outside the room. He crawled out under the bottom sash and, when outside, put the sashes again in position. A firm tug on the ends of the string, with knees braced against the wall, and the catch was levered into the slot. Another firm pull on one string only, and the whole six feet of string was drawn outside. The last operation, however, was apt to fray the string, owing to the tightness of the sashes.

The other two examined the catch. It was not quite home admittedly, but to all intents and purposes the window was fastened.

"Well, I'm damned, sir!" said George. "Whoever'd 'a' thought it?" And when he'd received his tip and the others had departed he was still a trifle incredulous.

"Of course, it's difficult with well-fitting sashes and stiff catches," said Franklin. "Those at The Grove are very loose; what you'd expect in an oldish house. What did you think of for the shutters? Knife?"

"That's it. First close the shutter which has the slot. Then put the heavy hasp of the other in position and while you close the shutter keep it there with a knife blade. Just as the shutter closes, pull away the knife and down goes the hasp into the slot by its own weight."

"Now we might see where we've got to," said Travers when they were once more before the fire. "Still, we'd better have a drink first," and he pushed the bell. Two minutes later they got down to it again.

"If all the suppositions are correct," said Franklin, "we've done ourselves a good turn. We've eliminated the South African nephew and all question of a confederate. That means a long start on the Yard. They'll put the maid and the housekeeper on the grill again and exhaust that letter clue."

"One peculiar thing did occur to me about that exit by the window," said Travers. "The murderer was careful how he got into the room, but he took his time about getting out. Perhaps I don't make myself clear, but what I mean is, you expect a murderer to be anxious about a quick getaway, not an elaborate one."

Franklin took out his notebook. "I made some notes on that as soon as I worked out your window problem. The main deductions are these:

(a) He was sure he wouldn't be seen entering, and by leaving by the window he did what seems to be a spectacular and wholly unnecessary thing, and for the sole reason that it mattered more about his being seen when he left than when he entered.

(b) Therefore, he was somebody who would not have called any particular attention to himself had he been seen entering. He could probably have given some excuse and then, presumably, could not have committed the murder. The "Marius" letters would then have turned out to be a damp squib.

(c) He must therefore have been somebody whom the maid could have identified. Therefore he must have been somebody with whom she had come into contact during her short period of service at the house.

(d) Why then did he not disguise himself? The answers seem to be:

(1) Because he couldn't conceal certain physical defects or deformities.

(2) Because he couldn't have got rid of the disguise, for some reason or other, sufficiently soon after the murder.

"Now, then," he went on; "when you add to these suppositions the facts that the murderer knew the house well, that he was a person of considerable education, and that he claimed to have a sound motive, what need is there to go beyond the four nephews?"

"The motive of course being the keeping of the money in the family."

"That's it; and the fact that the deceased was a pretty disreputable specimen who might have smirched the family name rather badly."

"But what of the caller of the Wednesday night? South African nephew or not, he's a flesh-and-blood person."

"I'm going to see Adams about her account of him. But assuming that one of the four did it and laid the false trail, why shouldn't he have been the caller—in disguise, of course? I admit that for that purpose he would have had to stay at the hotel as T. W. Richards—at least, that's a possible theory. That I can go into at once."

"How will you tackle the alibis?"

"I shan't. What I'm proposing to do is to rely on the Yard. If there's one thing we can be certain of it is that the Yard will turn these alibis inside out, and if they pass them as correct then it's as sure as anything on God's green earth that correct they are. I've got hold of the information, by the way, that Superintendent Wharton is taking over the case. He's a first-class man, and I owe him more than I could ever state. I believe he's actually gone to France already about one alibi. Also I rather suspect that Eaton, whom you mentioned, is doing at least one other. He and I have done each other a good turn or two in our time, and I ought to know all about those alibis pretty soon. Also, if the Yard haven't tumbled to it already, I might exchange that information about the window for what I wanted to know."

"There is just one thing that occurs to me," said Travers. "If the case merely depends on the alibis of the four nephews it isn't going to be the Perfect Murder. And when you get a man of education like Marius stating implicitly that he doesn't see how he can be caught, well, the two aspects are rather at variance."

"We shall have to wait and see if Marius always spoke the truth. By the way, why the 'Marius'? Is there any clue in that?"

"As far as I remember," said Travers, "Marius was a bloodthirsty old Roman who once remarked that the state would be all the better for a little bloodletting. This Marius is apparently of the same opinion. What are you going to do to-morrow?"

"Find out about the alibis, if I can. After that it all depends. Marius is only human, and he must have made a slip, for all his boasting. It's up to us to find that slip."

Travers smiled. "It's good of you to say 'we,' but I'm afraid it's your show. Seriously, what can I do?"

"That remains to be seen. Go on as you've started and we'll set Durangos alight."

"God forbid!" said Travers hastily. "But there is one thing I can do. If you want a home from home, come up here and do as you like."

Franklin had started to express his thanks, but he was too late. Travers had pushed the bell, and Palmer had appeared with the celerity of a genie.

"Oh, Palmer; whenever Mr. Franklin comes along, look after him and see that he has everything he wants."

"You *will* keep me informed?" he asked as they stood in the corridor waiting for the lift.

"You needn't worry about that," said Franklin warmly.

"Good! And just one thing. It's easy to give advice, but don't let this case worry you. Cheek on my part, I admit. What's mostly curiosity on my part is damned hard work for you and the devil of a lot of responsibility. Still, I've got another intuition. You're going to work wonders in this case. I know it."

Franklin looked like a man who has done the first nine holes well under bogey. "Good-night, Mr. Travers. You don't know how—"

And he didn't; for at the first symptom of gratitude Travers had fled.

CHAPTER VIII
THE NET IS SPREAD

(A)

Now, of course all this was perfectly preposterous. What precisely Franklin thought about it the following morning is hard to say. In any case, he was at the mercy of chance, and for him one gamble was as good as another. But when Ludovic Travers came to survey it in the cool air of reason after a seven hours' sleep he was forced to smile at himself. As he had felt at the time, it was all too easy. Scott had probably been laughing up his sleeve when he handed over that Constable Hotel letter, and Eaton must have tumbled to the fact that to get out of that room was ingenious but easy. He had most likely thought it a trifle that could be settled by a minute or two's reflection. Either that or the pair of them, friendly enough out of harness, had seen no necessity to give information and disclose methods to an outsider and a dilettante at that.

But whatever the cause there was something in the morning's judgment that was much at variance with the evening's optimism and its *couleur de rose*. Things reassumed a right perspective. The inefficient or unseeing of Scotland Yard became once more the inevitable, the majestic, the far-seeing forces of law and order. And just what had those forces been doing in the last twenty-four hours?

Chief-Constable Scott, with a self-operating alarum as good as Napoleon's, had woke up just after five. He brewed a pot of tea and made a slab or two of toast before arousing Eaton. Then Adams was called, and by the time the breakfast was over she made an appearance, once more in the pathetic rôle which seemed her chosen lead. But Scott's questioning had no effect on her story of the previous night. She stuck to it, and nothing could prise her loose. She admitted, however, having read the "Marius" letters and discussed them with Mrs. Cardon; an interesting insight into two hostile minds and what had constituted a ground of common interest.

Mrs. Cardon descended with the obvious idea of ingratiating herself with authority and was much less difficult. She gave a history of all visitors—much the same as she gave later to Franklin—and a comprehensive account of his nephews. But though she stood by the deceased in determined fashion it was not difficult to judge that her views would undergo considerable alteration when she discovered that there really was no will. The information supplied was of no great value; it was too discursive, too prejudiced, and too unsubstantiated. She admitted discussing the "Marius" letters with Adams, but neither of them had for a moment imagined they were ever likely to be concerned.

By this time the finger-print experts had arrived for a final look round by daylight. Meanwhile there followed for Scott a certain amount of telephoning. The whereabouts of Harold Richleigh, which overnight had been discovered to be Norwich, had made possible the killing of two birds with one stone. Eaton left for Liverpool Street, and then, by the light of a sunny dawn, Scott surveyed for himself the scene of the murder and found nothing new. When Orwell arrived he arranged for the departure of the maid, her attendance at the inquest, and the isolation of the house. Then there had to be the examination of the chauffeur who last drove Richleigh to Tottenham. Moreover, every scrap of local gossip had to be brought in and sifted, and Steward was once more to be questioned.

Leaving this legacy behind him, Scott left for the Yard. Here he got Superintendent Wharton's account of the Constable Hotel end of the business and compared the signature of T. W. Richards with the T. W. R. of the letter. The following was further decided on. Wharton was to leave for France by the boat train in order to examine Frank Richleigh's alibi. According to his brother, he was tramping the Aude Valley—the nearest address he could give—and was due at Quillan by the following day to receive the posted brushes. Before his departure for France Wharton would arrange inquiries into the dossiers of Adams, Cardon, and the deceased and see to the continuance of the search for the South African nephew. It was recognised that Wharton himself should take the case over. In the meantime Burren should be given all necessary information and proceed to Enfield for a further interview with Ernest Richleigh, while Scott acted as clearing house till the superintendent's return.

To confine ourselves then to the new and immediate drama—the alibis of the four nephews—and to follow up this drama chronologically, it would be as well to begin with the statement of Mr. Ernest Richleigh as given by him to Chief-Inspector Burren.

The Rev. Peter Richleigh of Little Martens, Suffolk, had three sons. The living was a good one and the further possession of a private income enabled him to send two of these sons to Cambridge. Of these two, Thomas turned out a bad egg; his sending down was over a particularly disreputable piece of business. He had then been lost sight of for many years, and what he had done in the interval nobody knew. Ultimately he had reappeared as the proprietor of a billiard hall in Tottenham in partnership with a man named Lewin. Next had come some bother over a fire, but the Company had settled and with his share of the proceeds Thomas Richleigh had acquired a hairdresser's shop. The shingling craze did him the best possible turn. He acquired another shop, "Mariette" by name, and both concerns were in the nature of little gold mines.

The second son, Charles, took orders and at his father's death succeeded to the living. He had four sons, the four nephews in question, and of these more will be said. It should be mentioned, however, that on his early death his son Charles succeeded in his turn to the living.

The third son, Peter, ran away from school and after an adventurous early manhood finally settled in South Africa, where he made good as the proprietor of a general store in Cape Town. From time to time he communicated with his brother Charles—for Thomas he always had a peculiar antipathy—and on his death with his nephew, the new vicar. After the war, however, he realised his property and returned to England, where Ernest Richleigh advised him in most of his reinvestments. At first he made his home at Little Martens, and as to the final disposal of his money, he made no secret of it at all. Charles, his favourite, was specially mentioned, but each of the nephews was well looked after.

Then something happened. It was felt that the estrangement of the two brothers was, at their time of life, at the best a pathetic and unnecessary business. In the bringing together of the two Ernest, as the legal adviser of both, acted as go-between. The brothers met, and Peter went to the Grove for a short visit. This first became lengthy and then apparently permanent. Moreover, Peter Richleigh changed in an amazing way. Considering the old bachelor he was, he had been a cheerful and even genial companion at Little Martens. Now he cut his nephews dead. The letters ceased, and those from Charles were unanswered. He refused to see Ernest, and when in 1921 he fell from the second landing of No. 122 and injured himself so badly that he died a few minutes later, it was found that a will drawn up a week previously by a local solicitor had left all his property unconditionally to his brother Thomas.

Thereafter Ernest had for some time refused to act for his uncle, but later he had resumed his former relationship feeling that the least he owed to his brothers was to keep an eye on their interests. From time to time, however, Thomas had done his best to set the four by the ears. He had tried policies of isolation and ingratiation, but with poor success. Ernest confessed, however, that when he set himself to it, his uncle could be an entertaining character. Further, he was head of the family, whatever else he was. Add the passing of time which cures most ills, and you will understand why from time to time the nephews called on him and were in varying degrees of friendship, if not affection. Besides all this, as Ernest frankly owned, human nature is what it is. Thomas Richleigh received £30,000 from his brother's estate and from all sources his income was not less than £2,500 a year. One can forgive much for that!

About the dead man and his doings the lawyer was very frank. He was mean to a degree, and yet with eccentric variations. For his guest at cribbage he would put out choice of gin, whisky, or port, and yet cheat flagrantly for the possible gain of a few coppers. A letter to the press about local tradesmen got him into hot water from which his nephew dragged him with difficulty. He was fined for abusive and blasphemous language directed at the local Salvation Army who had disturbed his Sunday sleep. He got himself into trouble with the housekeeper who preceded Mrs. Cardon, and, the affair not only cost him several hundred pounds, but still persisted in the form of an allowance to mother and child. Mrs. Cardon had changed, or concentrated in herself, those tendencies, and for some years there had been no open scandal. But Burren guessed how the new domestic arrangement must have been watched by the nephews and by Ernest in particular.

As for the four nephews, their history was briefly this: Ernest, now forty-seven years of age, was senior partner in the firm he had entered as a boy, thanks to the interest taken in him by an old friend of the family. He was, *inter alia,* a churchwarden, captain of Muffley Hill Golf Club, president of the local Rose Society and—an O. B. E.

Charles, aged forty-five, had led a life so uneventful and blameless that nothing could be said about him. He was, however, a cricketer of note and still wielded a stout bat. He was a magistrate and married, his two daughters being at Cheltenham.

Harold was the adventurous outcrop, a cross between his two uncles. He too had quitted the job found for him—a bank in Ipswich—for something more romantic, the stage. The worst that could be said against him was that he was generous to a fault and had no enemy except himself. He had at first done well, and the critics had noticed him. Then his wife died, and his descent was rapid. Drink had helped, and the rut in which after a few years he found himself was one from which there was, for one of his temperament, no chance of escape. From time to time his brothers helped him financially. At the moment he was playing unimportant parts for Rupert Pyne's No. 3 Company, then in Norwich, and whose repertoire was principally Shakespearean.

Frank Richleigh, then thirty-seven, had had a far from brilliant career at Cambridge. He had at first found a job with a private school at Eastbourne where his cricket was his soundest qualification. From there he went to one or two old-established country grammar schools, and finally to Muffley Hill, where he taught some mathematics and a little geography. At the moment he was enjoying a grace term in recognition of his ten years' work. He was said to be a man of brilliant but eccentric intellect, and his hobby was sketching. He had exhibited several times at the shows of the New English Group. In the war he had had a good record of service in Gallipoli and Egypt, but his health was not good, and he invariably spent his winter holidays on the south coast.

Three things remain to be stated. Ernest Richleigh had read and discussed the "Marius" letters, but he had never taken them seriously. Secondly, his alibi, as Inspector Veer had hinted, was foolproof. He was not a frequenter of the cinema, but on this occasion he had accompanied his wife and daughter to the Rialto, Enfield, where immediately on its general release there was being shown the super-film, *Paradise Lost*, a picture that had broken all records at the Pantheon, London. He had arrived at 6.00 p. m. and in front of his party had discovered a friend, the curate of St. Ethelbald's, with whom he exchanged criticisms during the performance.

Lastly there emerged what Burren considered more than a suspicion. It looked exceedingly likely that there had been between the four brothers some sort of an understanding; a league, as it were, of defence. Whether that league had gone so far as to contemplate a division of Thomas Richleigh's money, whichever of them got it, was mere conjecture. But in Burren's mind was the vague feeling that all was not what it appeared on the surface and that churchwardens and standers in high places were intensely human and touched with the same frailties that are more generally assumed to beset only their weaker brethren.

(B)

Travelling by Ipswich and Haughley, Detective Inspector Eaton arrived at Bury St. Edmunds before 11 a. m. A taxi from the station yard landed him in Little Martens in another quarter of an hour, and as by an odd coincidence the driver was a native of that village, by the end of the short journey Eaton's knowledge of the Richleigh family, and of the present incumbent in particular, was considerably augmented.

Leaving the car to wait beyond the gate, Eaton made his way over the gravel drive to the front porch of the creeper-clad and rambling vicarage. The first thing that caught his eye was the shutters, hung back by their hooks from the south windows. He studied them for a second or two, then rapped at the door.

"Mr. Richleigh in?"

"Yes, sir," and the maid drew back to admit him. But the caller advanced to the threshold and no further.

"I wanted to see him last night, but I was told he was out."

The maid looked surprised. "Oh, no, sir! Mr. Richleigh was in all the night."

"Now I wonder how they came to make that mistake," said Eaton and stepped into the hall. "No name. Just say it's very important."

The room into which he was admitted had its fellow in hundreds of villages. The vicar, too, was of no unexpected type. He was clean-shaved, plump, of medium height, slightly fussy, and wholly clerical. His smile was dental, conventional, vicarial, and somehow condescending. His voice was reminiscent of visiting days, and his consonants clear cut as facets. His proffered hand drooped effeminately.

"How do you do, er—"

"I'm Detective-Inspector Eaton of the Criminal Investigation Department," said the other.

The vicar looked rather helpless.

"I take it, sir, you've not seen the papers this morning?"

"I'm afraid I haven't. You see they come by bicycle, and we don't get them till noon."

"Then I'm sorry to say, sir, I've some bad news for you." He saw the other's face start in alarm and added hastily, "Your uncle, Thomas Richleigh, has died suddenly." He noted the relief and went further. "He was murdered last night."

"No, never!" The vicar was genuinely distressed, and his vocabulary failed him badly. But he remembered his position. "Sit down, inspector. I am, as you may know, a magistrate, and, er—"

"I understand that, sir, and know you'll do all you can to help," and in as brief a time as possible he gave a comprehensive account of the happenings of the previous evening.

"Terrible! Terrible!" moaned the vicar. "I think I ought to go to town at once to see my brother."

"That's for you to say, sir. I told you what we got from Mr. Ernest Richleigh. The inquest's to-morrow, by the way," and he rose as if to go.

"You'll take some refreshments? A glass of wine and a biscuit?"

The detective glanced at his watch. "Well, that's very good of you, sir. Perhaps I will."

So the bell cord was pulled. As the maid entered, the vicar gave an exaggerated frown to caution silence, and when she had finally gone, "Shouldn't like this to get about, Mr. Eaton."

"There's just two things you can help us in, sir. Did you read those extraordinary 'Marius' letters in the press?"

"Well—er—I did see them. I didn't consider them as things of which undue notice should be taken."

"Well, sir, when 'Marius' talked about committing a Perfect Murder this is the one he meant. It was he who murdered your uncle!"

This was a shock. The look on the vicar's face was indignation, incomprehension, and even alarm.

"Do you know of any enemy of your uncle who might have committed such a crime?"

The vicar shook his head helplessly. "I can think of nobody. He was a man of very material passions; a gross man in many ways. We are not all cast in the same mould."

"That's true enough, sir." He finished his glass and again rose. "Just one other thing, sir, and as a matter of pure routine. As a magistrate you will realise the importance of the question and, in your own case, its pure formality. The time of the murder was, as I told you, 7.30 p. m. You, I imagine, were in the house here all the evening."

The vicar flashed a look from under his eyebrows which told of the struggle between outraged dignity and the whole duty of magistrates. His voice had in it just the exact formality and reproof which the question demanded.

"I always compose my sermons on Thursday evenings. Mrs. Richleigh was with me as usual during their composition."

"Thank you, sir. A pure formality, as you recognised." Then his eyes wandered to the windows. "By the way, I couldn't help noticing your shutters as I came by. Just like a policeman to notice things like that. Not much protection against burglars?"

The vicar's reply was conclusive. "We are not troubled by burglars in this part of the world."

"Well, you're lucky, sir," was Eaton's reply as he made his final exit. Two minutes later he was on his way back to the station and listening to the chatter of the driver.

"Yes, sir; I've seen the parson whatcher call knockin' 'em about. His old father was a rare good cricketer too."

"Well, you wouldn't think it to look at him," was Eaton's comment on the son. Then drawing a bow at a venture, "Wasn't Mr. Richleigh in Bury yesterday?"

"I didn't see nothin' on 'im, sir. He allust put up at the Griffin when he do come in."

"That reminds me," said Eaton, with another glance at his watch. "I've got to see a man at the Griffin." And hazarding a guess as to its locality, "You might pull up there, will you?"

Luck was with him. The vicar *had* been in the town the previous day. Where he had been did not matter; the certain and undeniable thing was that the ostler had put his pony in the trap and he had left at 5.30 p. m. So much for the alibi. With two minutes to spare Eaton caught the local to Thetford and an hour and a half later was in Norwich.

(C)

Having made his report to the Yard as arranged beforehand Eaton got from the station sergeant his bearings for the Classic Theatre. In five minutes he was before the door of that dingy haven of the classics. The large bills attracted him with their notices of the repertory programme and the names of the company in letters proportionate to the size of their salary. The previous day had been early closing; with a consequent matinée—*Twelfth Night*—and in the evening had been *Macbeth*. The name of Harold Richleigh did not appear at all, nor was his photograph with the numerous others in the vestibule.

Eaton peered through the grille of the box-office. "Can you possibly tell me," he asked the "young lady" in charge, "where I can find Mr. Harold Richleigh?"

The novelette was put down gradually. "Mr. Harold Richleigh?"

"Yes. I wanted to see him last night, but I understood he wasn't playing."

She consulted a programme. "Oh, yes, he was. He was doing the murderer!"

"The devil he was!" began Eaton, and then caught the context. "I beg your pardon. I'm sorry to trouble you, but it's really most important."

She rose languidly and, having locked the entrance to her cage, found up the address. And at 73 Catlow Street an unmistakable landlady opened the door.

"Could I see Mr. Richleigh, please?"

The landlady gave him a shrewd look. "I'm sorry, but he's out."

"That's a pity. I really wanted him last night, but they said I shouldn't find him in."

"He was in till six and then again at eleven." Eaton's face expressed such intense disappointment that she gave some further help. "I expect you'll find him at the Dog and Pheasant. That's where they usually get to. He said he'd had some good news."

"Another dead end," thought Eaton and set off again. He found the hotel and with a sure knowledge of his man pushed open the door of the billiard room and entered. The air was dense with smoke, and by the light of the arcs at least a dozen men could be discerned. There was the noisy back-chat of hilarious and lubricated voices as the game of snooker concluded. Everybody seemed to be talking at once.

"As before for you, Tom?"

"I never thought he'd get that black!"

"Five Guinness's, George! No, make it six."

"Bring me a packet of Gold Flake!" and so on. Eaton followed the marker out of the room and then buttonholed him. "Just slip back and give Mr. Richleigh the tip he's wanted badly outside. Is there a private room here, by the way?"

But when he got Harold Richleigh to himself it was clear that the difficulty was not going to be to make him talk but to stop him. He had stopped sufficient drinks to make him eloquently benign and a lover of mankind—with one exception, his uncle. He was a man whose face told its own story, the one that Burren had heard. What he had once been could still be guessed, in spite of the boisterous vulgarity of his person. A family likeness could be discerned; the coarseness of the face could not conceal that.

The wheat of his communications, separated from the mound of chaff, was, however, a poor handful. He had seen the midday paper, and a damn good effort somebody had made of it. For tuppence he'd have done the job himself. That bitch of a housekeeper was the one to watch. The old swine had only got what was coming to him. People didn't fall downstairs by accident, and so on, *ad nauseam*.

Eaton couldn't follow all the allusions, but from the sum total he got an impression or two. But one fact was again clear, and the stage manager confirmed it. Harold Richleigh had played the first murderer in *Macbeth*. So much for the alibi.

That Eaton was depressed during the long homeward journey goes without saying. As far as he could judge, the four nephews were already eliminated and the case of the Perfect Murder was still to be begun. Where to begin it was the problem that occupied his mind. Admittedly it might not be his affair, he might be taken off the case altogether. But somebody would have a long row to hoe, and what was more, somebody was by no means unlikely to be asked soon by the one above him to show results. And as that badgered one would in his turn make demands, to put it charitably, on his subordinates, and they again on theirs, it seemed as if the Perfect Murder Case would be a memorable one for a good many.

"If ever I have a son," thought Eaton, "I'm damned if I call him 'Marius'!"

CHAPTER IX
THE FOURTH ALIBI

(A)

WHEN IN his earlier years Superintendent Wharton had satisfied himself that the man who could offer something extra would sooner or later get his chance and had followed a natural bent by specialising in French, he did himself a good turn. The chance came in the well-remembered Simone Case. His superiors were so impressed with the fact that he had repeated in the vernacular the long conversation between the brothers that he was thereafter a marked man. His French, it must be confessed, was fluent, his vocabulary adequate, and his accent not too insular. But that was all. He certainly could not think in it and it is doubtful if he could have sworn in it with any degree of fluency.

The journey to Toulouse was a good one, and in the slower parts of the final stages the time passed quickly enough; most of it in conversation with a delightful old gentleman who was going on by road to Foix the following day, and who recommended the Grand Hôtel des Pyrénées, where he himself was spending the night, as the only one in Quillan that was worth the name.

The hotel certainly looked comfortable enough. In the lobby a pleasant-faced woman of fifty greeted the other traveller with that welcome which the regular visitor deserves. "You have a room, madame?" inquired Wharton, his fellow traveller standing by ready to put in a good word if necessary.

"Why, yes. Monsieur desires it for how long?"

"My affairs are rather uncertain," replied Wharton diplomatically. "To-night and possibly to-morrow."

Madame's, *"Bien, monsieur!"* was as amiable as if he had said, "A month." She called, "Maximilien!" and when the general man appeared indicated the guest's bag and gave him his orders, all, however, in the patois of the district—as unintelligible to the Englishman as if it had been Chinese.

But when Wharton picked up the pen to sign the register and ran his eye down the names there stood out something that he hardly expected, at least so soon; the name "F. Richleigh" and the address, London.

"You have another Englishman here?" he observed to madame.

Madame leaned her plump elbows on the counter and discoursed at some length. The gentleman had arrived that afternoon by road, all dusty, pouf! like that. He was a real Englishman; the clothes, the boots, the pipe. He spoke very little, not like monsieur. Oh, yes; English were fairly frequent in that part. A table for two? Why, certainly it could be arranged. For monsieur, room No. 3 and dinner in a quarter of an hour.

He had a hasty clean-up and in ten minutes was sitting in the far corner of the lobby, well behind a copy of the *Journal.* In a few seconds he was rewarded. There came into the room what could have been only a fellow countryman, in tweed plus-fours and brogues and with that air of aloofest detachment which is always misinterpreted by the foreigner. He had a likable face, tanned by weather and full of personality. To Wharton's eyes he looked good; something which one might gladly claim as English in its happiest sense; something clean and wholly reliable.

Madame's voice was heard, and she too came into the lobby. Richleigh rose to offer his chair and at madame's *"Ne vous inquiétez pas, monsieur,"* looked rather awkward. You could almost feel the flush on his cheek. He stammered, shook his head, and in final confusion produced in an atrocious accent, *"Je ne comprends beaucoup français, madame."*

Then, happily, the bell rang. People appeared as if by magic, and everything was bustle. Wharton moved off last. He was feeling uncommonly hungry and in the air was a hungry smell.

But as he sat down, his companion at the table looked surprised, and no wonder. There were plenty of empty tables, and why shouldn't he have been left to himself? Still, he maintained his air of aloofness, and when his soup arrived ate it leisurely like a man who wants a meal but has plenty of time in which to enjoy it. At closer view the face was still pleasing and the eyes remarkably arresting. They were big and brown and somehow plaintive, and at their corners were little wrinkles. Wharton wondered what the voice would be like and set the ball rolling.

"I hope you didn't mind my planting myself at your table, Mr. Richleigh?"

There was nothing aggressively English about Wharton, and he was not in the least surprised to see the other's quick start at the sound of his native tongue fired at him across that four feet. The answering voice had in it considerable charm, for all the reserve it expressed.

"My name *is* Richleigh. How did you guess that?"

"Saw it in the register." He paused to dispatch the waiter for a half bottle and then explained further.

"I really came to give you some news. However much it surprises you, we'll just chat in the ordinary way. No need to shout it to the whole room. You've seen the papers, Mr. Richleigh?"

"Can't say I have. What *is* this news you're talking about?"

"The murder of your uncle!"

Richleigh looked startled out of his life. He opened his mouth to speak and then changed his mind. He stared at the detective until the latter felt as if holes were being bored in him. Then what he did say was astonishing enough.

"Then it *has* come out?"

"Just what do you mean by that?" asked Wharton, with a look that never left the other's face.

The two stared at each other like cat and dog. "Exactly who *are* you?" asked Richleigh and you could hear the anger in the voice.

"Superintendent Wharton of Scotland Yard, come to acquaint you with the murder of your uncle, Thomas Richleigh, of 122 The Grove, Woodmore Hill, and to ask you what you know about it."

The other collapsed like a punctured tire, but from relief. Then he smiled! "By jove, Mr. Ward! You had me scared stiff. I thought it was another uncle you were talking about."

"Just a minute," said Wharton. "Let's get this clear. Your uncle Peter has been dead these ten years."

"That's true," said Richleigh. "I'm sorry I said what I did. I don't know how to explain," and he looked really worried. "I suppose I'd better tell you. None of us—my brothers and myself—ever thought my uncle Peter met his death by fair means, and sooner or later we thought something would come out. That's what I was thinking of."

Wharton sat back in his chair. For a moment the tension had been severe, and both men felt it. Then Wharton smiled, the kind of smile that might have been given by a lion who had missed a particularly plump but evasive Christian.

"If I understand the facts, Mr. Richleigh, the one who knows the answer to that problem will never be able to tell it." Then his smile became more friendly. "And the next time you're asked what you know about a murder don't say you did it!"

"You must have thought me a callous sort of person," observed Richleigh. "It ought to be rather a shock to a man to be told his uncle's been murdered. Could you tell me—er—I mean will you—?"

Wharton went over the story and left very little out. "You see the kind of man we're looking for, Mr. Richleigh; somebody of good education and with a perfect knowledge of the house. Is there anybody you can think of? Anybody with a sufficient grudge against your uncle?"

Richleigh shook his head. "There were times when a lot of people, including myself, might have wished him dead. It sounds a rotten thing to say, Mr. Ward—"

"Wharton," corrected the other.

"I beg your pardon—but my uncle was a pretty awful outsider. That's a charitable way to speak of him."

Wharton noted the hard look that came over his face and saw the curl of the lip.

"You saw my brother, Mr. Ernest Richleigh?"

"Oh, yes. He helped us a good deal, but like yourself he could only go so far and no further."

"What about the housekeeper?" suggested the other. "An unscrupulous vulgarian if ever there was one."

"I think we know quite a lot about her," hinted Wharton. "Did you see much of her, by the way?"

"Well, I suppose I did. I used to call on my uncle fairly frequently, when she was out if I could manage it. I don't feel very happy at the moment about those visits. I used to hate 'em like sin."

"I expect you did," said Wharton. "But there is one question I have to put to you, and it's the one we've had to put to every interested party including your brothers and Mrs. Cardon. Exactly where were you on the night of October the 11th?"

Richleigh looked at him suspiciously. "You surely can't imagine—"

"We imagine everything," interrupted the other. "You would be the last to question the law and its methods."

"I'm sorry," said Richleigh. "It was rather ridiculous of me. October the 11th. Let me see. I crossed on the 5th and stayed in Paris till the 7th; got to Toulouse the same evening and to Carcassonne on the 8th. I wrote a letter to my brother Ernest from there and posted it the following morning. I was anxious to sketch part of the fortifications and found I'd left some brushes behind."

"Expensive ones?"

"They were, rather; about thirty bob the pair, and they were a special sort. However, I did a pencil sketch which I've got upstairs in my rucksack. Then I left there on foot and got to St.

Hilaire on the 10th. Next day I tramped to Limoux and got a sore heel, so I didn't go on. That would be the 11th, when I was at the Cap d'Or Hotel. Next day I got as far as Couiza, and to-day I got here."

"Well, that's perfectly plain, Mr. Richleigh. There'll be no trouble about checking up on that."

"I'll tell you what we'll do," suggested the other. "If you care to hang on till the morning we'll take a car and run back. You see," he explained, "I suppose, like everybody else, I did French at school, but I always loathed the beastly stuff. Wish to God I'd stuck to it a bit better. I suppose you talk it like a native?"

"Well, hardly," laughed Wharton, remembering the patois.

"What I thought was that you could do the talking and see for yourself—that is, of course, if you are agreeable."

So it was left, and Wharton was grateful for the offer. Englishmen abroad are of a set type, and though it was extremely unlikely that two would have been at the same place at the special date, yet the matter could now be settled once and for all. And there for the moment it was left.

(B)

By the time they started on their journey the following morning Wharton knew as much about Frank Richleigh as some who had known him for years. As a companion he was reserved and even shy in manner; unexpectedly well informed but not dogmatic; perfectly mannered and, as far as Wharton could judge, without the least trace of pretension or conceit.

Of the work he had been doing the last few years it was plain he had a poor opinion, and he spoke of it as a tired man and a disgruntled one. On the question of cricket he was an enthusiast, and for him the year began and ended with summer. As for the holiday he was on, it appeared that the authority by whom he was employed had introduced the scheme as a means of retaining in their service what had always been itinerant people. After ten years' work, then, he was free from July to January. The August he had spent chiefly at Lords and the Oval, and had the weather turned out less fine in September he would have left earlier for his tour in France.

It was, moreover, his first holiday in that country and had been taken partly at the suggestion of a colleague and partly as the result of a visit to an exhibition of paintings by Henri Lecru, whose Aude landscapes had not till then been known to him. Later in the year, after exhausting the Aude country, he was proposing to make for Marseilles to do the bits between there and Toulon. But he confessed that the death of his uncle might make a difference. He might even give up his work in London and live abroad permanently. But that, of course, would depend on the will.

The journey to Couiza was a short one. "You'll recognise the head boss," said Richleigh as they pulled up before the modest front of the Hotel de France. "Black beard; big as a shovel." And conveniently enough, just inside the door he was.

"My friend Mr. Richleigh here," explained Wharton, "has lost a rather important letter and he thinks he may have left it here yesterday morning."

The proprietor accepted the statement in good faith. The hotel was searched, but there was no letter. Perhaps if M. Richleigh could return something would have been discovered about it. The general circumstances seemed to Wharton sufficient confirmation of Richleigh's statements, and they moved on to Limoux. This time the business was more important.

The Cap d'Or, a quiet, solid-looking building, lay at the far end of the town, nestling over the rushing, shallow water, and behind it the hills rose sheer. As Richleigh explained, his heel had been sore, and the first hotel he came to had been the one for him.

As the two entered, Richleigh was recognised. The face of the podgy lady who was conversing with the girl at the desk became a mass of smiles. Richleigh smiled too, rather sheepishly, and then the girl of the bureau smiled also. Madame began a, *"Quelle chance de vous revoir!"* Richleigh continued to smile but said nothing.

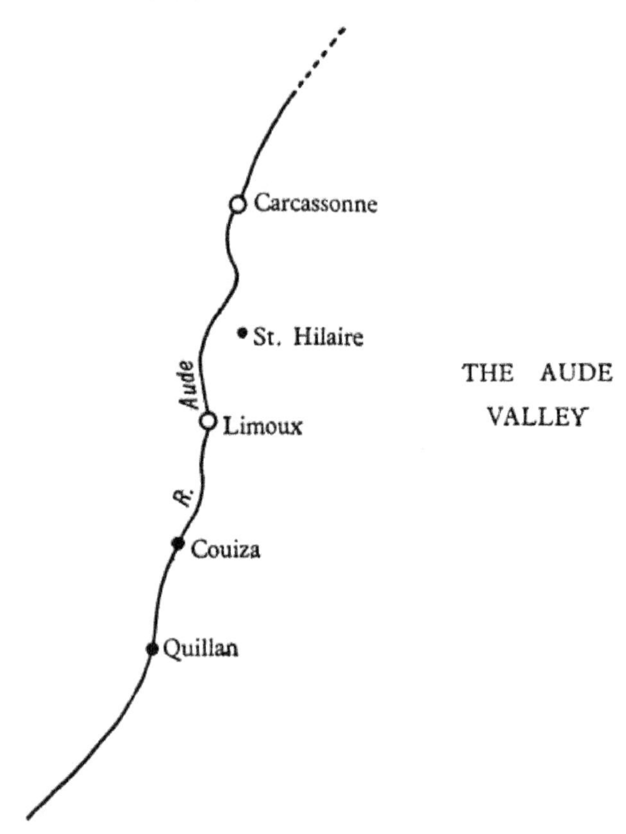

Wharton waded in. "M. Richleigh and I have been having an argument, madame. I said he was at St. Hilaire on the 11th, and he insisted he was here. Now we've decided to let you settle it."

Madame burst out laughing. "Monsieur is wrong. You recall on Thursday, Marcelle, the coffee and how he would pay." She seized Richleigh's coat and examined it. "You can't see the mark. Look, Marcelle. Only the merest trace." All this was very familiar and friendly and rather like the examination of a returned relative. "And the heel? It is better?" And all the time there was Richleigh looking, as he afterwards considered, very much as an ass.

"That's all right, then," said Wharton when they got outside. "What happened to the coffee, by the way?"

"Oh, I upset the gadget they brought it in and made a mess of the cloth and my coat. The women cleaned it up for me."

Wharton looked up at the clock in the Square. "Well, my train goes in half an hour. Too early for a drink?"

Apparently it wasn't as far as Richleigh was concerned. Over the table they talked of things that had to be done. Wharton took a message for Ernest Richleigh, and the other mapped out roughly his tour in case he should be wanted. His present intentions were to continue his holiday as if nothing had happened.

But as soon as the car had disappeared Wharton profited by his prevarication. It was immaterial to him whether Richleigh knew the times of the trains, but there still remained much more than half an hour. At the hotel he again interviewed madame. Was she certain of the date? Was it a Thursday? The result was such a flood of confirmatory evidence that Wharton left finally with the absolute conviction that Frank Richleigh would not again be troubled by the police.

Next came the journey, by another car, to St. Hilaire. He remembered suddenly too that he had neglected to ask Richleigh the name of the hotel at which he had stayed. But he need not have worried; the Hôtel des Voyageurs seemed the only one possible. And in response to his question about an Englishman who had spent the night there on the 10th the reply of the proprietor and the description he gave of Richleigh were so convincing that the matter seemed definitely settled. There ended, though Scott didn't know it for some hours, the case of the four nephews. In the ten minutes that were left he sent off a telegram. Scott might as well know at once how things stood.

Then began a journey that was long and yet fully occupied. Assuming that the other alibis were correct, where was the best place to recommence? Had Thomas Richleigh's former housekeeper still a grievance? Had she relatives? What about the neighbours of the dead man? Had he made a will? What about Steward? What of Richleigh's earlier years, that period when he had been lost sight of? Had he made enemies then? Had he been blackmailed? Had Peter Richleigh really a son, or had that letter been planted, as Scott had suggested? Who wrote the "Marius" letters? What could be got from them by an exhaustive study?

Add to these the weighing up of the value that might be obtained by press publicity, the wondering what had happened in his absence, and the preparations for the next steps in the campaign, and you have an idea of how Wharton occupied his time on that journey. At four o'clock the following afternoon he was in Chief-Constable Scott's room, going over it all again.

CHAPTER X
FRANKLIN STARTS TO WORK

(A)

As Eaton came out on the pavement he stood irresolutely for a moment as if undecided which way to go. It was then that he caught sight of Franklin.

"Hallo, Jack! I thought it was you. How are things going?"

"Can't grumble," replied Franklin. "And you? You're looking pretty fit."

"That's not my fault. Had about eight hours' sleep in three days. Which way were you going?"

"Anywhere that will suit you," was the reply. "What about some food? Or were you going home?"

"Not I, while the government pays. You know anywhere about here?"

Franklin did; as a matter of fact he had it all ready for the contingency. Five minutes brought them to the Jolly Fishermen and the side door that led to the dining-room. On the way he explained his appearance at the inquest on the twin lines of busman's holiday and that where the carcass is there will the vultures be gathered together. Eaton had heard a rumour that the other was setting up in business for himself, an idea that Franklin could not very well deny. He did admit, however, that as a freelance he was interested in the case, if only to the extent of wondering how things were going. As far as the question of beating the Yard at their own game was concerned, well, he wasn't such a fool as that.

They found a secluded corner and over a typical hotel lunch waded at once into shop.

"Well, what did you think of the inquest?" asked Eaton.

"That you fellows didn't give much away."

"There wasn't anything to give away. Or were you referring to the parcel?"

Franklin decided that ignorance was the safest line. "Parcel? What parcel?"

Eaton told him. "You see," he added, "Adams would have been marked for life if that had got out. After all, the public wanted to know if he was murdered and who did it. Well, they know he was, and for the rest they know as much as we do."

"Exactly! You know who didn't do it."

Eaton lowered his voice and leaned forward confidentially. "Between you and me, Jack, I'm not so sure of that. As far as I can see the only people who did it are the ones who couldn't have done it."

"Now, look here, Tom," said Franklin with perfect candour; "before we go any further there's something you ought to know. I'll discuss generalities with you as long as you like. I may not want to solve this case as much as you do, but if you give me information and I make use of it, I ask you, is it fair to you?"

"I don't see it," said Eaton. "Here's you and I who've done each other a good turn or two in our time. I'm off duty, and if I like to talk over this case as a private individual, why shouldn't I?" Franklin was about to speak. "Just a minute. Two questions. Is it the duty of every citizen to help the law?"

Franklin smiled. "Go on."

"And am I at liberty to pick your brains if I get the chance?"

"You certainly are; such as they are."

"Well, that's my funeral. Now you've put me off. What was I talking about?"

"The people who couldn't have done it."

"Well, who could have done it? He was well educated, laid his plans well, had heaps of nerve, and knew the house from floor to ceiling. Who's that suggest?"

"The four nephews."

"What about a confederate of Adams or Cardon?"

"Impossible! And in the latter case unnecessary. She had nothing to gain by murdering him. Further than that, under the sort of cross-examination you blokes would have given, either of them would have blown the gaff. But what about Steward?"

"He's definitely out of it, you take my word. He had no more to do with it than I had."

"Well, you ought to know. But what's wrong with the four nephews? Everything fits in."

"What's wrong? I'll tell you what's wrong. I don't know about the one in France because the 'General' is doing that himself and when he's finished with it you can bet your life it's final. But the others; everyone's got an alibi as tight as a drum, with at least two sound and perfectly independent witnesses. I did two of 'em myself, and I got Burren's account of the other. Listen to this, for example," and he gave an account of his two visits.

"Hm! As you say, that complicates matters," said Franklin sympathetically. "But if the alibis are perfect, why worry? You've only got to start all over again, and we're used enough to that in our game."

"That's the trouble. There's something wrong somewhere; you know, when you're off the right road and something inside you says, 'Damn it all, this can't be right.' That's how I'm feeling." And he nodded his head disconsolately and continued to munch his bread and cheese.

Franklin went a step farther. "You've got something on your mind. Look here, Tom; I'll strike a bargain with you. You know I went round to that house, and I don't mind telling you I saw something that may be useful. Answer me one question and I'll put my cards on the table."

"Good enough," said Eaton. "Fire away!"

"What's been done about T. W. R.?"

"To-morrow's papers will have a full description as given by the staff of the 'Constable.' There may be a composite photo made up from it. Also T. W. R. will be asked to come forward and make his statement. And that's all I know except that after he stepped out of the hotel he hasn't been seen."

"Well, that's a sound enough answer. Now listen to this," and he gave an account of the method of leaving by the window. "Try it yourself with some good catgut: it's easier. And have a look at the brass catch and slot of the west window and you'll see the friction marks. They come out as polish. Put that across the General when he gets back and see what he thinks of it."

Eaton clicked his tongue with annoyance. "Fancy missing that! Of course that shrubbery would mask his exit. But why no footprints?"

"Concrete path and then rain. But anybody could have missed the window. What about some coffee, by the way? You in a hurry?"

"Why should I be?" laughed Eaton. "I'm doing pretty well."

Franklin gave the order, and as they filled their pipes they had a look round. Then, when the coffee came, Eaton made up his mind.

"Look here, Jack; I've got to get this thing off my mind. You're the only chap I'd tell it to, it's such stark lunacy. You may possibly think the same thing when I've done; still, here it is. I've seen three of those brothers at close quarters, and I've formed certain impressions. As soon as I saw Ernest Richleigh I summed him up in my own way, right or wrong. Then last night I had a long talk with Burren and heard what he'd got to say about him.

"Then I've seen the second brother, as I told you. He's a parson, and he couldn't have done it, but yet I got the same impression about him as I did about his brother. Then I saw the third, the actor, and he couldn't have done it, but various things he let slip and things other people told me strengthened the impression I'd formed about the other two.

"And it's this. It's my private opinion and I can't get away from it, that though none of them did it, yet those four brothers did away with Richleigh. I believe they've had, and have got now, a sort of league of mutual help; that they held a sort of committee meeting and decided that if the family name was to be saved and this woman Cardon kept out of the money there was only one thing for it. Then they schemed it out and decided to lie like the devil and stick by each other through thick and thin. That's what they did, and that's what they couldn't have done because Harold Richleigh would have blabbed when he was drunk, and also the alibis are too perfect. Now have a good laugh!"

But Franklin did not laugh. He looked very much in earnest. "My God, Tom, that would make a fine play! Think of Charles Richleigh as the scourge of God and with the fanaticism of a mad Puritan; Harold, partly fuddled and game for anything; the lawyer with the brains, and the schoolmaster with the pluck. Can't you picture it?" and he gestured into space.

"Can't I? I've done little else since I thought of it, and last night, when I got the chance to sleep, it wouldn't let me."

"I tell you what, Tom," said Franklin. "Let me think it over. It's full of problems, but the chief one is how they could have made four perfect alibis with a wrong 'un among them. They couldn't have had a confederate. People can't be hired to commit murder nowadays. But could one of their women folk have done it? But, of course, that's ridiculous."

"Don't ask me," said Eaton. "I've got to get that nightmare out of my system or end up at Colney Hatch. Still, I bet I come back to it, for all that." He knocked out his pipe and stared gloomily at the dust.

"Something you can do for me," said Franklin, reaching for his overcoat. "Ring me up about that French alibi, will you? If I'm not in, just leave a message. Some sort of code, if you like."

"Same old address?"

"That's right. By the way, where does Adams hang out nowadays?"

Eaton consulted his notebook. "No. 5 Tinker's Lane, Epping. Not a bad job, a tinker's."

"I know," laughed Franklin. "Wind on the heath, brother, and the wheel's come off the caravan. You for headquarters? Then we'll take a bus for Finsbury Park."

Whether his brains had been picked or not Franklin was uncommonly pleased with that morning's work. He knew a good deal more than when he started. For one thing he had full details of three of the alibis and the promise of the fourth. Later might come news of T. W. R. who was certainly, like the visitor of that Wednesday evening, a flesh-and-blood person. And while waiting for the remaining alibi it was on that pugnacious visitor to The Grove that he decided to concentrate. Though the brothers had alibis, if he could prove that one of them had either impersonated T. W. R. by staying in that name at the hotel or had drawn that red herring of a threatening visit across the trail, then there would be time to consider further the theory that Eaton had advanced.

(B)

It should be borne in mind that in the department of which Franklin had taken over control some days previously, the usual inquiry work was going on. There had indeed been an unusual rush of business, and, automatic as most of it was, yet Franklin's second in command was living laborious days.

Franklin himself kept one reserve off general routine: Potter, an ex-sergeant of police whom he had signed up on the day of his arrival and whom he knew for not only a sound workman but a tactful one. He proposed to go to Epping himself for an interview with Adams. If she could be more explicit, could remember some characteristic or peculiarity of the caller, there would be something solid to build on.

Potter was sent to Norwich by the 2.40. His chief mission was to find out everything possible about the movements of Harold Richleigh from the 1st to the 3d of October. Any general bearing on the case might also be collected, and a photo of the actor would also come in handy. On the Sunday he was to call at Little Martens and find out the whereabouts of the vicar at that time and particularly on the night of the 3d. Again he was to get a photo if possible. Potter, of course, kept what he thought under his hat, but all the same he couldn't see the point of all that photo business. When he knew Franklin better he would know that the gathering of photos was his particular fad when on a case. He liked to have his suspects with him on the premises, so to speak.

The other nephews, Ernest and Frank, had almost certainly been in town on the night in question, and he proposed to handle them himself, Frank through his eldest brother. But first of all must come the interview with Adams and her first-hand account of the caller of that Wednesday night.

Things started badly. Franklin timed his arrival at Tinker's Lane for 5.00 p.m., a likely hour for tea and a family reunion. But the house was shut up. From a neighbour he learned that the father had received a telegram during the dinner hour; that he had gone to a football match at Tottenham, and that Mrs. Adams had accompanied her daughter to the inquest from which neither had yet returned. To wait in the hope of Mary Adams's early return seemed a waste of time and he decided therefore to go round to Enfield by Waltham Cross and try to see Ernest Richleigh.

There was no difficulty about finding Ridgeway House, and shortly after 6.00 he was in the lawyer's small workroom. When he learned that the caller was on business connected with his uncle's murder Richleigh's manner was most abrupt. It might have been a deliberate pose that he was assuming, but he certainly seemed sick to death of the whole affair and resentful of any attempts to connect him, even in the remotest capacity, with it. Franklin realised that he had to be handled carefully.

"Please understand, Mr. Richleigh, I'm entirely at your mercy. I'm here merely as the representative of an interested party, and there's no reason why you should answer any question I put to you. On the other hand, what I do want to ask is just one question which is liable to affect my client but which, we hope, will never be a public matter. I can't tell you more than that."

Richleigh had watched his man as a cat watches a mouse. The impression he formed was evidently a favourable one. "What *is* your question? And is it the only one?"

"It *is* the only one. I admit it is a compound one, and I repeat that you are in no way forced to answer it, as you very well know.

To the best of your belief, where were your brothers on the night of Wednesday, October the third?"

Richleigh looked surprised, or was it relieved? "My brothers? Why, all four of us dined here that night!"

It was the other's turn to be surprised. Why had Richleigh recognised that suddenly spoken date? And before he was aware of it he put into words the thought that came next. "May I ask what time they arrived?"

"You may, but you'll be breaking your word."

"I beg your pardon, Mr. Richleigh. That was unpardonable of me. May I bid you good-night and thank—"

"Don't apologise," interrupted the other. "I don't know what you're getting at, Mr. Franklin, but I think one thing ought to be clear to you. Those of us who bear the Richleigh name are getting precious little out of this unhappy business but notoriety and possibly scandal. I think we shall emerge from both."

Franklin could find no comment, but he nodded in assent.

"Just a minute," said the lawyer. "I'll see if my daughter is about," and he went to the door and called, "Dorothy!"

An answering voice was heard upstairs, and then a girl of some eighteen years entered the room. At the sight of the stranger she stopped short and threw a questioning look at her father.

"Dorothy, you remember a few days ago—the third to be exact—when your uncles all came to mummy's birthday party. What time did Uncle Charles get here?"

"I don't know, daddy. About half-past six, I think. That's it, daddy; don't you remember? Uncle Harold met the train at Liverpool Street, and they came together."

"Yes, dear; that's right. And Uncle Frank?"

"Just as we were going to start. Don't you remember we scraped the mud off his trousers where he slipped down."

"That's right, dear; about half-past seven. Thank you, dear." He waited till she had left the room and then turned to the other with no word but with a face that was eloquent.

Franklin had nothing to say. At the outside door Richleigh put out his hand with a dismissive and final "Good-night."

"Good-night, Mr. Richleigh, and many thanks for your courtesy. If everybody I had to interview were as helpful, life would be more pleasant."

Framed in the doorway, his features unrecognisable against the light, Richleigh made a quick reply. The tone was elusive, and a minute afterwards Franklin tried in vain to recapture it.

"If every person you interviewed, Mr. Franklin, had as little to tell, life would be more prosaic."

Now you would have thought that with so unexpected a windfall of information Franklin would have been extraordinarily pleased with himself, but he was nothing of the sort. He was vaguely disturbed and exactly why, he could hardly determine. He too had the feeling after contact with the lawyer that all was not what it seemed. Even that gesture of resignation had smacked of the theatrical, and the whole man had been too watchful, too careful lest something should escape more than the quota he had assigned himself. Yet you could not come to grips with it. The position held by Richleigh was impregnable; he did not commit the murder. And yet there it was—something in the background.

As for the visitor to The Grove, three nephews were let out. The fourth was abroad, and if he were not, there was little possibility of checking his movements. He would have every right to resent questioning about a date which had no apparent connection with the crime itself. Still, Adams should be asked about that caller as if Frank Richleigh were the person concerned. He arrived later than his brothers. His dirty trousers might mean that he had had a fall when running to make up lost time.

But the chief thing that kept cropping up in Franklin's mind was that uneasy feeling: the suspicion that Eaton had not been chasing moonbeams and that his theory was not so mad as it sounded. For all their alibis, the Richleigh brothers would pay for watching.

CHAPTER XI
FRANKLIN IS BUSY

As FRANKLIN ARRIVED at Liverpool Street to catch the Epping train, there caught his eye the multi-coloured posters of the Sunday papers. His own had contained nothing that he did not know already, but two of the others, the *Weekly News* and the *Workman,* gave promise of sensational disclosures if their splash bills were to be believed.

THE STORY OF MY LIFE
by
ROSE CARDON

and—

LIFE AT 122, THE GROVE
by
ROSE CARDON

said the one, while

THOMAS RICHLEIGH AS I KNEW HIM
by
MARY ADAMS

announced the other. Franklin invested in two penn'orth. If they did nothing else, the papers would pass the time on a tedious journey.

His first hasty look through was, from the point of view of information, distinctly disappointing. But, as he recognised, it was all very well for him to be superior. The public wanted anything it could get about the murder; it wanted something to get its argumentative teeth into, and the press supplied it. If that wasn't thundering good journalism, what was? He had to pay, too, his homage to the adapters who, out of the brazen utterances of Rose Cardon or the more perky periods of Mary Adams, had produced something so slick and palatable.

The story of the housekeeper was illustrated by three photographs: a flattering one of the woman herself, one of herself and her husband—the latter in the uniform of a private of garrison artillery—and a stilted studio effort of Thomas Richleigh. The story itself was interesting. What it would be like stripped of its verbiage and reduced to hard facts Scotland Yard would doubtless soon be aware.

The things which were new or which he considered sufficiently important Franklin summarised in his notebook—

(*a*) William Cardon was killed in action at Bethune, in 1918.

(*b*) Mrs. Cardon first met Richleigh five years later. The meeting appeared to be connected with the hairdressing business at Tottenham.

(*c*) She stated her implicit belief in the existence of a will but gave no very definite reasons.

For the rest, there were several hits at the expense of certain indefinite people whom Franklin knew to be the nephews. Mary Adams was mentioned patronisingly.

The account given by Adams was specially discursive. The adapter here was a genius, since what he wrote came from precious little; moreover, he had to bear in mind the ramifications of the laws of libel. She did, however, make the statement that she had no sweetheart and that there was no truth in the rumour that a young man was with her in the kitchen on the night of the murder. There were also various innuendos concerning the dead man and his relationships with the housekeeper. The only other interesting thing was that the reciting of that article accounted for the absence of Mary Adams the previous afternoon.

Franklin wondered too what Mrs. Cardon would say when she read her rival's effusion. If Scotland Yard, thought he, could put those two women, well chained up, at the opposite ends of a room and could then listen in, there shouldn't be much untold. Modern methods of interrogation were all very well, but there were occasions when subtle variations of a Third Degree were more to the purpose.

Still, the reading passed the time pleasantly. It was 10.00 o'clock when he knocked at the door of 5 Tinker's Lane. It was opened by a small man with a drooping moustache whose shirt sleeves and unlaced boots told of recent rising. Inside the cottage could be heard the voice of a woman scolding a child.

"May I see Miss Adams?"

"And what might your business be?" was the reply, given with such an impertinence of tone and look that Franklin read in it almost the exact amount the daughter had been paid for her journalistic outpourings.

"It's exceedingly important and connected with yesterday's inquest."

"Are you from the papers, young man?"

"It doesn't matter where I'm from," replied Franklin, taking a pound note out of his case and passing it over. "I want five minutes with your daughter, and I'm prepared to pay for it."

With no explanation the man went into the room and was absent for a minute or two. When he came back he maintained his air of cheap importance. "You can come into the kitchen if you like. Round the back way."

There was nothing to be gained by indignation, and round to the kitchen Franklin went. Mary Adams, with a pose of girlishness, was talking baby language to a kitten, and her manner was more than offhand. This was more than Franklin could stand. She at least could be put in her place.

"I shall be very glad if you can give me some information, Miss Adams. Before we start, I might as well inform you that I know *all* the events of last Thursday night."

There was a dramatic change. A look of fear came into her face, and she stared at the detective without a word. Then he went on: "This is of course in confidence between you and me. I have no intention of making known any private matters—the parcel of silk stockings, for instance—but I must request you to give me all the help you can."

There was still no answer.

"You informed the police that on the night of October the third a man came to the front door of No. 122 to see Mr. Richleigh. At exactly what time was that?"

"I don't know exactly, but I'd washed up the tea things and I hadn't started getting the supper."

"Nearer half-past six or seven?"

"No, it wasn't seven."

"Well, we'll leave that. Now tell me exactly what happened when you opened the door."

"I saw a man there. He'd a soft hat on and a muffler round his neck and an overcoat—"

"Was it a cold night? You don't remember? Never mind. Go on."

"And he had glasses on because the light shone on them and they looked all funny."

Franklin relaxed the iron hand. "Good! That shows observation. What next?"

"I was going to let him in because I thought he was Mr. Harold Richleigh, and then I knew it wasn't him because he didn't wear glasses."

"Any other reasons?"

"He didn't speak like him."

"Well, why did you think at first it was Mr. Richleigh? Was he dressed like him? Had he any peculiar trick, say rubbing his chin, or anything else that Mr. Richleigh does?"

"Oh, no; he just looked like him." And in spite of all examination that was all that could be extracted. Insistence might have been dangerous. If she thought it so necessary she could easily have made up information.

"Well," said Franklin, "let's look at it another way. You know Mr. Frank Richleigh very well by sight, don't you? Now, then; have a look at that sketch. Does that resemble him at all?" and he passed over the *Weekly News* which he had folded in readiness.

She looked at it vacantly, so little did the picture convey to her. "It wasn't him."

"You never had the least idea that the caller was Mr. Frank Richleigh?"

"No; I'm sure, positive it wasn't."

"I suppose it was too dark to see his hair. But had he a moustache—a bushy one?"

"I don't think he had a moustache."

"What would you say his age was?"

"I thought he was about middle; you know, sort of about forty. He was all hunched up."

"Hunched up, was he? Just show me." And without any ado she hunched up her shoulders in the attitude of a man waiting in the cold. Franklin put the paper back in his pocket.

"What was the voice like?"

"Ever so angry. I thought he was going to make a row."

"Well, now, I want you to try to imagine something. Suppose you had been sitting in the kitchen and you had heard the man speaking to somebody else outside. Would you have thought it was a tradesman or a gentleman speaking?"

She made a face which registered intense thought and then produced, "I thought it was sort of refined like."

"Hm! Did you see his back?"

"I don't know. I shut the door hard. I was all scared like because I thought he was coming in."

"Did he shake his fist?"

"I don't think so, but he spoke ever so angry."

"Now, just one last question. When you were looking at this man and when you were listening to him, did you ever have the least idea that he might be Mr. Frank Richleigh?"

The idea was so absurd that she actually smiled. Franklin cut in with a quick guess. "But you thought the man was Mr. Harold Richleigh! And they're the same height, aren't they?"

"No, but Mr. Frank, he's all different."

But wherein the difference lay she was unable to explain. Franklin concluded they were the same build but had little facial resemblance, and there he had to leave it. But before he left the cottage he was careful to assure his future position, not only by the sincerity of his thanks but by the assurance that as far as he was concerned, the visit should be as secret as the grave. After all, he couldn't tell when he might have to make use of Adams again.

On the top of the homeward bus he reviewed his morning's work and failed to find it good. Of course, a good deal depended upon the amount of reliance that could be placed on Adams as a witness. Still, taking her at her best value, things had got no further forward. According to her, the caller of the Wednesday evening had not been either Frank Richleigh or the T. W. R. as pictured by the press. But that did not say definitely that Frank Richleigh was *not* the caller. It was suspicious, for instance, that he had arrived at that birthday dinner the last of the four, or say the three, brothers. He had had nobody to meet and had only to come direct from town.

And there was another important thing: If Frank Richleigh were the caller it must have been either as a practical joke or with some sinister motive; the laying, for instance, of that false trail of which the culminating episode was the T. W. R. letter. What he would do, then, would be to go to Muffley Hill Grammar School and make a few inquiries into the life and character of Frank Richleigh and find out if possible where he had been on that Wednesday night. Further, he would find out where he had been staying since his summer holidays and inquire there as to his movements. All sorts of things might be brought to light.

But that evening something unexpected happened. Potter returned a day before he was due and brought various bits of news with him. Harold Richleigh had thrown up his job and announced his intention of quitting the profession forthwith. He was not to be found at his rooms, and at the railway station he had not been noticed. Where he had raised the wind nobody knew, but gone he had, and the manager left to blaspheme at his leisure. Further, that job at Norwich was the first he had done since the beginning of September, when a tour of the East Coast resorts had come to an end. It was proved by the mouths of many witnesses that he had been in town most of that period. He had been seen in the Eagle in Coventry St. on the 1st and the

3rd of October. The address of his rooms in town was, 7 Harries Road, Pimlico.

Potter had thereupon pushed off to Little Martens. There he had an easy case. The vicar had been in his parish till the Wednesday morning and had caught the train which would land him in Liverpool St. at the time his niece had stated. As for gossip, there were people in the parish who thought him standoffish; his wife, however, had an excellent name. He had already mentioned that he hoped in the near future to replace the pony trap by a small car. Potter had also secured photos of both the brothers; Charles from a village cricket group and his brother from a theatrical advertisement.

"Thundering good work, Potter!" said Franklin, and promptly the pair of them went into the question of how to pick up the traces of the missing actor. Asked to suggest his own assistant for the job, Potter named a good man he could get and was authorised to fix him up.

The next thing was to arrange for the photos of the brothers to be enlarged and for three copies of each to be printed. Later, at his rooms, he found a message from Eaton, a hastily scribbled note.

"F. R. o/k as expected. See you in a day or two. Expect developments *re* window. S. there this afternoon.

"T. E."

"P. S.—I damn near signed it 'Marius.'"

CHAPTER XII
FRANKLIN IS EXCEEDINGLY BUSY

(A)

THE ONLY AID that Franklin had in timing his visit to Muffley Hill Grammar School was the recollection of his own school hours. He assumed the morning interval would be taken round about 10.30. The secretary who answered the bell let fall that he was ten minutes early. Mr. Richleigh, she said, was absent on a holiday and she did not know his whereabouts. His rooms were at 12 Station Road, but rumour said he had vacated these at the end of the summer term. However, if the caller cared to wait till the morning interval, somebody in the Common Room might give him the information he needed.

As it happened a couple of masters off duty were already in the Common Room. Franklin apologised for his intrusion but said he was looking up Richleigh, whom he had not seen for a very long while and who, he was disappointed to learn, was away from the school. Did anybody by any chance know his present address?

They were quite a friendly pair and drew him up a chair by the fire. "Who was it had Richleigh's address, Purcell? Walton, wasn't it?"

"Hanged if I know," said Purcell. "If you don't mind waiting—(Franklin's my name)—Mr. Franklin, the other men'll be down in a minute. You knew Richleigh pretty well?"

"Fairly well," prevaricated the other.

"Played cricket with him, I expect."

"He still plays a good game?" parried Franklin. "Oh, rather; jolly useful man to have on one's side. Rotten business about his uncle."

"Oh, that *was* his uncle. I thought the name was familiar."

"Oh, yes; that was his uncle all right. Pretty awful outsider, by all accounts. I never heard Richleigh mention him, did you, Burton?"

"He was a secretive sort of bloke," said Burton.

"But an awfully clever chap, don't you think?" suggested Franklin.

Purcell flashed a glance at his colleague. The look seemed to be a warning, but Burton didn't quite catch it. "A very original sort of chap. Rather too highbrow for this sort of work. Shouldn't be surprised if he never comes back." He turned to the other. "Lay you evens, Purcell, that Richleigh doesn't come back."

"Even what? Bobs, if you like."

But the bet was never registered. Somewhere a bell rang and a pattering of feet was heard. In a minute it became a rush as the forms hurtled down the stairs. Then the Common Room door opened and the staff trickled in. Franklin stood up and drew back from the fire.

"Don't move, Mr. Franklin," said Purcell. "There's plenty of room for everybody. Here's the chap we're waiting for. Oh, Walton," and he raised his voice by way of general introduction, "this is Mr. Franklin, a friend of Richleigh's. Have you got his address, by any chance?"

"How do you do, Mr. Franklin," said Walton, a man in the early forties. "Which address did you want? I'm afraid I haven't got his French one."

"French?" remarked Franklin. "What's he doing in that galley?"

"Oh, just globe-trotting," laughed the other. "We rather guessed he was going on to Marseilles and then to Algiers. He's hot stuff on Arabic. Had a Gippo here last term, showing him over the school." He paused for a moment, then, "Curious sort of chap, Richleigh!" And then again, fearing perhaps the dropping of a brick, "And a damn good chap in many ways." But Franklin noted the tone of the addition.

"I have the address of his rooms," said Franklin, "but I believe he left there in July."

"That's right. I believe he spent some of his time in the country with his brother—you know him, perhaps: the parson—and then he came to town for a bit. The Danvers Hotel, in Southampton Row. I saw him there the beginning of term, and he told me he was staying on till he went to France. For all I know, he may be there now."

"Well, I'm awfully grateful to you," said Franklin. "I'll run along and make sure. Please don't trouble to come out."

"Oh, that's all right," said Walton. "I want a breath of fresh air. Perfectly poisonous atmosphere you get in these Common Rooms."

But it was not until they got outside the main gate that Walton unburdened his soul. "Are you a close friend of Richleigh's, Mr. Franklin? You don't mind my asking?"

"Not in the least," was the reply. "To be perfectly candid, you can say what you like about Richleigh In front of me."

"Well, then; when you said you'd see him next term you can take it from me it won't be here. The old man's rather had his knife into him lately, and he's most unpopular with the men—"

"Surely not!" interrupted the other.

"It isn't all his fault, I grant you. Richleigh happens to have a small amount of private means; he's a damn sight more of a gentleman than some we've got here, and he used to keep himself to himself: three unpardonable crimes in our profession, Mr. Franklin. He and the rest of the staff rarely used to speak to each other, though he always got on well with the boys. If I might use a hack expression, I should call Richleigh soured by experience. He had a tongue like vitriol."

"How did you get on with him yourself?"

"Quite well. I think I was the only one he ever cottoned to, and he didn't tell me very much. Then there's been this scandal about his uncle, and I happen to know the old man has made up his mind to ask him to send in his resignation."

"I don't hold any brief for Richleigh," said Franklin, "but surely that's pretty damnable. If he likes to fight the case, wouldn't the old man, as you call him, find himself in queer street?"

"There are more ways of killing a cat than hitting it on the head," said Walton enigmatically. Then he gave a squint round to see if anybody was in sight. "Headmasters are strange beings. I'll give you an example. The old man smokes perfectly poisonous tobacco, and Richleigh remarked in the Common Room—

rather clever, I thought it—that he was the man who put the 'g' in Dunhill. Somebody made it his business to tell the Head, and he gave Richleigh the hell of a ticking off."

"I'd rather like to meet your Head," said Franklin. "He sounds interesting."

"Oh, damnably!" said Walton. "Well, you know your way—straight down the hill. Remember me to Richleigh if you see him, and give him the straight tip about the old man."

"Some band of brothers!" thought Franklin as he strode down the hill. In two minutes he was knocking at the door of No. 12 Station Road. The door was opened by an elderly woman.

"Is Mr. Richleigh in?"

"Oh, no! He left last July and took all his things with him. Did you want to see the rooms?"

"I'm afraid I don't; thank you very much. You don't know his address by any chance?"

"I don't know where he is, but I always send on any letters to his brother at Enfield."

"Well, it's an awful pity I missed him. He was with you quite a long time, wasn't he?"

"Just over five years. He *was* such a nice gentleman to have in the house. He gave me this picture when he went away," and she drew back to point out a water colour that hung just inside the hall door. "We *were* sorry to lose him."

"I expect you were," said Franklin, running his eye over the really fine bit of colour work. "That's the school, isn't it?"

"Yes; he did that himself. From the cricket field," and she ran over it an appraising eye of her own.

"You haven't got a photograph of him that you could spare?"

"Well, not by himself, but he left a lot of old groups behind when he left."

"The very thing!" Franklin reassured her, and in a minute or two had selected what looked like a really good picture.

And there ended the first objective and on the journey back to town Franklin had quite a lot to think about. That chap Richleigh must have been quite an extraordinary bird. Why did he leave his rooms if he had the intention of coming back? Surely not to save a paltry retaining fee. Or had he a pretty shrewd suspicion of how things stood at the school? Still, all that could be attended to later. The great thing was to get on with the next step.

What he was getting at was in a way very simple, though as a solution rather melodramatic. Frank Richleigh, as he had just learned, had stayed at the Danvers Hotel. Only a few yards away was the Constable. Why should he not have played truant for a night or two and left the Danvers for the Constable, there to pass himself off as T. W. Richards? Moreover, Franklin proposed to find out at what time Richleigh had left the hotel on that Wednesday night. If he had left early, say with ample time to get to Enfield by six-thirty, then he might also have been the caller of that evening.

The immediate question was, which hotel was it better to begin with? And the Constable, being next door to the Tube station, got it.

(B)

When Franklin was shown into the office of the manageress of the Constable Hotel he was rather surprised to see how young she was. "I was going to say, 'Are you the manageress?'" he began.

She smiled. "What is it you want to sell me?"

He looked confused for once. "I'm sorry. At least, it's like this. I expect you've been worried to death by the police, but I want to worry you again. I represent a particularly interested party, and I'm after information about the T. W. Richards who stayed here from the first to the third. He registered in the usual way?"

"Yes."

"Did he actually sleep in the hotel?"

"As far as we know, he did. There's no rule that a chambermaid should report in the morning whether a bed has been slept in or not. He had breakfast here each morning. You can take that as certain."

"Could I see the chambermaid?"

"There's no need. I was present when a Scotland Yard detective questioned her in this very office. She either didn't remember or else noticed nothing unusual."

"At what time were the breakfasts?"

"Impossible to say. There are four hundred breakfasts in this hotel every day."

"Any other meals?"

"None, and no extras."

"Well, I'm very grateful to you," said Franklin, preparing to go. "Could I speak to the porter on duty? Would you mind?"

"The one you want is not on duty, but I can tell you all you want. I think I know it all by heart."

"There's only one last thing," said Franklin when she'd finished. "Could a person pop in and out of here say, to write a letter—without being detected? I mean, of course, if he were a stranger?"

"Frankly, I think he could," was the reply.

Franklin thanked her and hurried away to the next objective. This time it was a manager whom he approached.

"May I have a word with you in confidence? I'm a detective and want to ask about a guest who recently left."

"By all means," was the reply. "But of course the answers will depend on the nature of the information you want."

"I recognise that," said Franklin. "If there's anything you don't feel like answering, just say so point-blank. It's about a Mr. Richleigh who was here a few days ago."

"Richleigh?" The name seemed familiar. "When did he leave?"

"On the 5th or about that date."

"Just a minute," said the manager and went to the hall desk. When he came back he had the statement in his hand. "Here we are. August 28th to October 5th, inclusive," and he handed it to Franklin.

"I see Mr. Richleigh was here from the first of this month to the third. Is there any means of finding out if he actually slept here on those dates?"

The manager was on his dignity at once. "None whatever. It is no concern of the management whether a guest actually occupies the room he pays for. If we started inquiries of that sort we might get ourselves into serious trouble."

"And quite right, too. I just wondered, that's all. The dates are frightfully important."

"Just wait a minute," said the manager. The wait was nearly ten minutes, but was worth it. "You can take it for certain that Mr. Richleigh *was* in his room on those nights. By the way, is he anything to do with this murder case?"

"Hallo!" thought Franklin. "Somebody's jogged his memory." Then aloud, "Well, he is and he isn't. He's a relative and left England long before the murder. Would you mind if I spoke to the hall porter? I'd rather like to know something about his leaving."

"Turpin!" called the manager. "Just come here a minute. Do you remember a Mr. Richleigh who stayed here all September and left on the fifth of this month? No. 277."

"Youngish man, about my height. Used to go to all the cricket matches when he first come."

"Turpin's a marvel for faces and numbers," said the manager.

"I suppose this isn't him," said Franklin, pointing out the photo of T. W. R. as constructed by the Sunday paper.

"No, sir," was the instant reply. "That isn't him."

"Is he on this cricket group then?"

The porter found him like a shot. "This is him, sir. The one sitting down in the middle."

"And when exactly did he leave?"

"On the fifth, sir, and he gave me half a quid. He and I used to talk quite a lot about cricket, sir."

"Any idea where he was going?"

"Going to France, sir, where I copped my packet!"

"Just one more question. The Wednesday night before he left he went to his brother's at Enfield to attend a party. Do you happen to know for certain what time he left here?"

The porter thought for a second or two, then, "Yes, sir. He left here pretty late. I remember it now, sir; on the Wednesday night like you said. Mr. Richleigh, he said to me, 'Get me a taxi, George, and make it snappy. I'm due at Enfield at six-thirty,' he said, 'and it's past that now.'"

"And was it?"

"Just on seven, sir."

Franklin slipped him his tip, thanked the manager, and departed. Outside the hotel he looked at his watch. A bit of lunch on the spot or at Durango House? He decided on the latter and boarded a bus. But no sooner had he set foot in the entrance when Grigson, the senior commissionaire, spotted him.

"Excuse me, sir, but there's an urgent message for you in the hall office."

The message was from Potter.

"Come Eagle at once. Am holding H. R.

"W. R. P."

Ten minutes later, lunch forgotten, Franklin was entering the saloon bar of the hotel.

(C)

In the corner of the lounge sat the two, Potter busy on a plate of sandwiches and at his elbow a Guinness. Opposite him, full face to the bar, was a man who at the distance of thirty feet looked like a hard-bitten man of the world: a trifle shop-soiled, perhaps, but still presentable. His waistcoat was unbuttoned, and his bowler was tilted to the back of his head. His face was a brick-red, but a nearer view showed its puffiness and the bagginess under the eyes. Yet it was the face of one who could still assume and demand a certain respect. So much and more Franklin noted as he moved along, as if in search of a friend. Then he caught Potter's eye.

The latter stood up, his face beaming with surprised happiness. "Well, if it ain't old George! Put it there, my boy! Where did you spring from?"

Franklin showed equal pleasure. “Well, I’m damned if it isn’t old Tom. Well, this is a treat. What are you going to have? Hi, waiter! Now, then. What is it?”

“Just a minute,” said Potter. “Meet my friend, Mr. Richleigh.”

Richleigh waved his hand and then staggered to his feet. With both hands on the table he bowed solemnly. “Pleased to meet you—er—George. Richleigh, that’s me—Richleigh. You have this one with me.”

“No, no, no!” protested Franklin. “Pleased to meet you, Mr. Richleigh, but this one’s on me.”

So the drinks were ordered, and the three sat down. Potter finished off his half-emptied glass.

“Mr. Brown here—old Tom Brown,” remarked Richleigh and surveyed the other two with stiff and glassy look. Then he laughed foolishly. “Did me a good turn.”

Potter hastened to explain. “You know that pickpocket, George, the one we ran up against at Kempton? Damned if I didn’t see him hanging round Mr. Richleigh here at the door. You ought to have seen him hop it when he caught sight of me.”

“That’s right. Good fellow, old Tom.”

The drinks arrived and with them two plates of sandwiches. Richleigh protested that he wasn’t hungry but was finally induced to make an attempt to eat. It was plain, however, that he had had far more than he could carry, and unless he could be got outside he looked like presenting a problem.

“What are you doing this afternoon, Mr. Richleigh?” asked Franklin. “Is there a football match on, Tom?”

“No use for football,” observed Richleigh. “Man must play for his school and all that. This professionalism” (the word rather floored him) “is no class. Not the sort of thing to do.”

Before the others were aware of it he stopped a passing waiter and ordered another whisky. Then he resumed his speech. “I’m going to my brother’s place, near Enfield. Very good place; near the country.”

“Enfield?” said Franklin. “Isn’t that near where the murder took place the other day?”

Richleigh took his whisky and threw a shilling on the tray with a gesture of dismissal. He held the drink to the light, then tossed it off—neat. He got on his pins once more and bowed jerkily.

"My uncle," he said, much as a butler might say, "The vicar, m'lady!" and then dropped down again. The two watched him with very different feelings. To one, there sat a man who might blab out anything. The other saw something unbearably disgusting, and when Richleigh let out an expression that was foulness itself, irrespective of its reference to the dead man, Franklin finished his drink and left the remainder of his sandwiches.

"You coming, Tom?"

"Right ho, George!" replied Potter, taking the hint.

Before Richleigh could speak the two were outside in the bar. Franklin motioned to the waiter and slipped him half a crown. "That man we were drinking with—don't let him have any more. Get him to push off."

He went out to the street, followed by Potter. "My God! What a bloke! Keep an eye on him and see he gets to Enfield. Ring up Inquiry Office if anything happens; otherwise report to-morrow morning."

When later Franklin sat down to think over his morning's work, the more he thought about it the less he liked it. Frank Richleigh had definitely been proved *not* to be the caller of that Wednesday night, and T. W. R. was also a perfectly independent person. But Harold Richleigh could never have impersonated him, and the other two brothers seemed equally impossible. Who then remained to suspect as the author of the Perfect Murder?

He took pencil and paper and wrote idly as ideas came to him.

> THE FOUR NEPHEWS. Considering their alibis, ridiculous.
>
> EATON'S THEORY. Plausible but unworkable.
>
> T. W. R. Who was he? He had been at the hotel and had left perfectly normally. Why, then, had he disappeared and where?

THE CALLER. Who was he? Why did he announce his threat if he meant it to develop into murder?

Of these the last two seemed also extremely unlikely to provide him with the chance to pick up any sort of a trail. He had exhausted the available information, for one thing. What else, then, was left? The will? But had there been one? The statement made by Mrs. Cardon seemed positive enough. If, then, there had been one and the witnesses could be found, it was just possible that a provision might have been told them or they might have caught a glimpse of a name when signing. Then if that will had been taken by the murderer from the room or the dead man's person there might be some new matter. At any rate, that will should be the first business in the morning.

But because he was by nature a tidy person who hated the sight of loose ends he decided to finish off smoothly the business of the last two nephews. Was either Ernest or Charles in need of money? If not, then there would no longer be any sense in paying the slightest attention to Eaton's theory. So Potter's instructions were written out for a return to Little Martens and the new man's for a round of gossip at Enfield.

For himself he proposed an hour that night with Ludovic Travers. He rang up House Exchange and got through to the Finance Office. A secretary answered. Mr. Travers had been called away that morning to a conference in Brussels. When would he be back? It was hard to say, but not before a week. Yes; his man always went with him.

So he resolved to see Wharton and let him know how he stood with his new job. That at least would remove any misunderstanding if the General found it out for himself. But at the Yard he had an hour's wait, and even then it was not known when he would be free. But as he was turning the corner into Whitehall, he ran against Burren, and the two adjourned for a cup of tea and a chat; a meeting that provided more unexpected information.

The rest of the evening he spent at a revue. Whatever happened he was determined that until he had slept on it the Case of the Perfect Murder should trouble him no more.

CHAPTER XIII
A STROKE OF LUCK

(A)

Before setting off for Tottenham, Franklin read up again from the press files the account given by the driver of the car which took Thomas Richleigh, on the two Wednesdays preceding the murder, on his weekly collection of dues. Richleigh, it appeared, had always insisted on the same driver and the same car, and as far as could be gathered from the press account, what happened on one journey happened on all.

The driver, for instance, called at No. 122 at 5.00 p.m. and drove direct to The North London Hairdressing Company, the manager of which lived above the shop. He assisted his passenger to the door, and when the manager appeared, returned to the car. With an evening paper he there made himself comfortable for an hour. On the reappearance of his fare he drove to the establishment known as "Mariette" where the husband of the manageress was the ministering angel. Then came another hour's wait and a drive to Pell's Restaurant, where the commissionaire always lent a helping hand. In about half an hour the fare generally appeared again, the small black bag containing his money being held tightly in his hand. The usual hour for return was 9.15.

As Franklin saw at once, there was ample opportunity and time for making a will at either of those two flats. And where else could it have been made? Had Richleigh drawn one up at his house there would not have been available the necessary witnesses, since Mrs. Cardon was a beneficiary. Franklin was, moreover, strongly of the opinion that there had been a will. Certainly Richleigh must have intended to make one. He had seemed to be completely under the influence of his housekeeper, and sooner or later he would have had to show it to her as evidence of good faith. Or was he so ignorant as to assume that she would regard an indefinite promise of marriage and his bare word about a will as equivalent to the benefits of marriage itself? Or again, was he merely fobbing her off, knowing that if he married her and then died intestate, she would inherit?

Then the lucky hit occurred. He really did need a haircut, and the saloon would be empty or almost so, at 1.15. Moreover, as he calculated, barbers are not reticent people, and in a judiciously ordered conversation something might be dropped which would prove quite as important as the later interview with the manager.

Franklin squirmed as the icy fingers of the solitary assistant tucked the wool strip into his neck.

"How'd you like it, sir?"

"Well out of the neck and ears and trim it on top. You been here long?"

The man looked at the private door before replying. "About three weeks, and I'm going Saturday."

"What's the trouble? Too much work?"

"No, sir. Fed up. The chap whose place I took was a perishin' marvel. All you get is, 'Fred did this,' and 'Fred did that,' and I'm fed up with it."

"What was the idea?" asked Franklin. "If he was such a marvel, why didn't they keep him?"

"It isn't the manager; it's the customers. Because he'd been here ten years they got the idea nobody knew nothing but him. Ought to be in the West End, he did!"

"Where is he now?"

"Where is he?" Then followed a nasty laugh. "Three doors up the road. Pokey little hole. Three customers in the shop and one of 'em's got to stand; *if* he can find a chair."

A useful man to interview, thought Franklin, with his ten years' knowledge of the shop and probably of its proprietor. Moreover, according to the further statements of the lugubrious one, the present manager had been in his job only a year. Also everybody in the shop was fed up with the murder, what with the police coming round and people staring outside. Might as well be in the monkey house at the Zoo.

From the description that was given him Franklin managed to run his man to earth in an A. B. C. two doors from the shop. He sat down at the same table, but not until the waitress had brought his small order did he attempt to get into conversation.

"Are you by any chance Mr. Strode who used to work at Mr. Richleigh's shop lower down?"

The other gave a sharp look and hesitated before replying. "Yes, that's me."

"If you would be so good as to spare me a minute or two I'd like to ask you a question."

The look he got was aggressive and suspicious. "I'm not saying anything to anybody except in front of my solicitor."

Franklin was puzzled. "I don't follow you. I don't know anything about your solicitor. What I want you to be so good as to do is to give me some information about the late Thomas Richleigh."

"Are you a detective?"

"I am, but that's neither here nor there. I'm not a policeman, if that's what you mean. Look here, Mr. Strode; I give you my word that I don't know a thing about the matter to which you seem to be referring. Not only that: anything you tell me shall go no farther."

He seemed to be an unassuming, decent sort of fellow, and his speech had only the rarest trace of accent. A bit obstinate, perhaps, and decidedly a man with a grievance. His reply, however, was an unanswerable one.

"I don't know who you are or what you want, but I'll tell you one thing. People say if you speak the truth you can't go wrong. Don't you believe it! If there's no witnesses his word's as good as yours."

Franklin leaned across the table and spoke with all the earnestness he could command. "I don't know what this matter is, Mr. Strode, but if you tell me your side of it I give you my solemn word it shall go no farther."

Something in the words or the speaker must have made some impression on the barber. At any rate, he decided to tell his story.

"Well, mister, I hope what you say is true, but this is what happened, if I was on my dying bed. It was on a Wednesday and not many in the shop and I'd run out of wool, so I slipped up the stairs to get a fresh tin off the landing, and then I heard the manager coming up the stairs. 'What are you doing here?' he says, and I told him. 'You keep down in the shop,' he says. 'Too much money laying about in that room.' 'What do you mean?' I says. 'You know what I mean,' he says, and then I told him what I thought of him. 'That's enough of your lip,' he says. 'You can pack up and go on Saturday.' 'You go to hell,' I says. 'I'm going now, and you'll hear more about this,' and I put on my things and walked out of the shop and I haven't been there since."

"Sounds a pretty low trick," said Franklin. "What was the idea? Jealous or got a grudge against you?"

Strode lowered his voice to a whisper. "Old Richleigh put him up to it. They meant to have me out, one way or another." He felt in his pocket and found a letter. "You read that!"

122 The Grove,
N. 22
27/9/3–.

DEAR MISS MALLOW:

I do not think you understand just what I wanted you to do. If you do not accept a chance of bettering yourself you will be very foolish. I would like you to come and see me at the above address on Thursday next, at about 7.00 p.m. would do. You can take it from me that you will be very much an enemy to yourself if you miss such a chance. There is money in it, and money is always useful.

I shall expect you without fail on Thursday.

Your sincere friend,

T. T. RICHLEIGH.

"You see his little scheme?"

"I think I do," replied Franklin. "Who is this Miss Mallow?"

"My girl; the one I'm walking out with. Known each other for years, ever since we were kids. He saw her round at the other shop one night and got a bit fresh. Then he raised her ten bob a week and got her to stay late one Wednesday, but she wasn't having any. Then she told me all about it and showed me this letter, and she and I put our heads together, and she writ him an answer, and she didn't half tell him off. Then she got the sack."

"I say, that was pretty low down. She got a new job?"

"Not half she hasn't!"

"And what did *you* do about it? You surely didn't sit down under a thing like that?"

"What did I do? Well, it was an afternoon off in any case, so I talked it over with Lil, and then I went to see a lawyer what her sister's typewriter for, and he told me to come and see him again and keep my mouth shut and he'd see what he could do. I wasn't half mad. Then I thought I'd go and have it out with the old swine himself but—"

Franklin gave a start. "That would be on Wednesday the third?"

"That's right. That's when it was. As I was saying, I went to have it out with the wicked old devil, but he wasn't in. I ought to have known that."

"Why?"

"That's the day he comes to the shop to collect his money. But I was that mad I clean forgot all about it till the girl at the door said he was out, and then it dawned on me."

"Would that be about seven o'clock?"

"You mean when I went round to the house? Yes, just about seven, I should think."

"And do you always wear your glasses?"

"I'd be as blind as a bat without them," was the reply. "Gas done that—in the war."

When Franklin got outside that shop it didn't take him long to make up his mind what to do. There was no need to interview the manager about that will. Scotland Yard would have done all that. Much better see the General and try to exchange the information he had just acquired and which would almost certainly be news to the Yard, for information about the will and any other crumbs which might fall from the great man's table. Not that it was a nice job to undertake. At headquarters he had no official standing, and there was no reason why he should be given preferential treatment. And it would depend too on what sort of a mood the General was in.

But when he thought of that wasted Sunday morning and the evidence he had wrung so laboriously from Adams he felt like twisting her neck. The voice, for instance, that had been "sort of refined like." But the fault had been his for expecting from that cheap little hussy anything that required intelligence. Later he was to learn that lack of the things he expected could prove for Mary Adams a really profitable business.

(B)

Wharton was in, so Franklin learned, but interviewing a man who had arrived half an hour previously with an urgent request to see him. But he had no more than five minutes in which to kick his heels before he was shown into the room. The superintendent was alone and writing at his desk; something important too, for he didn't even look up when giving his quiet, "Take a seat, Franklin, will you?"

In a couple of minutes he finished his writing. Then he rose, pulled out his pipe, and drew up a chair. "Five minutes if I'm hanged for it. Now, my boy, what's your trouble?"

Somehow Franklin's prepared speeches went by the board. "Well, sir, it's difficult to say. But I think I've run across some information that might be useful, and I've come to turn it over."

Wharton paused in the act of lighting his pipe and turned his eyes with sudden interest on the caller. His tone became brusque and official. "What sort of information?"

"I've discovered who the man was who came to see Thomas Richleigh on the night of October the third."

Wharton preserved his poker face but the tone of his, "And who was it?" admitted that the information would be news.

Franklin told him and in detail. Wharton was interested and when the dénouement came, considerably surprised.

"Well, I'm very much obliged to you. And about that will business you were mentioning, you can take it from me that there never was one. You've saved me some work and I'll save you some." Then he struck another match and got the pipe going well. Franklin guessed that something was coming, and there was.

"Now, then, young man; there's one or two things *I* want to ask *you*. And I want to know them pretty bad. We'll start at the beginning. Why didn't you come back to the Yard?"

Franklin sat with his elbows on his knees, his hat swinging idly in his hand, but his eyes never left the other's face. "Several reasons, sir; health, for one. If I'd come back I could never have stuck it; all hours. Then I got the offer of private work where I could be my own master. Just what it is I'm not at liberty to say—"

"You needn't," interrupted Wharton. "I know!"

"I expect you do, sir, but I'm not at liberty to disclose it."

"Well, I hope you'll make good," said Wharton more kindly. "I thought a good deal of you, young man, and I always said you'd end up higher than I shall. Still, you've got your own welfare to consider."

"You may think me impertinent to say so, but I'd give up a good deal rather than lose your good opinion."

"While you do what I expect of every man, that is go straight," said Wharton seriously, "you'll never lose that. But don't you think you've given cause for suspicion? You've been round here two or three times, you were at the inquest, you had permission to visit the house, and now you come round with information. Is that so or is it not?"

"I grant your side of the case, sir, but you ought to take my word for one thing: As soon as you got back from France I tried to see you and I've been trying ever since. And as soon as I saw you I intended to tell you what I've just told you."

That was the last of the frown on the General's face. "That's settled, then. But I'll tell you one thing young man. If I'd really thought all the things I hinted at, you'd have gone away with a flea in your ear. Now, then. What are you so anxious for me to tell you?"

Franklin hardly knew how to answer that *riposte*. "Well, sir, I really don't want anything, but if you answered one question it might help a good deal. Was there anything the least suspicious about that French alibi?"

"Nothing. It was bombproof!"

"Thank you, sir," said Franklin and rose to go. But the other had not yet finished.

"Before you go I want you to understand the position. You have an interest in this case. But the law can take no notice of you, although it can be grateful for your, and anybody's else's, help. To be frank, the law can do without you except as a helper. It will take no official notice of you and will never admit that information has to be purchased. But if you give information, like any other citizen, you will be thanked. Is that perfectly clear?"

"Perfectly, sir. Discipline is discipline."

"That's all right, then," and he held out his hand. At the door, however, he had a surprise ready. "I shall be at the Primrose Tea Rooms in the Haymarket at about four. If John Franklin happens to turn up I might be glad to see him."

As he went along the Strand, Franklin felt like a grubby urchin whose head has been patted by the captain of the eleven. If he had had a tail he would have wagged it. By a quarter to four he was outside the shop and watching both entrances. Prompt to time Wharton arrived, looking like a benevolent city man who can afford to take things easy rather than the one who had been hard at it for days. Franklin saw him seated and then joined him.

The last five minutes produced the excitement.

"Curious how things happen," said Wharton. "You've seen from the papers that we've been anxious to get into touch with a T. W. Richards. This afternoon I was puzzling my head about him when the door opened and a voice said, 'Will you speak to a Mr. Richards?' Would I not! And there he was, large as life. Glass and china buyer from Hone's of Manchester; just taken over the job, was recommended by a friend to put up at the

Constable Hotel. Spent a day or two in London looking over the wholesale houses and then, on the morning of the fourth, told the hall porter he was going to Liverpool Street. So he was, but only to meet his brother-in-law. The two went to Victoria and ultimately to Vienna, where Richards did more buying and between ourselves had a pretty hectic time. Then the first thing he saw in his paper was that the police were anxious to get in touch with him, so along he comes to find out why. He was shown a certain letter, but knew no more, and probably less, about it than you or I."

"An interesting thing would be," suggested Franklin, "to find out if any engaging stranger got into conversation with Richards and learned his plans; and above all if Mr. Richards could describe that stranger."

"As you say," agreed Wharton. "Unhappily Mr. Richards doesn't recall any such talk except at the Coliseum one night with a rather nice old gentleman with white whiskers." And with that he rose and reached for his hat.

Franklin rose too and motioned to the waitress. "No, no!" expostulated Wharton. "This is my show. One bill, please." Then he held out his hand. "Goodbye, my boy. Don't work too hard. Come and see me when you're not too busy."

Franklin began to speak, but the other smothered his thanks. He leaned forward and whispered in his ear, "You run on. I've got a little job of work here. Got to see if the whiskers were real!"

Franklin left the tea shop strangely chastened and subdued. No more information, then, from the Yard. But what a thundering good sort the old General was. One of the best, and straight as a gun barrel. A sudden glow of feeling swept over him as he thought of all the happenings of that afternoon.

And then later came the inevitable question: what was now to be done? All the side issues seemed to have been cleared away, and the stage would soon be bare of the former suspects who played there a brief part. But new characters must be found, and from where? And after an hour's hard thinking there seemed to be one answer only.

The earlier years of Richleigh's life about which Burren had told him—that period when he had disappeared entirely—why not try to see what had happened then? In those hidden years there might be material for a dozen tragedies. And after all, if one had to start all over again, that start had to be made somewhere.

CHAPTER XIV
SCOTLAND YARD IS ALSO BUSY

(A)

WHEN FRANKLIN made up his mind to set about unearthing the facts concerning the earlier life of Thomas Richleigh, he hardly estimated the enormous difficulties involved. His state of mind at the time was an optimistic one. Things had not gone so badly, considering everything, and the meeting with Wharton was further responsible for an outlook that took insufficient notice both of the means at his disposal and of the scarcity of clues. Richleigh had succeeded in keeping so completely to himself the happenings of those earlier years that nobody had the least idea how or where he had spent them. To Mrs. Cardon and her predecessor he had said nothing and had let nothing escape him. As to the facilities for the search and the time available, where Franklin could employ a minute the Yard spent an hour. They had moreover means and methods of approach that were wholly out of his reach.

During the weeks that followed the murder, the authorities, as will be seen, were exceedingly active, and they had to be. There were plenty of people who wanted to know what the police were doing and why they didn't earn their living. The case had been so challenging that it was felt the police should rise to it and the occasion. Those who had felt it incumbent on them to stand by Scotland Yard as the equal of any criminal investigation department in the world were having their patience sorely tried. Those who had disabled the benefits of their own country were annoyingly triumphant.

In those early days when nothing in particular was happening the case was in the nature of a windfall, and for some time the columns of the press were filled. There were the private investigations of certain papers, the glut of pictures, the trails that opened suddenly and as speedily were closed, the interviews, the anonymous letters and their false alarms, the rumours and—the rewards. The *Record* offered £500 for information that would lead to a conviction and the *Wire* outbid it by another £500. And then the nine days' wonder came slowly to an end. The columns became fewer, reduced themselves to paragraphs, became intermittent, and finally the great case rumbled faintly like the scant reverberations of very distant drums.

Then there came to light the presumed escape from the window, and again there were columns and pictures and stories of notable and baffling escapes. Then it all died away again. Then something else happened: Mary Adams was engaged within a week of the tragedy to play the housemaid in the Schwinder Bros. Film, *When the Cat's Away*. It must be confessed that she made a good job of it, thanks to a certain low-comedy perkiness and the genius of the producer. Be that as it may, the publicity agent saw to it on the film's completion that the public should recall the name of Mary Adams. This spasmodic and casual revival was almost the last.

By the end of December it was barely a memory, and then certain things happened. Of these one only need be mentioned. James Steward died of pneumonia, a chill which he caught in his garden carrying him off in three days. A statement was made and promptly denied, that worry over the Richleigh affair had hastened his end. In any event, the death of a man even remotely connected with the tragedy was a cause of revival of interest.

During all these weeks, however, the last thing the public really knew was what the police were actually doing. It was because the inquiry was largely local and subterranean that the thoughtless or garrulous inferred that nothing was being done at all. It might be interesting to see, therefore, without any nice estimation of reasons, exactly what Superintendent Wharton directed and accomplished. It was always said of him that he resolutely refrained from being clever; in the conduct of this case it must be admitted that he succeeded in being thorough. Part of this ground, it should be stated, particularly that which concerned Thomas Richleigh, was covered by Franklin.

(B)

At first sight the Perfect Murder Case seemed to abound in clues, but somehow, when one came to get to grips with them, they produced nothing in themselves. All that arose out of them was the increasing certainty that the murderer had planned with rare foresight. Take the parcel. Paper, label, string, and contents were of everyday type. Silk stockings are a handy present and the average male need not be embarrassed at their purchase. The result of inquiries produced therefore such a multiplicity of replies that a lifetime would have been insufficient to follow them up. So with the knife. It was not new and it was not old, and its maker turned out thousands like it every year. The purchase of the catgut which had been used in the escape from the window? Impossible, when thousands of strings are daily sold over the counters of music shops. And it was found to be equally hopeless to trace out the ownership of typewriters of the make used by the writer of the "Marius" letters.

As for the scene of the crime, it was gone over like a doubtful Old Master. Every inch was searched for prints and the garden and its paths hunted over for a dropped clue. Occupants of all houses in The Grove were questioned as to their movements on that night, in the hope that somebody might have seen either the murderer's entrance or his escape. The local police were questioned in the same way, as were the owners of those houses in Maple Terrace whose gardens ran down to the back of The Grove. Tradesmen were questioned as to deliveries made in the street during that evening; a fairly hopeless business, as it had been early-closing day. The booking clerks on duty at the local stations proved equally bruised reeds.

The matter of the shutters was gone into in great detail. Those at Little Martens Vicarage had been there as long as anybody could remember. Those at The Grove had been put in by a local tradesman to Richleigh's specifications, why nobody knew, unless it were for reasons of sentiment or a horror of being overlooked. Charles Richleigh could recall nobody who had ever experimented on his windows, nor could the maids or their predecessors for years back.

Then came the dossiers and with them some interesting disclosures. Life for Thomas Taylor Richleigh had been a sordid business. Thanks to an examination of fingerprints the police had been presented with a magnificent clue and a starting point, and had found it fairly easy to fit in the grimy pieces of the puzzle that had been his life.

After leaving Cambridge he had changed his name to Thomas Taylor. In the year 1883 he had joined the army, understating his age, and had ultimately reached the rank of colour-sergeant. On his regiment's receiving orders to embark for South Africa in 1900 he deserted and certain moneys of the sergeants' mess went with him. In 1902, under the name of Richard Thomas, he was convicted of blackmail. On leaving prison his return to respectability and his relatives began with the purchase, in partnership with a certain Hermann Lewin, of a billiard hall in Tottenham, the growing of a beard, and the resumption of his own name. The rest of his history the reader has heard.

But as far as helping the case was concerned all this proved a waste of time. The officer whose life he had ruined in that blackmail affair died abroad in 1905, and there was, as far as could be ascertained, no enemy whose rancour might have persisted to the time of the murder. His relationships with the late Hermann Lewin were perfectly satisfactory. Two other lines of research were speedily closed. Examination of Richleigh's accounts produced no evidence that he in his turn had been blackmailed. His marriage was, moreover, a myth and had probably been an invention of his own as a sort of cheap acquisition of respectability.

The dossier of Mary Adams proved to be such an innocuous affair that it is not worth quoting. The worst that any of her previous employers could say about her was that she was impertinent and flighty.

But that of Rose Cardon, *née* Barns, was far different. Life at No. 122 The Grove must have been for her a placid and lucrative business. That stream of infantile sentiment which had been printed as the story of her life was founded on fact. What it had told was in the main true; what it diplomatically neglected was much more interesting. The "lifelong connection with hotel life," for instance, was not incorrect—her father had been a brewer's drayman. For herself, beginning as general help, she had risen to the position of barmaid. She had kept her job—at the Three Acres, Edmonton—after the death of her husband till within eighteen months of chrysalising into a housekeeper. In that time something happened which led to much. In the Maternity Hospital, Hampstead Road, she gave birth to a daughter which died a few hours later. The father was Joseph Purland, a hairdresser of Tottenham, and three months after the affair he left the neighbourhood.

It was undoubtedly during inquiries about him that Cardon had come into contact with Richleigh, at that time a bit weather-beaten but still hale and hearty. The advertised salary had been £40, all found. As, however, at the date of the murder she had no less than £400 in Savings Certificates alone, the rest of the history of Richleigh's housekeeper need not be related.

Again, the predecessor of Cardon. She was still living in the village to which she had retired on the death of her father. She had no grudge against Richleigh and no relatives. She seemed a bovine, colourless sort of person who received her monthly allowance as something normal and wholly uneventful. The village knew her as a widow, and her son was still at school.

The affair of the will had proved a dead end; at least, the advertisement produced no witnesses. Had a solicitor drawn one up and found the witnesses from his office he must have been made aware of the death of his client and have come forward with evidence or produced the will to the executors. It had been assumed, therefore, that Richleigh had died intestate. Ernest, doubtless as the result of a family conclave, had applied for letters of administration and had ultimately been granted the necessary powers.

There still remained two possible sources of information. An enormous amount of local gossip was collected and sifted. Every person known to have come into contact with the dead man—tradesmen, employees, gardener, maids, bank manager—was questioned. But there emerged nothing except the confirmation of Richleigh as a pig-headed, truculent, and not over-scrupulous man.

There had also been the forged T. W. R. letter and the attempt to trace all the people to whom Richards had told his business. Of these the white-bearded gentleman who had later taken tea in those rooms in the Haymarket seemed the most promising. But he had been rather deaf, and as Richards admitted that their Coliseum conversation had been more in the nature of a broadcast, there was no telling who had listened in. And as for any clue afforded by the hotel paper, Wharton proved for himself that in half a dozen hotels one could enter lounge or smoke room unchallenged and write letters with as much security as if one were a director.

Then there were the letters, particularly the first. Because some part of the statements of Marius had proved true, that was no reason to believe the rest reliable. The likelihood was all the other way. No man would be such a fool as to put his neck too far into the noose. Probably the first trick acquired by any Stone Age schemer was to give his enemy certain truths so that he should not regard the balance as lies. Yet Wharton took a good number of opinions on that letter, from men of the world, sportsmen, psychopaths, neuropaths, and even the man in the street. All came up against the one stumbling block, "*If* the letter is true ..." Wharton got to believe with the jester that there is much virtue in "if."

Before the case was definitely put aside one last desperate trail was followed; desperate because it was as certain as anything in this world can be that the letter from the pseudo-South-African nephew was a flagrant forgery. The T. W. R. was an exact copy of Richards's initials, and there had never been another T. W. R. in the hotel. In spite of all this Wharton took a chance. But though the Cape authorities made an inquiry as minute as he could ever have expected nothing arose to prove that Peter Richleigh had ever married or had been the father of an illegitimate son.

But though the case was set aside it was not abandoned. From time to time, as they suggested themselves, minor inquiries were made. At any moment, too, something might turn up: some loose thread from another case give a labyrinthine clue, or some unguarded word or peculiarity of conduct call attention. But as far as Superintendent Wharton was concerned the case seemed to be over, and Abnett took over the remains. Did I say, "Took over"? That is hardly correct. He was about to take them over when something did happen.

Just what that was is a long story, and if not an incredible one, one at least that would strain credulity were not its individual happenings veritable beyond all question.

CHAPTER XV
DOUBTING CASTLE

It was in November that Franklin spent with Ludovic Travers an evening which was to be, as far as concerned the happenings that arose out of it, the most momentous of his career. He had been looking forward to the conversation as a relaxation, after too much of his own company and a tendency to become introspective, but it is doubtful if he anticipated in the least, even when he left the flat, the importance of what had been said.

"How are things coming along now?" Travers had inquired.

"Slowly," was the reply. "Nothing for days but trying to get back into Thomas Richleigh's life. I've had two men hunting Tottenham and Woodmore Hill for gossip, and Potter and I have got as far as when he first arrived in Tottenham, and I'm hanged if we can get any further."

"And how are Scotland Yard getting on?"

"No better. At least, if they had found out anything we should have heard something."

"Don't think I'm trying to hinder," said Travers, "but just what are you hoping to find in Richleigh's dossier? An enemy who'd found him out, or what?"

"To be perfectly frank, I don't know. I'm just expecting something to turn up."

"It's frightful cheek of me," said Travers, "bothering you like this. When I was a boy I was once taken over a famous racing stable and had all the horses pointed out to me. After that for years I used to open the paper always at the sports' page to see what was happening to them or their descendants. That's the way with this case. I pitchforked myself into it, and now I'm hanged if my curiosity will let me out of it."

The look of despondency did not clear off Franklin's face as Travers hoped it would. "Of course," he went on, "impatience is all very well for a layman like me. You fellows know results don't come by wishing."

"I wish to God they did," said Franklin. "The thing that's getting me now is the uselessness of it all. Take the old gang of suspects. Somehow, one felt at home with them. They didn't commit the murder, but they might have done. What I mean is that if I find another suspect, how on earth can he intrigue me like the original ones? Richleigh didn't go out, so how can there be a man who fits the case? It seems to me the first qualification of the criminal that he should be somebody known to the maid; somebody who had been in the house recently, therefore."

"I wonder if I might put it in another way?" said Travers.

"I read the other day, and perhaps you did, a preface written by Chesterton for a detective novel and in it he said how annoyed he always was if the murderer turned out to be some person whom he had never met before in the story; somebody dragged into the last chapter to explain improbabilities, or some relative turning up from abroad. I take it that's what you mean. If the murderer turned out to be some person with whom you weren't well acquainted you'd feel somehow as if you'd been swindled."

"That's exactly it. Now, take those four nephews. The more I think about it the more I think it's a pity one of them is not guilty. If you really think it out, the absolute certainty is that one of them *must* be guilty; but, then, what's the use of talking like that?"

"I'm not so sure," said Travers, perfectly seriously. "Suppose we disregard the alibis; which of the four would you name as the murderer?"

"Frank!" replied the other, without the slightest hesitation. "He had the education; he was sufficiently active; he knew the house, and the maid knew him; he was a sportsman, and his life was one of repression. He was a man who felt he could do better things and yet never had the chance. On the other hand, he was regarded by his colleagues as an incompetent. That's why he had such a scathing tongue."

"And the 'Marius' letters gave him his opportunity to make a show. It certainly explains the spectacular side of the whole business. And that reminds me."

He rose from the easy chair and found up a bundle of photographs. "These pictures you sent round. There's one of them. Frank, as a matter of fact, I've seen before somewhere. Where I should run up against him, heaven knows, but his face is perfectly familiar, somehow."

He held it at arm's length, and Franklin came and squinted over his shoulder. "Funny, isn't it? Something's on the tip of my tongue, and for the life of me I can't get it out." He threw the photos on the table. "Still, there we are. It'll pop up some time."

"Very annoying, that sort of thing," said Franklin. "By the way, did I ever tell you Eaton's theory?"

"You didn't, but I'd like to hear it."

If Eaton had been there he would have been pleased with Franklin's presentation. He might have been gratified too at the fact that Travers did not laugh; indeed, he seemed to regard it as perfectly feasible.

"Eaton struck me as a most original fellow," he said, "but this is better than ever. Why shouldn't Ernest have been mixed up in the business?"

"Too much to risk and too much money already. Rolling in it."

"And Charles?"

"Plenty of money too, though a bit on the close side. Potter says Eaton's opinion of him was all wrong. He's a rattling good sort, and those who've known him since he was a boy say he's the best-living parson they've ever run across."

"Harold, then? I suppose, by the way, he couldn't have been exaggerating the drunk business for purposes of effect?"

"Not he. If he could act like that he'd be a top-liner in town instead of what he is, and if he could make up his face the colour it's acquired, he'd be a consulting expert to the profession. Moreover," and here he couldn't resist a smile, "he was removed yesterday to a private home—for inebriates, I fancy—at Hertford."

Franklin joined in Travers's roar of laughter. "Pretty good reasons, especially the last." And then Travers thought the correct moment had come and decided to voice the idea that had been in his mind for a day or two.

"I want to put something up to you. If you've got all those ideas about Frank Richleigh without seeing him, what might you not have got if you'd seen him and lived with him for a week or two?"

"But what's the use? He didn't commit the murder. He's an impossibility."

"Damn the impossibilities. Look at it fair and square. Here's a case of a unique kind. A man of keen intelligence actually announces that he can't be caught. He flaunts before everybody the assertion that the police can have no chance. And why? Because he's found out a way to do something which nobody believes possible. He may have found the way to murder a man and not be there, or he may have discovered how to be in two places at once. And yet you people will persist in looking for the possible." Then he smiled. "Pretty cool of me, what? But why not give it a trial? Why not go and see this Frank Richleigh who fits the case so well?"

Franklin was silent for a good few moments. He sat looking into the fire as if seeking in the interplay of the dancing flames some answer to the enigma. Then he shook his head.

"I don't know what to say. It's all this time since the thing was done, and we're as far off as ever."

"True enough. That's why I feel so annoyed that anybody in this Twentieth Century should continue to propound his homicidal riddle and be so cocksure of getting no answer. That's why I'd give a candle as big as a wireless pole to St. James of Compostello if you could solve it."

"That's very nicely put," said Franklin. "And I'd give a year's salary for a substantial clue."

"There'll be one sooner or later. Infallibility is a mischievous doctrine. Besides, this Marius had too much to say. Like the lady, he protested too much. He isn't a superman or even your strong, silent man who does things. There's a yellow streak in him somewhere and an absence of discipline."

Franklin tossed his head. "Frank Richleigh every time."

"Then I'll rub it in again," said Travers. "Go and see him. Get into his company. Give him the chance to make a slip when you're there to see it or hear it."

"I'd love to," said Franklin, but his voice sounded hopeless and depressed. "But what's the use? I simply must dig for results. Suppose I presented my accounts for a visit to France on the lines you suggest; wouldn't any auditor who knew the facts strike his pencil through them? If it were my own money I were spending it might be different." His teeth clenched on his pipe, and the other noted the determined frown of the brows.

"And if the worst comes to the worst, I'll do that. The murder was done by a human being and, as you said, a fallible one. Sooner or later I'll find the flaw in his defence if it takes a lifetime."

"That, as we used to say, is the spirit," said Travers. But he felt that the situation was becoming a little tense. He replenished the other's glass, squirted the siphon, and then diplomatically edged the conversation aside.

• • • • • • •

Now the first thing that emerged from that evening's talk was the appreciation by Travers of the fact that the case was likely to be a trying one, under his peculiar circumstances, for Franklin. Moreover, he lacked that versatility of temperament which might enable him to turn aside from an obsession into some less exacting bypath. If Franklin should begin to take things, or even himself, too seriously, it might be disastrous for him.

That is why he determined to do an unusual thing. He was in the private room of Sir Francis Weston on a certain affair about which his opinion was required, and having completed the business in hand considered the moment a favourable one.

"I hope you won't think it unpardonable of me, Sir Francis, but I'd like to bring a confidential matter to your notice."

"By all means, Travers. What is it?"

"I'll come direct to it because it explains itself. Some time ago you asked me to see Mr. Franklin on a certain matter, and since then I've been extremely interested in the particular case in which he's engaged, and also in Franklin himself. I have your permission to speak freely, Sir Francis?"

"Do, please!" said the other, who was beginning to wonder what it was all about.

"Well—er—Franklin seems to me an exceptionally capable man but very highly strung. Not only that, but he's getting the idea that he's expected to produce immediate results; make good, as he'd call it, and he looks to me to be heading straight for another breakdown. I ventured to remind him that Scotland Yard was in the same boat as himself. The obvious error about your insisting on results and his impression that expenses were to be cut down to the minimum were hardly—well, were no affair of mine."

"I'm much obliged," said the other, so abruptly that Travers feared at first that he had put a flat foot clean in it. "As a matter of fact, I'm exceedingly grateful. I'll see Franklin at once."

"If I might venture to suggest it, Sir Francis, I would like him to think the initiative came from you."

"I think that can be managed. When I saw him the other day he seemed to be perfectly satisfied. Still, we mustn't let an impression of the kind you've been mentioning get about. Results are all very well, but I'll never stand for impossibilities being asked or expected of any man," and he picked up the paper-knife and waved it emphatically.

Travers murmured a throaty, "Quite so!" but the other put up a detaining hand. "Tell me as man to man. What's your impression of this case? A long business?"

"For what my opinion is worth, Sir Francis, I should say a very long business. It was an unusual one from the outset."

"Hm! Well, we can stand it. I'm very much obliged to you, Travers." And then with a touch of his dry humour; "Don't forget to record in your ledger one good deed for the day."

Travers, in confusion, clutched his papers and fled.

CHAPTER XVI

FRANKLIN MAKES A FRESH START

As the result of an unexpected interview with the Head of Durangos, Franklin was feeling twice the man he had been and very much on his toes. He had made up his mind to "damn the impossibilities," as Travers had suggested. He would no longer take things at their face value or receive his impressions at second hand. He had seen two of the nephews, and now he would see the other two. But because he had considerable respect for Potter's opinion, he decided for the present to leave Charles Richleigh out of it and concentrate on the schoolmaster.

First of all a difficulty or two had to be got over. He knew that at the time of the murder Frank Richleigh had been touring the Aude Valley, starting at Carcassonne. Further application to Eaton produced the information that his headquarters had been Quillan. The thing was, was he still there? Probably his brother Ernest was the only person in England who could answer that question, and to apply to him was impossible. Without doubt the lawyer would mention the matter in his next letter and the suspect would be put on his guard. Moreover, since Franklin had no good reason to assign for the request, the lawyer would at once become suspicious. To apply to Wharton would also be awkward, since it could only be assumed that Franklin was going to test alibis which Wharton had passed as bombproof. But he did try to get over that difficulty. Potter was sent to Enfield to get by hook or crook an envelope sent by Frank to his brother. It was likely to be difficult, since in winter odd paper is made to light fires and not put in dust bins.

Further, to go as an Englishman to so remote a spot would be to arouse suspicions at once. Franklin's French was sound but hardly good enough. Italian, on the other hand, thanks to his mother, was his second tongue, the use of which had brought him to the front in the Intelligence Department. He would go as an Italian, then, but in what rôle? Ludovic Travers supplied the answer. All that district was full of castles and gorges and cascades. Why not be the advance agent of a cinema company, interested in the making of a picture dealing with the exploits of, say, Gaston de Foix? Moreover, Travers taught him most of the patter and provided him with a book or two to read up in the train.

But when Franklin arrived in Carcassonne it was with no news of Richleigh's whereabouts. Potter had been unsuccessful. Still, Franklin wasn't worrying. It would be easy enough to pick up the Englishman's trail and not difficult to follow it. And the opportunity was a good one for checking that alibi. At Limoux he tried the first hotel he came to—the right one—and received all the confirmation he wished. Indeed, the confirmation was so strong and unanswerable that he made the first entry in his notebook! And that was not to be the last paradoxical entry he was to make before he returned to England.

Couiza told the same story, and then came Quillan and the Grand Hôtel des Pyrénées. Madame's face brightened at the mention of Mr. Richleigh.

"I'm a friend of his," said Franklin-Vittorini, "and it's most important that I should see him as soon as possible. He's not coming back here, I suppose?"

Madame called Maximilien, and the two had a machine-gun burst of conversation. It then appeared that Mr. Richleigh had stayed some days in Quillan before going on to Belcaire. In two days he was back, the district proving unfavourable from an artist's point of view. Later he went to Montlouis up on the frontier but that proved too cold and back he came to Quillan. Then he made his final adieux and left for Foix.

Was M. Richleigh still at Foix? Madame did not know. Could M. Vittorini go there that afternoon? Not if he wished to go by bus, he was told. But why not wait till the morning and do the journey in comfort and cheaply, by the auto? Franklin saw the force of the argument. He hoped also to hear a good deal about Richleigh in that hotel where he was evidently so esteemed a guest.

But at Foix the next morning he had an unpleasant surprise. Richleigh had stayed at the Hotel Terminus as the driver had told him but two days before, had left with all his belongings for a destination unknown. At the station, however, he was informed that an Englishman with a pronounced accent and dressed as described had taken a ticket for Toulouse. Franklin caught the next train and followed. Inquiries produced the reply that the Englishman had been advised, as he himself was, to stay the night in Toulouse and then reserve a place on the *rapide* for Marseilles.

By this time Franklin was getting annoyed with his Cook's tour across France. He might have been tempted to abandon the chase, since the alibi had received proof as strong as holy writ, had not two things driven him on: a certain obstinacy in his make-up and the ironical solace that at the end of the journey the impossible was waiting to be damned.

At Marseilles it took him two days to discover that Richleigh had left by a slow train for Toulon, after having claimed from the *consigne* a large suitcase. At Toulon, however, the luck ran out. Richleigh might have changed his clothes in the train; at any rate, there was no news to be picked up about an Englishman who might definitely be said to resemble him. Moreover, he was surprised to hear that his fellow countrymen were a long way from uncommon in that part of the world, particularly at the beginning of the Riviera season.

To search the Riviera would have taken months, so, having secured a room, he made a further attempt to obtain information by sending a long and urgent wire to Ludovic Travers. Two days later he received the reply:

"Exact whereabouts unknown. Try Poste Restante Marseilles, Toulon and Hyères."

At the post office there was no letter for Richleigh. The only thing to do, therefore, was to push on to Hyères, since returning to Marseilles would have meant a longer journey. Having choice of tram or train for the short excursion, he chose the former and took with him a guidebook about the coast. And at the post office he was lucky.

Had they any letters for a M. Richleigh? Yes; there was one. Franklin took it and noticed the Enfield postmark.

"I beg your pardon," he said, handing it back. "This is not the name. I want Ritchley," and he spelt it out.

Next came a visit to the *chef-de-police* and a display of his credentials. Might he have permission to exercise surveillance at the post office? The references must have been formidable and satisfactory, for he received a letter for the postal authorities and the services of a plain-clothes agent as a relief during meal hours.

The very first day produced results. He had just returned from lunch and relieved his assistant when all at once he caught the clerk's eye. At the desk was a man; hatless, wearing a brown coat and grey flannel trousers, and with face burned to so dark a brown that Franklin scarcely recognised him. He opened the letter at once, read it quickly, smiled once or twice, put it in his breast pocket carefully, and then went out, with Franklin at his heels.

For some distance Richleigh followed the tram lines; then he turned off down a long avenue. For the next quarter of a mile a bare hundred yards separated them. It looked a certainty that he was making for the station, but suddenly, just short of it and at an unseen fork in the road, he stopped and consulted his watch. Then he sat down on a seat that seemed to mark some sort of a bus stop. Franklin pulled down the brim of his hat to give himself a slightly more un-English air, and strolled to the corner. Five minutes passed; then ten; and what Richleigh was waiting for Franklin had no idea. Then he tried his first bluff. In his best manner he approached the Englishman and addressed him in fluent Italian. Richleigh seemed rather self-conscious. He shook his head, tapped his chest and remarked, *"Anglais!"* Franklin replied with more Italian. But just then a bus drew up at the curb, and Richleigh, obviously relieved, got in.

Franklin got in too. Where he was going he had not the least idea, and there were his belongings, too, at the hotel. Still, he took the back seat and hoped for the best. The difficult thing would be to follow Richleigh when he descended without drawing attention to himself. Also there was the question of what fare to take. Still, the conductor took his five-franc note and gave him a ticket. "One stage only," thought Franklin, "and about three miles." But he was a long way out. The bus went due west; then swung south by the side of a vast stretch of salt pools. On the raised causeway were mountains of salt, tiled in against the rain. Then came a halt at a hamlet; a mile or two along a narrow isthmus; hillier country with entrancing views of landlocked bays, and finally a sharp descent, a sudden bend, and then—the sea!

The passengers alighted, Richleigh among them. Down below them was the stone jetty, and anchored by it could be seen a small motor launch, the *Cormoran*. Looked down upon from the height the scene was like an Arthur Watts drawing. Above by the bus was an inn with its tables set out on the stone-flagged square. Here one or two of his fellow passengers paused for a hasty drink; the others moved down the slope towards the boat. Then the bus circled ready for the return journey, and three passengers, obviously from the *Cormoran*, got in. Franklin, after his short leg-stretch, did the same, and from the window looked across the sea. In a second or two he had to make up his mind. Was he to follow his quarry or keep out of sight?

Then in the distance he noticed something. The light might have been deceptive, but there, three or four miles away on the horizon, lay what could only be an island. It seemed the faintest mark against the skyline; a kind of whale almost hidden in the mist. Farther east, too, another island could be discerned; or was it two?

Franklin decided to stay where he was. After all, islands don't run away. And then the last packages were stored on the *Cormoran* and she cast off, chug-chugging steadily. Standing on the deck was Richleigh, his face towards the island. Then the sound of voices was heard; the driver and his conductor left the inn; the parcels were put in the back, and the return journey began.

"Where does it go to, that boat?" asked Franklin of his neighbour.

The man looked surprised. "To the Island of Porquerolles!"

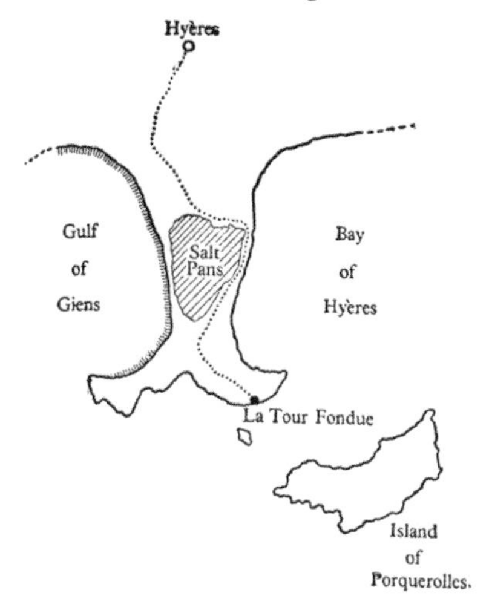

"Really!" said Franklin. "And how does one amuse one's self there?"

In many ways, as he learned. In the season there was swimming and always there were fine walks for those who liked that sort of thing. On the island was an excellent hotel, owned like everything else there, including the *Cormoran,* by the gentleman who possessed the whole island. A service of autos like the one they were in travelled daily from Hyères, and the times could be got from the conductor. Was the island worth visiting? Why, certainly! It had a Moorish Castle, a Pirates' Cave and the most magnificent of views. Monsieur was English, perhaps? Italian? But how interesting! M. Papini of the hotel—l'Hôtel des Îles d'Or—was Italian also. And from then to the end of the journey the two of them jabbered away, and in the half hour Franklin got as much information as a much longer study of the guidebook could not have given him.

Back in Hyères there was plenty of work to do: visits to the police, to the manager of the principal cinema, and to a bookseller, where he was advised to take the Abbé Ferrat's book on the Island of Porquerolles. There was money, too, that had to be spent on new clothes; not that he wore anything aggressively English. Still it would be safer to remove tailor's tabs and laundry marks and to acquire a little more Italian sartorial colour.

Then, too, his original scheme concerning Gaston de Foix and a historical picture had to go by the board. Finally he decided that M. Vittorini would have to be the representative of an Italian company with headquarters in Turin. The picture he would make play with should be a melodramatic affair, dealing either with Algerian corsairs or modern spies, but requiring in either case highly romantic backgrounds. All of which done, he left instructions to be called at 7.00, went to bed, and slept like a dormouse.

CHAPTER XVII
THE ISLAND OF PORQUEROLLES

(A)

NOTHING that happened during Franklin's short stay in the Island of Porquerolles solved entirely the mystery of the Perfect Murder, and yet everything that happened contributed to its final solution. And, curiously enough, it was the small and apparently irrelevant happenings that contributed most.

Take, for instance, the journey to La Tour Fondue. When he awoke a stiff breeze was blowing, and somewhere in the back of his mind was the indefinite feeling that all was not what it should be. Then he realised just what the mental disturbance was—the crossing from the mainland. The sight of the tiny *Cormoran* setting her nose to the sea had made him wonder how she would stand it on a rough day. He himself had always been a bad sailor. How people could for pleasure go down to the sea in small boats was beyond him.

He caught the early bus and from his seat by the driver put more than one cautious question. The reason for the breeze? A mistral coming. Would the sea be rough? Perhaps a little, but to-night! To Franklin the pace of the auto seemed a crawl, with that sea getting worse every minute, but when the jetty was reached there was the *Cormoran* bobbing up and down at anchor and nobody showing the least excitement, in spite of the little white flecks showing in the channel. There were half a dozen passengers besides himself; four of them women.

"A bit rough," he remarked to the deck-hand, who with bare feet was moving like a tightrope walker. The man shook his head and pointed to his tongue.

"That's Muet," said one of the passengers. "He's deaf and dumb."

Out in the middle channel there was a heavy swell. The *Cormoran* sank in the troughs and rose like a cork to the crests. Slowly the island came in sight, its houses discernible. As the captain collected the fares Franklin, with a rare assumption of seamanship, remarked that they were having a good crossing. Was the sea ever so rough that the *Cormoran* could not make it? Only once, the skipper assured him, and during the previous winter. Besides, the *Cormoran* carried the mails and was therefore on government service.

The village seemed quite a large one, and above it towered what looked like the keep of a mediæval fortress. Almost at the water's edge stood the hotel, a three-storied building with wide, glass-covered veranda in front. Franklin picked up his heavy suitcase and ploughed through the sand to the side door. Boarded off from the main dining-room was an office, and in this the manager was sitting.

"You have a room, monsieur?" said Franklin, giving his hat a flourish.

The manager admitted that he had, but with no particular enthusiasm. For how long would it be wanted? Franklin proceeded to explain. It might be two or three days or then, again, it might be a week. His report to his employers would have to be final but all depended on how the picture fitted the scenery. One could not tell until one saw.

"But you could not make pictures here," said the manager. "The permission of the patron would have to be obtained."

"We do things differently in Torino," retorted Franklin with a grandiose gesture. "All that can arrange itself."

"Monsieur is from Torino?"

"I was born there and my mother too."

M. Papini shook hands fervently. "There was something about you, signore, that I could not place; something distinguished and very different. There is a room, the best in the hotel, facing the sea. It is yours for one night—for two—for as long as you like."

There was nothing wrong with that. The manager escorted his fellow countryman up the stairs to the first landing, where the room stood at the handier end of the corridor. Its narrow end faced the sea, and the longer side looked over a pine-covered slope.

"Superb," said Franklin. "It is good to be among friends."

Across the road, facing the square and the eternal eucalyptus trees, was a café-restaurant, and there the two went. M. Papini forgot the urgency of his accounts under the spell of the enchanting voice of his guest: a man who had travelled much, who knew London like the back of his hand, and who now represented interests of first-class importance.

"The world is a small place," said Papini, "and the war changed many things."

"It is the habit of wars," said Vittorini sententiously. "This island too; always with those Moors on its doorstep and their galleys smelling their way round its coast. Those were not very good times."

"And now you come to begin it all over again," laughed the other, "what with your Algerians and pirates and Christians. The hotel could accommodate a good thirty at a pinch; but of course you would give ample warning."

Vittorini finished his apéritif and announced that he would have to get to work. Where was that Souterrain des Pirates—that pirates' cave?

"At the other end of the island," was the reply. "If you are a good walker, half an hour or perhaps more. And you must know the way."

"Body of Bacchus!" exclaimed Vittorini. "Am I an athlete to walk there and back? Is there not an auto?"

"Not on the island," the other assured him. "*M. le patron* had one to cart the stones from the quarries, but in a month it shook itself to pieces on the roads. Teeth of a Turk! What roads!" and he spat.

The other mopped his head for the sun was warm and the spot sheltered. "You have somebody in the hotel who will show this place? I will go in the afternoon. There will not be so much sun."

M. Vittorini was lucky. There was at the moment in the hotel an artist, an Englishman, who went out all day making sketches and returned for lunch. Perhaps he would show the place. And now another apéritif? But M. Vittorini excused himself. He must unpack his bag and write a letter or two. So with a ceremonious salute the two parted, both well pleased for the reasons which in neither case appeared on the surface.

At lunch M. Vittorini turned out to be a gross feeder. He tucked his napkin well into his collar and enjoyed himself thoroughly. From his seat facing the door he watched the entrance of Richleigh, whose face seemed tanned almost to Negro blackness. And when the coffee arrived he made his way to the bureau.

"A thousand pardons, but this Englishman who would take me to the cave?"

Papini got up delightedly and led the way to the Englishman's table. As soon as the film expert saw him he smiled as if he recognised a lost relative, and explained in a stream of rapid Italian that he had seen the other the previous day at Hyères. He also ventured to pat him on the back. Richleigh looked as if he had tumbled into a circus tent.

The manager explained in French which had to be funereal. Vittorini cut in with pantomimic explanations of his own and a word or two of English. "Feelm! Cinema! Feelm!" and altogether it must have been amazingly funny to watch. Then a map of the island was fetched and the Souterrain des Pirates pointed out, and after further pantomime and linguistic explosions there finally dawned on Richleigh just what was wanted. He smiled and nodded, and then, *"Quelle heure?"*

Vittorini held up two fingers. *"Deux heures!"* Then further smiles, a pat on the back from Vittorini, and all was settled.

(B)

Franklin was glad of that half hour's respite after lunch. The walk was going to be a ticklish thing and would need some preparation. That it would be necessary to keep at high tension he realised; that it would be as grotesque as it was he hardly imagined.

There was a man once, and the story is implicitly true, who met a Bedouin boy in the Sinai Desert. One knew no Arabic and the other no English. Yet the two had a really interesting conversation wherein the Englishman learned, among other things, that the youth had two brothers and two sisters. His father had been killed outright by a Turkish shell; his mother had had a leg blown off and had died almost at once. The two sisters had disappeared. One brother had died of—apparently—dysentery and the other was in the Camel Corps.

From the wealth of gesture, direct acting and facial distortion that went to make up that conversation may be gathered some idea of the forty minutes' walk—nearly all uphill—which this latest mono-lingual couple attempted. In most ways it was far more difficult. One could scarcely roll on the ground and make noises! The matter to explain was moreover fairly technical. But all the same, to any continuous observer, this new pilgrims' progress must have been extremely diverting. M. Vittorini had his three languages at command, if indeed the English he exhibited could be allowed to count, consisting as it did of occasional words spoken with strange accents. As for Richleigh, he struggled with much the same handicap in French, and endeavoured, more or less vainly, to make the other understand a kind of baby or pidgin English.

Imagine something like this. The path through the *bruyères* or among the pines swerved to the right. Vittorini would smile comprehensively, shoot out an arm and say, *"Alla destra. Droit.* Eengleesh?" and, "Right!" would bellow the other as if noise were a deciding factor in understanding. A few yards farther on the mainland would be visible. Another smile and, *"Lontano. Lointain,"* and this time no reply. However a smile all the same and then Richleigh, tapping a tree trunk, "Pine!" "Ah!" would exclaim the other, *"Sapin!"* and Richleigh, "That's it—'pine.'"

As they swung round the headland and down to the beach Richleigh gave a sudden exclamation. "Look out there! Your foot!" Vittorini turned round to smile and came a fearful purler over a root.

"I say, I'm dreadfully sorry," began Richleigh, and then, at the sight of his companion's trousers, "Oh, hell!"

But beyond a cut knee and scratched hands no harm was done. For another five minutes they moved along the top of the cliff, and then, at two pines which hung towards the sea, Richleigh stopped.

"Le Souterrain des Pirates?" inquired Vittorini. The other nodded and pointed down.

Then came the pantomimic masterpiece. By hook or crook the exact object of the visit had to be explained. Vittorini turned the handle of a machine; he directed through an imaginary megaphone; he was a corsair with turban and scimitar; he rowed at the galley oar; in short, he sweated blood. At intervals he repeated, "Feelm! Cinema!" and was finally rewarded by seeing a look of comprehension come into the other's eyes. Indeed, Richleigh repeated some of the performance. Vittorini beamed approval and pointed down to the cave. Then the descent began.

For thirty feet downwards they zigzagged by a series of rough steps cut in the rock. Then came twenty feet at a steeper angle with the steps cut more cleanly. Richleigh went first, lowering himself gingerly, since the spray from the roughening sea made the going treacherous. Once Richleigh called, "Give me your foot!" and the other thought it best to halt and see what the message meant.

But when they reached the foot of the stairs there was nothing to see. There was an opening, but no bigger than a cupboard, and as for the cavern where the corsairs once had their stronghold, a landslide had filled it in. In front too, towards the sea, were rocks and boulders; only the deep sheltered bay with its tiny entrance showed what the spot might once have been.

Vittorini, having expressed his opinion on the uselessness of the sight for his purpose, pointed upwards for the return journey. "You go first," said Richleigh, and seeing the vacancy in the other's eyes took the lead himself. And as Vittorini took the last step he saw what he had not previously noticed: a castle perched at the very extremity of the island and not more than a mile away. He pointed it out.

"Moors. *Château,"* explained Richleigh.

"Ah! Le Château des Maures!" said Vittorini with obvious satisfaction and waved an invitation to proceed. And this time the climb was worth while.

Poised sheer above the Mediterranean and on almost the last yard of foothold was a massive square tower. Around it were walls, enclosing what had once been courtyards and rooms. Then the sun came out for the occasion. The grey sea became purple and shot with emerald currents; the pines took on a distant blue; the bare fields showed a rosy madder and the rocks revealed their fissures and a delicacy of greens and grey. *"Che hella vista!"* exclaimed Vittorini, and turned to his companion. But Richleigh was not there.

In a minute or two he appeared from somewhere behind the great tower carrying a portfolio. From this he took a sketch and handed it to the Italian. And the fellow could paint. There was a superb poster effect with primary colours on a broad canvas.

"*Magnifique!*" was his comment. Richleigh smiled, replaced the picture, and produced another; a water colour as dainty and finished as a Rutherston fan.

Then M. Vittorini did a strange thing. He pulled out a roll of notes, retained the sketch, and indicated that the artist should help himself. Richleigh blushed, then shook his head. He replaced the sketch, went through the motions of painting another one, and solemnly presented it to the kindly critic. Vittorini was overjoyed. He promptly wrote out an address, loosed a flood of thanks, and patted the artist on the back. Then he consulted his watch, held up ten fingers, pointed to the sea, and went off to explore on his own account.

Though not discernible from the summit, there was a path that led sheer down the cliff to a narrow beach where once the long galleys had thrust their noses. But this was of small interest to Franklin. What he wanted was a minute or two's relief from the strain of that infernal mimicry; the chance to be himself for the space of just one cigarette. When he made the ascent again, there was Richleigh, sitting on a mound of broken rock, smoking his pipe.

"*La pipe,*" said M. Vittorini observantly, and pointing to his own packet of Marylands, "*Spagnoletti!* Cigarettes!" And with that, mad conversation began afresh.

They made the return journey by a rough road that ran clean through the centre of the island. The eastern side, he gathered, was uninteresting, being nearly all under cultivation. Not a soul was seen till the green-shuttered villas came in sight and the village began. The dusk was coming on, and on the mainland the lights began to twinkle. In the air was the smell of the south; the leaves of orange trees, smoke of wood fires, the whiff of a cigarette, and the faint odour of garlic. On the square the men were still throwing their balls and arguing fiercely. At the hotel door the two parted, with thanks and smiles and amiability. Franklin felt his brain whirling and as tired as if he had played a day's chess.

But when he got to bed that night it was not to sleep. There were things that had occurred that afternoon that set his brain working with full activity, and after an hour of it he got out and wrote up his notes. And just before he did go to sleep the last thing he had in his mind was the way Richleigh had appeared to look at him from the dinner table; with eyes quietly observant and yet wholly cynical.

(C)

The morning dawned cold but clear, and by nine M. Vittorini was up and on the quay, taking a constitutional and watching the progress of the *Cormoran* till she came in. Then from the small shop on the Square he bought a paper which the launch had brought in and on the counter saw a *Daily Mail.*

"It is ordered, that paper?" he asked.

"Yes," was the reply. "An Englishman at the hotel has ordered it."

"Really," said Franklin. "Does one find English often on the island?"

"Not very often. But at Easter sometimes one or two arrive. And always they ask for an English paper."

For half an hour he smoked his pipe and read his paper and then came an interview with Papini. The Moorish Castle was a magnificent site, but was there anything else that might be useful? Papini suggested the Plage d'Argent, a crescent of silver sand that lay to the west; the same road as the previous day but by a path that left the main road.

There was no sign of Richleigh, but Franklin was not sorry. A morning like that afternoon would be too much. One could pay too great a price for surveillance. So he set out briskly along the road; cut through a pine wood that lay to the right, and came out on the rocks that overlooked a bay.

Then the noise of a motor boat attracted him: the *Cormoran,* perhaps, setting off for another crossing. But the noise was too close for that; it was almost beneath him. With a perfectly natural curiosity he leaned out over a projecting rock and peered below. In a motor boat, large enough for half a dozen passengers, sat Richleigh alone. The engine was shut off and what Franklin saw made him draw back further behind his shelter. Then in a minute or two the engine chugged again. For a few yards the boat lazed at five or six knots; then, turning to the open channel, it leaped into action and became a black streak in the white spray. As it rounded the headland and met the heavy water it slowed down, and long after it was out of sight its engine was plainly audible.

The visit to the Plage d'Argent was abandoned, and in five minutes Franklin was back at the hotel. He reached his room unobserved and found he was in luck. The bed had been made and in the corridor was no sign of a maid. Now from which door had Richleigh emerged the previous evening? The second surely. He tried the handle. To his surprise the door opened. The room, moreover, was empty, swept, and garnished.

Like a flash Franklin was here and there. The contents of the open suitcase, two drawers that opened easily, the articles on the dressing table were all hurriedly glanced at. On another table lay odd books and papers: a *French Made Easy* and a guidebook, *Porquerolles et les Îles d'Or*. He flicked over quickly the leaves of them both and on the inside of the back cover of the latter saw something that interested him. He went quickly to the corridor and regained his room. Then as furtively the book was replaced. After that for the best part of an hour he busied himself with his pocket time-table and what he learned from it must have been disquieting, for he looked worried, and more than once he paced the room.

In the cool of the evening came an apéritif at the café-restaurant Papillot with his host. Could one hire a motor boat on the island? he asked. Usually yes, was the answer. For the moment, however, the one worth hiring had been taken over by M. Richleigh, Papillot, moreover, who owned the boat, gave them to understand that Richleigh had taken it for an indefinite period. He and Le Muet were going out fishing that night if the sea was quiet enough.

Then Richleigh himself passed and was called to join them. Had M. Papini a book about the island? Papini passed the question on to Richleigh, who was only too pleased to slip into the hotel and get his. When it came Vittorini studied it intently, though its importance consisted mainly in the fact that what he looked for didn't happen to be there.

That was Franklin's last day on the island. Physically he was feeling so fit that he could have pushed over the proverbial church. After lunch the next day, and still in perfect weather, he crossed on the *Cormoran*. At Hyères he paid a flying visit to the Syndicat d'Initiative—the information bureau for the benefit of travellers. From Toulon he wrote to a cousin in Turin, asking him to send to England any package which might arrive for him. He thus made sure of receiving from Richleigh the promised water colour in spite of the false address he had been forced to give.

The following afternoon he made the crossing in vile weather from Calais. At Dover a bitter wind was blowing and sleety rain lashed against the carriage windows. It seemed incredible that only a day before he had been sitting in the *Cormoran,* hatless and full of the exhilaration of life, with the sun as warm as on an English day of June, and the pleasant smell of the pines still in his nostrils. And as the fields of Kent swept by in the rainy mist, he smoked his pipe and thought of the Island of Porquerolles: its woods, its beaches, its sun, its food and good fellowship, and certainly not least, of that most painstaking of guides, that most poetical of painters, that most interesting of personalities—Frank Richleigh.

CHAPTER XVIII
FRANKLIN SEES DAYLIGHT

"You certainly look the better for it," said Travers as they drew their chairs up to the fire after an excellent dinner. "You sure it wasn't Vienna?"

"Vienna?" repeated Franklin, rather puzzled. "Oh, thyroid gland." He laughed, and the laugh was a cheerful one with some new confidences in it. "If the new department gets on its feet I hope all the crooks will decamp to the Riviera."

"Especially in November," added Travers, waving his hand towards the window against which the rain was pelting. "And now what's all the really sensational news?"

Franklin got out his notebook. "I don't want to appear as Holmes with you as Watson, but if you don't mind I'll go over the principal points as I made them. Almost as many as Woodrow Wilson's. I told you about the island generally and the humorous business with languages, but these are the special things that arose.

"A. Fundamentally the situation hasn't altered. Wharton was correct about the alibi and we may take it that Frank Richleigh did *not* commit the Murder. But, I had one idea. His alibi grows stronger every day. When Wharton interviewed the people concerned he brought clearly to their notice the events into which he had to inquire. They've told him that certain dates were correct. As soon as I asked the same questions they answered me more readily than I imagine they did him. If anybody else asks them those questions in a year's time, they'll have the answers still more pat, since the questions will have been impressed on their minds on two previous occasions. If therefore the original alibi was false, it's too late now to prove it so."

"Just a minute," said Travers. "I'm going to enjoy this without disturbance. Fill your pipe and let's get down to it. And fill your glass."

"Not the glass," said Franklin, stoking his pipe. "But if I give you some information that's really interesting, you shall fill it for me afterwards. That's a bargain? Good! Now listen to this. I wanted to see, on your own suggestion, how I reacted to Frank Richleigh. The situation was unusual on account of that comic business I told you about, but the impressions I gathered were these. Richleigh is an attractive fellow in many ways, but he seemed to me to have qualities that more than counteracted his better points. In other words, I didn't like him. Not only that, but in those conversations we conducted in gibberish and sign language, I'm as sure as that I'm sitting here now—"

"Waiting for a drink!"

"Yes, waiting for a drink; that on at least three occasions he tried deliberately to catch me out by making sudden remarks in English to see if I responded. You must take my word for it, but I could repeat it with much more emphasis."

"You thought he saw the nigger in the woodpile?"

"I thought he was on the lookout for the nigger; that's the important thing. Perhaps Wharton stroked him the wrong way, but suspicious he was, and that's certain. And though I say it as shouldn't, I'm positive he got no change out of me. That's point B. Now comes C. I also tried a little catch or two on the same lines but in French. And as a result I'm perfectly convinced that Frank Richleigh knows much more of that language than he pretends."

"You really think so? But of course it would be much easier to fake ignorance and a horrible accent than one would at first imagine. And he couldn't have forgotten so hopelessly what he was taught at school."

"Point D. Richleigh had given at the paper shop on the island a special order for a *Daily Mail*. One morning he got his paper and went in his motor boat to a lonely spot and pulled up there for a minute or two. Then he looked through that paper feverishly, like a man who wants desperately badly to see if anything's there. He scanned every column from front page to back. Then he put the paper away like a man relieved and hared off in the boat. There was the report of a Test Match in that paper, but he didn't stop to read it."

"Hm! Anything else?"

"Plenty! Point E, for instance. I found in a book of his some pencilled notes of times of trains from Victoria to—not Carcassonne, as you'd expect—but to Hyères, with an added time for the bus to La Tour Fondue and actual arrival at Porquerolles. He'd never done that journey, and when later he had to lend me that book he rubbed out those notes with scrupulous care. Further than that, I inquired at the Syndicat d'Initiative at Hyèeres and showed them Richleigh's photo, and one of the clerks was sure that he was a man who called there in the summer! In other words, I'm pretty sure I could prove to you that in spite of what he pretends, Richleigh had planned as long ago as the beginning of his summer holiday to go to Porquerolles, and moreover actually paid a visit, at least as far as La Tour Fondue, to spy out the land."

"Preparing a bolt hole, you think?"

"Why not? Porquerolles is a lonely place, but marvellously handy for bigger places—Toulon and Marseilles—where the ships start from. Then point F, which I thought of in the train. If you think back into the mind of the public and the press, doesn't it strike you that everybody expected the Perfect Murder to take place at night, say round about 10.00 p. m.?"

"Now you come to speak of it, I think we all did."

"And what happened? It took place in the early evening, at 7.30, to be precise. Suppose the murderer had wanted to catch the 8.50 from Victoria he could just have managed it."

And having made that point he watched the changing expressions on the face of Ludovic Travers as he sat looking into the fire. "Not only that, but *if;* I grant you the 'if' is an insuperable 'if'; still, if Frank Richleigh committed the murder he would not have wanted the maid to see him escape. He would not have been able to disguise himself effectively for the simple reason that he couldn't have removed the disguise in the time available after the murder—that is if he wanted to catch the boat train for France."

But Travers kept back his questions. He merely nodded, then, "Good! What next?"

"One point only, and it occurred to me when I was returning home. You've referred to it to-night without knowing it. And like all the other points it's not worth tuppence as far as a jury is concerned. When I left Porquerolles the weather was gorgeous, the sun was shining and the air was like a tonic. Three months and they'll be bathing again and having sunbaths. Still, you know it all better than I can describe it: the unlimited leisure, scenery by the acre, the simple life if you want it and plenty of the other thing if you don't. And all for forty francs a day, with the exchange at 125! Then England—listen to it for a second—rain and wind and fog and sleet. My God, thought I; if I had enough money would I be such a fool as to stand another English November? Then I went on without knowing it. If I were a schoolmaster, a member of the most unappreciated, unromantic, and unremunerative profession there is; if I had ideas I couldn't use, tastes I hadn't the time or money to cultivate, colleagues whom I despised intellectually and who regarded me as a fool; a headmaster bound stiff with red tape and his own importance; a job I couldn't leave because I was too old; if I'd lost my savings in a bad investment, as Richleigh had, and lastly, if I'd a chest which gave me a bad time every winter; then, I put it to you, wouldn't I do a great deal to—to—well, find my Island of Porquerolles?"

Travers got up. "You deserve more than a drink. You ought to put the decanter in your pocket."

"I know I got that speech off by heart. But seriously, is there anything in all those points of mine?"

"I think," said Travers, "and I think it in all seriousness, that if your words are nails driven by the master of assemblies, they look like being somebody's coffin nails."

Franklin thought that over, then took a pull at the drink. "Now you have a shot at the Aunt Sally!"

"I won't do that," said Travers, "because I've more than a suspicion that in this particular context I'm a bit of an Aunt Sally myself. Also destructive criticism is anybody's game. But I would like to know if Frank Richleigh really did pay that exploratory visit to the island in the summer."

"It would have been easy enough. Only two nights absent from the hotel, and he might have gone there before he came to town. But he couldn't have been in two places at once on the night of the murder."

"Has anything struck you as unusual about those alibis?" asked Travis.

"No," replied the other in astonishment.

"Well, perhaps not unusual but interesting. Who established the lawyer's alibi?"

"His wife, daughter, and a local curate."

"And the actor's?"

"All the company he was playing in."

"And the parson's?"

"His wife, two maids, and an ostler."

"And the schoolmaster's?"

"The proprietors of two hotels, a bureau clerk, and a waiter."

"That's just it. Three alibis remain constant irrespective of the passing of time. The fourth, as you pointed out, grows stronger and less vulnerable every day. Three are established by those who could never make a mistake; the fourth by utter strangers. Three take place almost on the domestic hearth; the fourth in a remote corner of another country."

"That's a sound enough argument. But the fact remains: that alibi can't be upset. Wharton knows it and I'd swear it."

"Probably it can't. And as you said, time is getting on. If it can't be upset to-day, it's far more immovable in a month's time. It's a geometrical, not an arithmetical progression, if you look at it from the point of view of a specialist in mathematics, like Richleigh. But could he be in two places at the same time?"

"If he could it amounts to unearthing a case of impersonation, and that would involve finding the impersonator. The whole idea seems to me to be *possible* only in the sense that in this world we hardly dare say what is really *impossible.*"

"I should say definitely it was impossible," said Travers. "Piccadilly Circus is supposed to be the hub of the English universe and all the world to pass by it; yet if you or I stood there for months and watched every face we should never find the perfect double we're popularly supposed to possess."

Franklin agreed. "But for all that, you admit that Frank Richleigh is seriously mixed up in it. If he didn't do that murder, he knows who did."

Both were silent, feeling that something was in the air. Travers sat, or rather sprawled, with his long legs stretched to the fire and his hands pressed together as if seeking the right word. Franklin seemed to look through the fire into some world of his own imagination. It was Travers who spoke first.

"What do you think you'll do now?"

"Go to Muffley Hill first of all and try to get into contact with as many persons as I can who knew Richleigh. I'll collect every scrap of gossip, every remembered conversation, and every impression. Potter's been down there a day or two in a quiet way. It was he who got the news about Richleigh losing his money. Still, I thought I'd go down there myself, while the iron's hot, so to speak, and get my own ideas. Then I hope to get other contacts, like the names of cricket teams he's played for. Then I shall go on to Little Martens and collect up the gossip there. And when I've finished I shall go over the reams of notes and get them correlated. By that time I shall have a pretty sound idea of what Frank Richleigh is really like."

"A long job!"

"As you say. What I feel, however, is that I'm no longer lost. I'm in a tunnel, and if I only have the patience to keep plodding on I must come to the end where the daylight is. Still, as I was saying, when I've finished in England I'm going to France again. I may have to take a film photographer with me for a blind, but I'm going to live near Richleigh for days. If I got those ideas I told you about in a few hours, what oughtn't I to get if I live with him for a week or two, especially when you consider all the new facts and theories I shall take over with me from England?"

"It reduces itself to what we said a good few weeks ago," said Travers. "It's a case that calls for the methods of Lecoq. Sooner or later something's going to be dropped—it may be something apparently insignificant—and then things are going to start happening."

"They'll happen all right," said Franklin. "What's more, if I'm sure you understand why I say it, I shan't report to you again till I've got something really worth reporting. When I've got some news as important as, well, say what I brought back from Porquerolles, then I'll come along with it like a streak of lightning."

• • • • • • •

For some minutes after Franklin had gone Travers sat before the fire. Then he pushed the bell for Palmer.

As a gentleman's servant, butler, major-domo, call him what you will, Palmer stood high in the estimation of St. Martin's Chambers. To his colleagues he could unbend and yet keep an essential and ultimate reserve. In some previous incarnation, according to Ludovic Travers, he had probably been a raven, black-coated and not unmindful of his young. As he stood there waiting for orders he presented a figure dignified and composed.

"Oh, Palmer, you busy for a minute?"

"No, sir."

"Sit down, then, and draw up to the fire. Look here—I'd rather like to have your opinion on something. Did you ever read up that Perfect Murder Case at all?"

Palmer was not in the least disconcerted. Conversations of that kind were by no means unusual. So he put the tips of his fingers together and gave as cautious a reply as possible.

"Well, I did read it, sir, and then again in a manner of speaking, I didn't."

"Not studied it in detail."

"No, sir; can't say I have. I did glance at the story of that housekeeper, sir, but not from what you might call the murder point of view."

"Sort of professional *esprit de corps*, what? Then it's no use asking you who did it?"

"I'm afraid not, sir."

"Hm! You back horses sometimes?"

Palmer was perfectly unruffled. "Sometimes I do, sir, and sometimes I don't."

"A very sound answer. However, suppose you do back a horse. On what principle do you work?"

"Well, sir, sometimes the Major gives me a tip and sometimes Mr. Henry does, and I put on my half-crown, and that's all there is to it."

"Except collecting the boodle. Then you never have a sudden intuition, by any chance?"

Palmer achieved a master stroke of diplomacy. "That depends on what you mean by 'intuition,' sir."

"Intuition? Well, an instinctive guess. You never had one in your life?"

"Oh, yes, sir. The trouble is they didn't turn out right."

Travers nodded. "Now, what about this? I try to sell you a bit of Waterford glass, like this stuff you've handled all your life, except that it's the cleverest fake there could be: feel, colour, marks, everything perfect. Yet you won't touch it. Why?"

Palmer's face lost its wariness and became more animated. "I don't know, sir, and you don't know, only something inside me would say, 'Leave it alone.' That's all, sir, and if I wasn't a fool I *should* leave it alone."

Travers smiled. "Good! Now let's have a last question. Suppose I had an intuition of that kind about something in which I was interested; say, for example, this murder case. Ought I in your opinion to trust that intuition?"

"Yes, sir; if you're a policeman."

Travers fairly roared. "Palmer, you're a philosopher. But to get to business. There's a little scheme I've got in my mind which I'd rather like your help in," and he explained it at some length.

And as Palmer left the room some minutes later with an expression of puzzled concern on his face Travers rang up the Academic Theatre, where he hoped to catch before his departure Roland du Fresne, the well-known actor-manager.

CHAPTER XIX

COMIC RELIEF AND A CROSS-WORD PUZZLE

SOME few days later, in the room of Ludovic Travers, at Durango House, the telephone bell rang. He picked up the receiver. "Hallo. Yes, speaking... Mr. Franklin has just gone to his office? Thank you, exchange. Put me through, will you?"

The conversation then ran something like this: "Hallo! That you, Franklin? Travers speaking. What's the news? ... Well, there's heaps of time yet. And look here, now—there's something most frightfully important I want you to do for me. Do you know Gregorio's night club in Charing Cross Road? ... Well, it's under the shop of Wilberforce, the sporting print man. There's a basement underneath and a door at the Leicester Square side. You go right down and show your card and I'll have the rest fixed up. You got that? ... Time? Oh, yes. Be there at nine sharp. There won't be anybody much about the place, and I've got an idea that something funny's going to happen. Are you there? ... I want you to follow this closely. Be there at nine sharp. If you see me, pay no attention whatever. If I leave the place without speaking to you, go away but don't follow. Don't even come to the flat. You got that all right? ... Good! Then, if I don't speak to you, be at the same place the same time on the following night. Can you manage that? ... I'm afraid it's a bit melodramatic, but it can't be helped. But it's awfully good of you. Good-bye!" and he replaced the receiver quickly and left the room.

A thoroughly perplexed Franklin presented himself therefore at 9.00 p.m. at the foot of the stairs that led to Gregorio's. He handed his card as directed to the black-coated shop-walker at the door.

"Mr. Franklin? Ah, yes, sir. Your coat and hat, sir. This seat, if you don't mind. Black coffee or white, sir? And a liqueur, sir? Thank you, sir."

From his comfortable seat Franklin surveyed the room. In length it seemed a good cricket pitch, but narrow in proportion. In the middle of the left side was the bar and elsewhere round the room was a continuous lounge seat and a string of tables. The polished floor looked a good one, but at the moment it was unoccupied. Indeed, the room was practically empty. At the far end a couple of girls were chattering over some kind of a drink and at the bar two elderly men were conversing in semi-whispers. In the far right corner the piano and deserted music stands alone marked the prospect of an orchestra. Franklin sipped his black coffee, sat well back in his padded seat, and waited for the ball to start rolling.

There was not long to wait. Voices were heard in the lobby outside, and before he was aware of it the familiar figure of

Ludovic Travers slid by over the slippery floor, heading for the bar. He nodded pleasantly to the elderly pair, thrust his head over the bar counter, and planted his elbows firmly. When the shirt-sleeved attendant placed a drink in front of him he made an inaudible remark to the pair, nodded, and finished it at a go. Then he looked round the room, and his eyes seemed to pass over Franklin without observing him, though that might have been an effect produced by the horn rims. Then he moved off to the far end of the room.

There, to Franklin's amazement, he promptly engaged in conversation with the women. There was a peal of laughter, and one of them moved along the lounge seat to make room for the newcomer. A waiter appeared, disappeared, and returned with three cocktails, at the sight of which Travers removed his glasses and blinked vigorously. Then followed ten minutes of mirthful chatter, of pretty somethings whispered into pretty ears, and occasional outbursts of giggling.

When the two departed to the roguish wag of Travers's finger the room was beginning to fill up. Travers again removed his glasses and after the usual polish peered round the room. There was another ten minutes of waiting, and then he looked at his watch. Then he left the room by a side door. Franklin, with his curiosity entirely unsatisfied, waited a few minutes, then called for his hat and coat and left also. What the whole business meant he hadn't the faintest idea, unless it was that much business had driven Travers mad.

Twice during the following day he 'phoned through to the finance department, but Travers was not there. Speculation was equally unprofitable, and there seemed to be nothing for it but to possess his soul in patience and go through the performance again. And the second night turned out to be in its preliminaries exactly like the first, except that the room was nearly full and the orchestra was present. Moreover, when Travers appeared he made straight for Franklin's corner, his face beaming with pleasure.

"Hullo, young feller. Nice sort of place to find you in!"

Franklin smiled. "I'm not the only whited sepulchre."

"So I expect. Now, what about a drink?"

"What do you make of it?" asked Travers as they sat watching the crowd. "Quite a modest haunt of vice?"

Franklin's reply was drowned by the band, which struck into the rhythmic lilt of "Mammy's Little Kitten," and he waited for a quieter moment. "Seems well conducted."

"By the way," said Travers, "I'm awfully sorry about last night. I hope you weren't too annoyed at not seeing me?"

"Oh, I saw you all right," laughed Franklin, "and—"

"You saw me!" exclaimed the other. "What time was that?"

"At nine-fifteen. That was when you came in, wasn't it?"

"Came in! Came in where?"

"Came in here," said Franklin jocularly.

"Here! My dear fellow, I was at the Portico at nine-fifteen last night, talking to Chief-Constable Scott, and I didn't leave till ten."

"Well, I'm damned! Just a second—here's the shop-walker. Look here. This gentleman says he wasn't here last night and I say he was. Now you tell us who's right."

"The gentleman *was* here, sir."

Franklin beamed. "You saw him and spoke to him?"

"Yes, sir."

"At about nine-fifteen?"

"About that, sir."

"Looks rather as if you were right," replied Travers with a perfectly serious face. "If so, it's a queer sort of business. Who else saw me, do you think?"

But at the bar the results were equally surprising; the attendant remembered the gentleman perfectly. Travers appeared to be flabbergasted, and Franklin couldn't help rubbing it in. "Somebody's been impersonating you. It's a pity your two charming acquaintances don't seem to be here!"

"Let's get round to the flat," said Travers, "and talk this over. We can get there in three minutes."

Palmer let them in and ventured a "Good evening, sir!" to Franklin on his own account. When they had settled down before a blazing fire, Travers reopened the discussion.

"You say you saw me at Gregorio's at nine-fifteen last night."

"I certainly did. You remember you made the appointment."

"What the soldier said is not evidence," retorted Travers drily. Then he looked straight at the other and his eyes twinkled. "I know you're going to take this the right way, so I'll own up. I was *not* at Gregorio's last night."

Franklin, who had expected the confession to be the other way about, was beginning to gather, somewhat hazily, that there was a catch in it somewhere. "I'll give it up. What's the answer?"

"What I told you. I wasn't there."

"Then whom did I see?"

"Palmer."

"Palmer?"

"That's right. He's the same height as myself but slightly fatter. Put my big ulster on him and button it tightly and he's the same. Then give him my glasses and stoop; add four or five rehearsals, and that Roland du Fresne, who doesn't come on till the second act, was round here making Palmer up and supervising the dress rehearsal, so to speak, and there we are. Add further that you never came within ten yards of my double and that the lights weren't all on, and what chance had you?"

Franklin took it very well. "Precious little, apparently! Well, I'd have sworn—"

"Of course you would. The disguise was perfect, and not enough grease paint to cover a sixpence. We tried it out with George the porter, and he gulped it down. And that reminds me. Have a drink."

"Only just swallowed the last. Do you mind if I congratulate Palmer?"

"He did put up an awfully good show," said Travers. "You sure you don't mind us behaving so disgracefully?"

"Not a bit. I rather enjoyed it. But there's one thing I would like to know, and it rather discounts the acknowledgment. Just *why* did you do it?"

"To tell you the truth," said Travers, "the first idea was to prove the easiness with which Frank Richleigh might have employed a confederate. Just as you'd have sworn to my whereabouts last night, so people may have sworn to his."

"There'd still remain to find that confederate."

"Oh, I know you can knock holes in it. I knew that before I did the damn-fool thing. But there was another reason. I was getting impatient. I knew you'd like to know I *was* impatient, so I lured you round here by means of a little comic relief. I really do mean relief, by the way. I know there's plenty of work to do, and I know you're like me—can't rest while it's there. And now you're here—you see I don't give you a chance to reply—what's the news from Muffley Hill?"

"I've spent a few days there. In some ways I'm satisfied with striking while the iron was hot."

"Anything happen?"

"It all depends. For instance, there was that disclosure about Richleigh losing his money a year or two ago. Also exactly at half term the headmaster received his resignation."

"Why the 'exactly'?"

"Well, it fitted in so precisely. He had to give a half term's notice and on the date—November the third—he couldn't have known that his uncle had died intestate. If he did, it must have been close work, and the date of the murder fitted remarkably well."

"That's what strikes me most about the whole business," said Travers. "Everything goes according to schedule. Everything for Frank Richleigh turns out the best in this best of all worlds. He hasn't even troubled about coming back to England. *II a de la chance; ce jeune homme-là!*"

"A damn sight too much luck for my liking," said Franklin. "The one man who gets the most out of it did *not* commit the murder."

"What else did you find out?"

"Not much really. Still, it was curious how everybody in his profession spoke badly of him and everybody outside it liked him and spoke well about him. I saw a good many people too: his landlady again, his tobacconist, the school groundsman, some of the senior boys, and his doctor."

"How on earth did you manage that?"

"Called to see him with an attack of indigestion. I couldn't very well give him an address, and it looked rather curious when I paid him on the spot. I got the conversation round to my old friend Richleigh whom I'd just seen in the south of France. 'Best place for him,' said the doctor. 'Really?' said I, and that's all there was to it. I couldn't very well drag him in again, and so bang went five bob."

"Didn't get your money's worth?"

"Can't say yet. Then I saw the headmaster on the plea that Richleigh had mentioned to me that he might possibly be free at Christmas and I thought of taking him on as private secretary! He was about the most pompous old ass I've ever struck and simply seething because Richleigh had got his notice in first."

"He was definitely going to dismiss him, then?"

"So he hinted. So did the other man, Walton, whom I told you about. But it sounded fishy to me. Something else I got from a man in the Common Room is rather interesting. You know the tone of that first 'Marius' letter—how generally superior and ironical it is, and I told you about Richleigh's sarcastic tongue. Here's another example. Richleigh was sitting by himself in the corner when he suddenly said to the music master—poisonous sort of chap called Jenston—'What was that you were playing to the Fourths this morning, Jenston?' 'A man of your tastes ought to have known,' was the reply. 'But if you want to know, it was the "War March of the Priests." 'Sorry,' said Richleigh. 'I thought it was a procession of the unemployed.' I may be wrong, but the more I think about it the more I place Richleigh as the writer of that letter."

"Hm! Anything else about Richleigh's temperamental make-up?"

"I don't know that there was. Oh, yes; there was one other thing. According to the Head, Richleigh had the very devil of a temper. You couldn't see a sign of it except a sort of quiet, white-hot smoulder. He'd never known him actually lose his temper but once, and that was in his very last term."

"What was that about?" asked Travers. "You mustn't mind my pestering you like this, but I do think we can't hear too much of Richleigh from every conceivable angle. What did he lose his temper about?"

"Something perfectly stupid—at least, it seemed so to me. This chap Jenston called him a certain nickname in the Common Room, and Richleigh knocked him tail over tip. The Head heard about it; quite by accident, so he persisted."

"Wonder what the nickname was?" asked Travers, almost to himself.

Franklin told him.

Then a surprising thing happened. Travers sat up with a jerk. "Do you mind saying that again?"

Franklin repeated it. Travers rubbed the pebbles of his glasses with a vigour that threatened disaster. But he did not blink. His eyes remained tightly closed. Then he sprang up and fetched the photos. He held that of Frank Richleigh to the light for a good half minute, and then what he said seemed little to the purpose. "Fancy not remembering that! Here's a crossword puzzle for you. Find the name of the murderer in nine letters. And the answer's not 'Richleigh.'"

Franklin gave it up.

"I'm sorry," said Travers. "Perhaps I was going too quickly. Here's something easier. Richleigh was a teacher of mathematics. Wouldn't he know that things which are equal to the same thing are equal to one another?"

Franklin still looked puzzled.

"I expect you think I'm mad," said Travers. Then he gave that rare smile of his. "I've got to think about it. It's no use diving off the deep end. Could you come round to breakfast in the morning? Say about 8.00?"

"I certainly can," said Franklin, watching the other's face in an attempt to find some clue to the tremendous thing that had so startled Travers and galvanised him into action. "You found something good?"

"For breakfast?" and they both smiled. "About the usual. There may be something extra, but don't count on it."

And with that Franklin had to be content.

CHAPTER XX
SPADE WORK

"I HAD TO SLEEP on it," said Travers. "It was a question of appealing from Travers drunk to Travers sober. When it struck me suddenly last night and I realised whom Richleigh's photograph reminded me of, it looked a certainty that the answer to that crossword puzzle was 'Gene Allen.' What it looks like this morning you've heard. And you really think we can go ahead?"

"I'm bursting to start now," said Franklin. "This bit of investigating may be a gamble, but it's something you can get your teeth into."

"How do you propose starting?"

"Well, there seem several methods of approach. We've got to find out who got that job. You say the queue you saw was a big one?"

"I should say that roughly a couple of hundred men were lined up, and a dozen more arrived while I was actually there. That's no guide of course to the final numbers, but I imagine all the serious applicants would be early birds."

"The two main lines I thought of were to see if a man of type asked for happens to be missing, and also identification of the man by means of the queue."

"Don't you think the first will be frightfully difficult? What I mean is this: Suppose you had been picking out a man for the purpose. You get from the queue a final selection of three or four, all reasonably well qualified. Everything else being equal, what would be your final test? Surely lack of relatives or dependents who might make inquiries in case of disappearance?"

"That does seem to be so," admitted Franklin. "Still, Potter could get on with that."

"As for the other," suggested Travers, "I think I can save you some time. Why not consult all the files of the press for photographs? Some enterprising photographer would surely have taken that queue. Then try the art departments of the papers. Above all, go to the three principal publishers of film gazettes; I'll give you the addresses of their offices, by the way. See if any of their men took that queue. Get all the pictures you can; make enlarged facsimiles of the heads, and then go to the film studios and try to get identification. Stage managers, theatrical agents, and stage-door keepers ought to produce something."

"Is it worth while trying to find out at the same time if any actual film company did insert that advertisement? If it should happen to be a genuine one the whole theory'll be upset."

"Why not? After all, it's no use working on a false hypothesis. But if they didn't, by that much more we're nearer the mark. I'll give you a list of companies in half an hour. I imagine there are no private concerns."

When Franklin got to Durango House he had visited the advertisement departments of four of the dailies which had printed the advertisement. In each case the records showed that a typewritten communication had been received, with the necessary payment for two appearances. There was no heading except the name of the office, and the signature read—

F. W. BUNTING,
(Manager).

and below in a bracket—

Comedy Films Limited.

It was the custom to accept small ads of that type for the "Men Wanted" column without any check, except in obviously peculiar circumstances. The machine used was *not* a Rolland Portable.

The list of the registered companies made Franklin whistle. Seventeen of them! And Comedy Films Limited *not* included: an omission that solved the problem of the genuineness of the advertisement. Three men were forthwith set to work at compilation of photographs from the press. The three companies that published gazettes Franklin proposed to interview himself, and a long and trying business it turned out to be.

From the fact that all had offices in Wardour Street he had anticipated a minimum of trouble, whereas of the thousands of feet of film actually taken to cut down into those five-minute gazettes he had no idea. The rest of the day was spent with one company only, and it involved a visit to the studio mortuary at Reigate and the running over miles of film. The actual shot had not been considered of sufficient topical interest to incorporate in either of the bi-weekly editions, and a series of events of more importance had helped to crowd it out. But the important thing was that Franklin obtained some really superb pictures. For the immediate present therefore he intended to leave the other two companies alone and work with the material at hand, especially as he was assured that other shots by different companies would in all probability have covered the same ground.

While Potter and his colleagues began the round of the cinema studios, armed with enlarged facsimiles, Franklin spent a day in tracing back from the office address. The room in which the interviews had actually taken place was a shop, the lease of which had expired. The agents—Harkness and Co. of Bedford Gardens—had let this lock-up shop to the special inquirer who gave his name as F. W. Bunting.

Asked for a description, the clerk gave what sounded like a cross between Rudolph Valentino and an anarchist. He had worn a very wide felt hat, horn rims and side whiskers. He limped slightly, had a pronounced stutter, and spoke in a high-pitched voice. He had worn yellow gloves, which he kept on while signing the agreement. Harkness and Co. did not know the man whom their tenant had employed as commissionaire for his queue. They did not even know the purpose for which the shop had been used. They did know that the key had been returned a day before the expiration of the agreement and that the shop and its annexe were in perfect order.

"How much was the rent for the week?" asked Franklin.

"Twenty guineas," replied the clerk calmly.

Franklin gave an involuntary start of surprise. "And how did he pay for it?"

"Cash down. Treasury notes."

Franklin departed with many thanks and a tracing of the signature of F. W. Bunting. He was not surprised to find that there was no resemblance whatever to the writing of F. C. Richleigh, which he had got from a chit in the headmaster's desk.

In two days' time there was found a man who had not only lined up in the queue but had also entered the magic door. He was, moreover, able to give information which led to the finding of others. According to him he had entered from the side door in the passage a room unfurnished except for a curtain hung across the front window, a chair, and a table at which sat a Spanish-looking gentleman. The light was not at all good. The instructions and questions received by him were approximately these:

Name?
Address?
Married?
Stage or film experience?
Teetotaller?
Turn face to the light. (Suddenly flashed on.)
Now profile.

During these last two there was some examination of and comparison with what were probably photographs. The whole proceeding took no more than three minutes. The man at the table then said in rather a high-pitched voice, "Thank you, Mr X If you are wanted you will be told not later than tomorrow. Through that door, please."

The applicant then passed through a kind of annexe into a court which led direct to Holborn. Two men he knew had gone through, but he did not catch up with them. As far as Franklin could judge, this particular applicant bore a considerable likeness to those photos of Gene Allen which he had been able to obtain. He was married, with three children, had both stage and film experience, but had frankly confessed he was not a teetotaller.

An examination of certain other members of that queue produced some interesting evidence. Some of the applicants had been rejected almost immediately. The procedure varied apparently with the degree of resemblance to the required type. A man whose claim depended on temporary distortion of features and accessories of clothing was not asked the first three questions. He was simply and frankly told he was not of the type required.

Some of the men were, moreover, shown a photograph of Richleigh which Franklin had adorned with side whiskers and horn rims. Most of them identified it at once with the man at the table. Franklin was for a moment inclined to be triumphant till a little sober reflection tempered his jubilation. From a shop he obtained photographs of the late Rudolph Valentino, Owen Nares, and Forbes Robertson. These he adorned in a similar way and then tried identification. The results were what he feared. So much for the magic of horn rims and side whiskers.

Something else that came to light was that at about 11.30 that morning the queue had suddenly been moved forward at a quicker pace. The applicants had been passed through the room, subject to a rapid inspection, at the rate of two a minute. Then, just after noon, a large card appeared in the window.

> "The position advertised for has been filled.
> "No further application can be entertained either to-day or to-morrow."

All this took several days, and then at last the clue came. Potter found at Elstree a man who had important news to tell and promptly handed him over to his chief to deal with. The tale he told Franklin was this:

His name was Arthur Lester and in the course of his career he had done comedy turns in pierrot troupes, run a show on the halls, and worked for the International Film Company at Elstree. He had seen the advertisement for an actor to take Gene Allen parts, and having the gift of facial manipulation, had thought a long shot worth attempting. Having determined to be at the head of the queue, he breakfasted early in Holborn and in the same restaurant met a man with whom he had worked before—Frederick Price, a quiet chap and a good sort generally. Price owned up to his intentions; indeed, as Lester admitted, his chance was a good one. At the studios his nickname was Gene, and he had more than once filled in a waiting interval with really good imitations.

When the two arrived, however, at 8.00 a. m., there were at least forty in front of them. Still, they fell in and made at the same time a definite agreement that they should afterwards meet in the restaurant and compare notes. When their turn came to enter, Lester went first. His bluff was speedily called, and he passed out into the courtyard. There he waited for a quarter of an hour, but Price did not appear. When he did not turn up at the restaurant he decided that it was useless to wait longer. In his opinion Price had got the job. In any case, he had neither heard anything of him nor seen him since. As far as he could recollect, the last job Price had had was in the summer, with Clifford Cartwright's Entertainers, who had touched the west coast.

All this information, which Franklin paid for handsomely, seemed well worth the money. The next thing to do was to get Clifford Cartwright's office from the telephone directory. There he obtained the address of Price at 11 Marshall's Avenue, Camden Town.

Hot on the trail Franklin rushed off by practically the next bus. He knocked at the door and asked the elderly woman who opened it if he could see Mrs. Price. He was told that he had made a mistake. Her husband's name was Sheffield. No, the people on the second floor were not called Price; their name was Rogers. She herself had been there only a short time and who the people were who had had the flat before her she didn't know. She thought, however, the name *was* Price, now she came to think of it. The side door, if he wanted the top flat.

The Rogers family appeared to be all in and having tea. Mrs. Rogers knew Mrs. Price quite well; a quiet little woman from the country. She hadn't been married many years and had no children. Mr. Price hadn't been to the flat for some days before his wife left. She had sold up the furniture and gone away; to some place in Norfolk, she believed. Pressed to recall the place, she was unable to do so but thought she would recognise it if she heard it. Franklin tried the few places he knew, then went out and bought a cycling map. Mrs. Rogers put her finger on the spot at once—Thetford.

Asked if she knew why Mrs. Price had gone away, she said she didn't know but had a shrewd suspicion. She had seen her crying, and putting two and two together had concluded that her husband had left her. She admitted that she knew Mr. Price was an actor and frequently away on tour, but all the same she had thought it peculiar.

Franklin refused to celebrate. He told himself that at the best he had merely unearthed a promising trail. There was nothing discovered yet that would be of the least value in a court of law. Richleigh himself was at the moment wholly unconnected with what discoveries had been made. But he did ring through to Ludovic Travers.

"Where did you say this Mrs. Price had gone to?"

"Thetford. Little town in Norfolk." He almost added, "Do you know it?" but remembered in time the weird extensiveness of his listener's knowledge.

"Thetford! That's very unusual. Look here; if you can wait till after an early lunch to-morrow and will let me come along I'll run you down in the car."

Franklin jumped at the chance, and the next day saw the pair of them leaving the Bell yard for the last piece of spade work. The ostler had had no knowledge of a Mrs. Price, so they tried the post office. No postmen were available, but one of the clerks on duty happened to have some idea.

"If the mother's a widow it'll probably be one of those cottage-villas on the Euston Road. I should try the first one and ask there."

Off again, then, for the very last lap. Franklin knocked at the door of the tiny villa, and there opened it a woman of less than thirty years, in white blouse and dark skirt.

Franklin lifted his hat. "Would you mind telling me where a Mrs. Price lives?"

The woman looked at him strangely, a look intent and nervous. Then her gaze wandered to the taller figure in the background. Her reply, when it came, was a fitting end to the long search.

"I am Mrs. Price."

Then she waited.

CHAPTER XXI
A PUZZLE IS SOLVED

(A)

FRANKLIN HESITATED too. What he might have to tell this sad-faced woman would be difficult for him and tragic for her. But exactly what he was to learn was farthest from his thoughts.

"May we come in, Mrs. Price? We hope to have some news for you."

She gave a quick start and made as if to ask a question. Then she let her hand fall to her side and drew back to let them pass.

In the living-room the furniture was of the simple country type: Windsor chairs, oak bureau, deal dresser, and kitchen table covered with a green cloth, The kettle was steaming on the hob, and before the fire a cat was lying on the home-made rug. On the mantelpiece two brass candlesticks shone white as silver, and between them were a Staffordshire figure and a copper lustre goblet. In a wicker chair sat an elderly woman, darning stockings by the late light of the window behind her.

"Do put that away, mother," said Mrs. Price. "You know your eyes are bad enough as it is. Here's some gentlemen who say they've got some news for us."

The mother too looked startled when she saw the strangers. She hastily put down her work and got to her feet.

"Now, don't you go running away, mother," said her daughter, rather petulantly it seemed to Franklin. "Will you sit down, Mr.—"

"My name's Franklin, and this is Mr. Travers. I think we *will* sit down, if you don't mind, because what there is to say may take a long time." He saw the growing alarm on their faces and added quickly, "But I don't want you to think it's anything serious. As a matter of fact, I want you to help me."

"I'll go and make a cup of tea, Milly," said Mrs. Wilford.

"You stop here, mother," said the other firmly. "And light the lamp, mother." And then to Franklin, "Is it about my husband?"

"It is, but nothing serious, I hope. I shall be glad if your mother would stay. Mrs. Wilford, isn't it? They gave us your name and address at the post office."

"That's right. Milly—Mrs. Price—is my only one," and she sat up stiffly in her chair, making a brave concealment of her disquiet.

"If I might explain this visit," said Franklin, "perhaps you'll understand better. I happen to be a private inquiry agent, Mrs. Price, and nothing to do with your husband. But I did happen to discover that a man I'm looking for had employed your husband and that both had disappeared together. From a friend of your husband I got your address at Camden Town, and then from Mrs. Rogers of the top flat I got your whereabouts as Thetford. Now you see what I want. If you can tell me where to find your husband, I shall probably find the man I'm looking for."

"I don't know where my husband is. I haven't seen him or heard a word for weeks."

"I'm sorry to hear that. Please don't think, Mrs. Price, or you, Mrs. Wilford, that I want to inquire into any private business. I know little about Mr. Price and want to know nothing that's secret in any way. All I'm very anxious to do is to find the man who employed him."

The tears came with a rush to Milly's eyes, and in a moment she was sobbing quietly. "Please, Mrs. Price ... Oh, I'm sorry," stammered Franklin and turned to Travers helplessly. The mother came quickly across and put her hands on her shoulders. "There, dear! Don't worry. Don't cry, now," and to Franklin, "She'll be all right in a minute, sir. It was rather a shock after all that time."

The sobbing slowly ceased, and Milly dried her eyes. Then she spoke. "Show the gentleman that letter, mother. It's in my bag."

Mrs. Wilford fetched it. "Would you like a cup of tea, sir? I'm going to make one."

"Thank you, Mrs. Wilford. I should, very much. I expect we all should like one." And while the mother set about it he read the letter. Then he handed it over to Travers. But neither could make head nor tail of it.

"Who is the 'Aggie' to whom your husband is writing?" asked Travers.

"That's what I'd like to know," was the determined answer. "Some woman or other who got him in a mess. And she's welcome to him, for all I care."

"When did you actually see your husband last, Mrs. Price?" asked Franklin.

"When was it, mother? About the end of August, I think. He'd got back from a tour which hadn't done very well, and they said there'd be at least a month before anything else was on. Then he saw an advertisement in the papers and said he was going to try that."

"What was the advertisement, do you know?"

"I don't know. He never used to talk things like that over with me for fear it should make me worry if he didn't get it."

"He was a good husband?"

"Oh, yes; he was everything he could be, and no wonder, when he had that other woman. I never saw him after that day. Then in about a week a letter came saying he thought he'd got a job up north but he had to keep it quiet. And he gave me an address I could write to, and the letter had ten pounds in it. Then I thought I'd go along and see this address, and when I got there it was only a tobacconist's near the Elephant, where they took in letters. Then a few days later another letter came with ten pounds in it, and it was full of all sorts of rubbish, and I couldn't make head nor tail of it, and I was so angry I threw it in the fire.

And then I didn't hear any more till this letter came, and that had twenty pounds in it. Mother sent it on from here. The other one came here too."

"What did you think when you got it?" asked Franklin.

"What would you have thought? He'd got hold of another woman and put the letters in the wrong envelopes."

"Your husband was well educated?"

"He went to a grammar school, didn't he, mother? And he was always reading."

"What sort of books?"

"Oh, silly detective novels. He had them on the brain. I used to hate them. Never talking when he was home and always sitting over the fire with a book!"

"Do come and have your tea," broke in Mrs. Wilford. "It's all getting cold."

"Excuse me one minute," said Franklin, passing the envelope to Travers, "but might I point out something? I expect it's really of no consequence at all, but why is the envelope addressed to *Miss* Price?"

Mrs. Wilford abandoned the pouring-out and came over. The two women took the envelope to the light and pored over it.

"Do you know, Milly," exclaimed Mrs. Wilford, "I really think the gentleman is right. I never noticed it."

The daughter was puzzled, and with good reason. "You'd never see anything with your eyes, mother. But what did he want to do that for? He hadn't got any sister—*or* brothers."

"Don't pay any attention to it," said Travers, seeing that tears were dangerously close. "If you write quickly there often isn't any difference between 'Mrs.' and 'Miss.' You expected to see 'Mrs.', and to all intents and purposes it was."

They moved over to the table, and both men tried to turn the conversation into other channels. There are simple country people, uneducated and humbly bred, who acquire unknowingly a natural dignity. Such a woman was Mrs. Wilford.

"I suppose you're a native of this part?" asked Travers.

"Oh, yes, sir; I've lived here all my life."

"Really! Then I expect you know Hainton?"

She smiled at her daughter, who smiled back. "I ought to, sir. I was parlour-maid at the vicarage before I married."

"I say, that's extraordinary!" exclaimed Travers. "I spent most of my holidays there when I was a boy. Geoffrey Wrentham and I went to school together."

"Well, now, that *is* funny, sir. This Mr. Wrentham's father was vicar in my time. But I remember Mr. Geoffrey being born, sir."

With that the stiffness vanished from the conversation. But for all that Franklin could see that from the daughter's mind there was never long absent the object of his visit, and with it a fear and a dread.

When they rose to go he had a favour to ask. "May I take a copy of that letter, Mrs. Price?"

She glanced at her mother. "If you look after it and send it back you may take it with you."

"You can rely on that," said Franklin, putting it away carefully in his pocketbook. Then he had a last question to put.

"I hardly like to ask you this, Mrs. Price, but perhaps you'll forgive me. I've heard a lot about your husband, and everybody spoke well of him. Will you take my word for it that there's more in this letter than meets the eye? Tell me, did you ever know your husband do what the world calls a dirty trick?"

She shook her head.

"Did he ever give you reason to suspect he was carrying on with another woman? I mean, did you trust him and he you?"

She made a gesture of assent, and the tears came into her eyes. Franklin would trust himself no further. He glanced at Travers, and the two of them said good-bye. But at the door there was still another word.

"We're more than grateful to you, Mrs. Price. Don't lose heart. We shall find your husband, and when we do all this will be cleared up. This time next year she'll be laughing to think how worried she was; won't she, Mrs. Wilford?"

The mother took the hint. "I hope so, sir, from what you've told us."

But as they made their way back to the town neither was feeling very cheerful. The kindly hospitality, the simple courtesies of that small home hurt like the pain from a blow. The amplitude of the information received made everything worse. One day, and *both* knew it as surely as if the event had already happened, it would be the lot of somebody to visit again that small home and leave behind him a woman with a grief that might be beyond even the relief of tears.

(B)

"A pitiful business," said Travers. "I might be unconcerned about the removal of a man like Thomas Richleigh, but this second murder! Those women, too. Wonder what they've got to live on? We shall have to see about that, Franklin," and he made a hasty note.

Franklin stared almost morosely into the fire. Ostensibly he had stayed on for a short talk and a nightcap; in reality the talk had lasted an hour, and that in spite of the conversation during the long journey home and the meal that followed it. In his hand he held the letter, and on the table between them lay the envelope and a powerful reading glass.

"Have we got any further? That's the problem. Price took the job, that's a certainty; but have we any evidence that connects Richleigh in any way?"

"Not a ha'p'orth," said Travers. "Tags don't help much either, or I'd say, 'Rome wasn't built in a day.' And things have worked out better than we could reasonably have expected."

"I admit you're positive, and so am I. The thing that gets me is why Price should have been such a fool as to put those letters in the wrong envelopes."

"If he did. From what you've told me and the direct answer his wife gave to that very pointed question of yours, the thought of Price and amorous adventures don't go well together. What I want to know is, why did he send two letters *via* his mother-in-law and not direct?"

"My opinion," said Franklin, "is that he knew his wife would be worried and anxious, and he'd assume she'd go down to the country for a bit with her mother. The money he sent would last a long while in a small town like that. Sending the letter to Norfolk made delivery a certainty. If she were there she'd get it, and if she weren't, her mother would be sure to send it on."

"But why the 'Miss'? We're both agreed it reads like that."

Franklin was suddenly alert. "I've got it. You remember the question put by F. W. Bunting? 'Are you married?' Price gathered from the tone of the voice that if he wanted that job he'd better say, 'No.' But he had to write to his wife at all costs, and so, on the spur of the moment, he invented an unmarried sister."

"That's it," agreed Travers. "But why didn't he write to his wife and explain? He might have given her the most emphatic cautions as to secrecy."

"Ask me another. Perhaps he gave his word and, like a fool, stuck to it. Perhaps the rewards were too high to risk. After all, he sent his wife quite a lot of money in a very short time. He must have been getting what was for him a fortune."

"Everything might be true," said Travers, "but where does Richleigh come in? Let's have another look at that letter."

"'DEAR AGGIE:

"'I was very glad to get your letter—'"

"But he hadn't had one I Of course, he'd have to make that up to explain the second letter."

"But he couldn't make it up," said Franklin. "If he got a reply to his first letter it meant that he'd have given her an address. What he probably did was to write himself an answer in a faked handwriting and send it to the address where he'd been told his sister might write to."

"I don't know," said Travers. "We shall have to get far more information before we can reconstruct all that's behind those letters. What's next?"

> "'—but sorry to hear about your rheumatism. If you take my advice you will on no account do as you suggest; go and stay with Tom's wife. Stuck down in the mud as it is, Great Oxley is no good for rheumatism ...'

"Now why the devil does he write all that screed about rheumatism?"

"Why not go down to Great Oxley and find out a few things?" suggested Franklin.

"Just a minute; I've thought of something!" and Travers sprang up and went to the library. In two minutes he was back.

"There's no town, village or hamlet in the British Isles of that name. Now let's look again."

They spread out the separated portions and on the back Travers put a strip or two of adhesive paper to keep the letters in true alignment. And then the discovery was made.

> "... Great Oxley is no good for rheumatism and nobody could ever ..."

"We've got it! Look at the initial letters of those words! GOING FRANCE."

The two looked at each other in startled surprise. Then the heads went down again. Travers ran his finger along till something else appeared—

> "... cure all rheumatic cases and so surely one needn't expect ..."

"Should have been two 'n's'," said Travers, "but that doesn't matter. Any more?"

The words went on again, pronounced with a grim impressiveness, until once more a message spelt itself.

> "... news ought to make a real record if everything doesn't..."

"Good God!" exclaimed Franklin and then was speechless.

"We'll try it again," said Travers, "and in reverse this time as well. No wonder the glass showed no secret marks."

But nothing else came to light. Travers wrote down the words—

"GOING FRANCE. CARCASSON(N)E.
NOT MARRIED."

and handed them to Franklin. "I'd give fifty pounds to see that letter full of rubbish which Mrs. Price put on the fire. It's a thousand to one it explained all the earlier happenings, and it might even have explained this very letter."

"If Price hadn't been too clever he might have been alive today. Perhaps I'm unjust; if he hadn't been too honest."

Travers shook his head. "There's still plenty we don't understand. Why did Price write the letter, do you think?"

Franklin thought for a moment. "For some extraordinary and binding reason, Price gave his word that he would communicate with nobody. Then when he came to think it over he knew his wife would be in a fearful state of worry. So he risked a very guarded letter and also told her where to write to. Then he had no answer to this letter and at the same time got the wind up about writing another in the same way. So he approached his employer and asked if he might write to his sister in Norfolk, provided the employer saw the letter and, probably, posted it. In the meanwhile the sums of money he sent were guarantees to his wife of his good faith. Then he wanted to write again, so he did what was just suggested; that is, wrote himself a letter to the permitted address, perhaps even to the employer himself. It would contain the remarks about rheumatism to which he refers. Then he got permission to answer it. Also he must have expected his wife to find out the hidden messages. If she were asked she might remember some private clue connected with the nickname 'Aggie.' Perhaps it was a joke they had some time or other. He certainly got the idea from a detective story, and if we could find the actual one we might get something else out of it. That's the best I can do."

"If I'd been Price's employer," said Travers, "I'd have been rather pleased about posting that letter. It says everything that would allay suspicion. 'Don't worry.' 'May be going abroad.' 'Turn up like a bad penny,' and so on."

Franklin looked at his watch. "I say, it's getting rather late. What about coming round very early in the morning?"

"Why not have a shakedown here? Palmer can fix you up. I suppose no one will worry if you don't turn up at your own place?"

"I think I will, if you don't mind. Now, then; what about going into the question of the sort of hold that his employer had over Price? Then we might start a general reconstruction of the whole thing."

"We might start off by referring to Price's employer as Richleigh. The mention of Carcassonne leaves no doubt about that. Now let's see. What sort of a hold *might* he have had over him?"

And so the argument began all over again. When it was settled, moreover, there still had to be a summary written, ready for presentation in the morning. And lastly, in spite of the lateness of the hour, Travers wrote a letter, and the address on the envelope was—

Rev. P. Wrentham,
The Vicarage,
Hainton,
Norwich.

CHAPTER XXII
THE DECKS ARE CLEARED

(A)

IT WAS NINE O'CLOCK the following morning before Franklin had finished his recital of those events which had ended so dramatically the previous night. Sir Francis Weston, whose worst enemy would not have denied him the possession of a keen imagination, was startled and impressed. He agreed that the case must be finished, however long it took to obtain the evidence, circumstantial or otherwise, that would be needed to convince a jury.

"The only criticism I have to offer," he said, "is that the evidence lacks correlation. Was Frank Richleigh F. W. Bunting, for example? What did Price actually do after he met Richleigh? Where did the conspirators meet? Get more evidence on those points and there's a case to present."

"A perfectly just objection," agreed Franklin, "but I think you'll admit one thing, sir. When the message was unravelled from the letter it definitely connected Price with Richleigh. The dates and the word Carcassonne showed that."

"I agree," was the reply. "But as I said, if you remember, from the point of view of the average jury. I think you're right; I'd bet a good many pounds you're right, but I'd bet the same amount that a jury wouldn't convict. Now about that other matter. You both agree that we've sufficient case to present to Scotland Yard?"

"Subject to the stipulations mentioned, I'm sure it would be the correct thing," said Franklin. "We give them a certain amount to do, which they alone can do, and moreover we don't antagonise them."

"What do you think, Travers?"

"Speaking as a layman, Sir Francis, I agree."

But when the company reassembled after breakfast, it was Chief-Constable Scott and not Superintendent Wharton who made the fourth. He seemed remarkably cordial; perhaps a shade more affable with Travers than with Franklin, but that was to be expected.

"Chief-Constable Scott agrees," said Sir Francis, "that the evidence I've just sketched out to him has extraordinary possibilities. The very reasonable conditions I've laid down—I say 'very reasonable,' gentlemen, because it isn't often one gets the chance of blackmailing the law—well, they're agreed to. Should the evidence turn out all that we expect it, the rewards offered by the press will be paid over to Mr. Franklin."

"If I might say something, Sir Francis—"

"Do, please."

"I would like to admit, and Mr. Travers agrees, that this case has so far been solved entirely by luck. There was no question of competing with Scotland Yard. We merely adopted an independent line of research and happened to have a lucky hit."

"That's very handsomely said," confessed Scott. "But in justice to yourselves I ought to add that in my experience luck and hard work were never far off each other."

"I think we ought to take this easily, gentlemen," said Sir Francis, and pushed the cigar box across the table. "But there is one thing we would like you to do, Mr. Franklin, and that is to read over again the statement you read to me."

"Very good; but of course you'll recognise that it's merely a very faint outline. This is the statement, sir, that Mr. Travers and I agreed upon last night:

> "There came a time in his life when Frank Richleigh realised one or two unpleasant things about the work he was doing. He disliked it, he was out of tune with his headmaster and his colleagues, and English winters, combined with sedentary work, were too great a strain on his health. He thought occasionally of the difference there would be when his uncle died. His own money and savings had been lost in an unlucky investment, but if things went well he might count on a legacy that would bring him in best part of £500 a year.
>
> "Moreover, he detested that uncle. He probably had an enormous shock when he first heard of the liaison with the housekeeper. That meant that he might have to go on working in that school for another twenty years."

"Excuse me a second," interrupted Scott. "Why shouldn't he have gone to another school?"

"Impossible!" replied Franklin. "He was what they call a man on his maximum. According to the findings of a committee—"

"The Burnham Award," said Travers.

"—the findings of this Burnham Committee, he was entitled to a certain salary, say in his case, £500 a year. If a headmaster wants a new man he gets him straight from the university or with only a year or so of experience, and so saves at least two hundred a year. That is why Richleigh realised he might have to go on working under the same conditions.

"The money, moreover, which he and his brothers considered should have been theirs at the death of their uncle Peter would now go to a woman of unquestionable vulgarity. He lived an introspective sort of life and brooded over all this until the idea of murdering his uncle got hold of his mind. The impending marriage with the housekeeper was one deciding factor; the fortuitous occurrence of his grace term was another.

"How he got the idea of impersonation—from a book, the cinema, or a press illustration—we don't know. He certainly had the idea in his mind when a colleague nicknamed him Gene Allen. At any rate, he realised how lucky he was. If any of us wanted a double we could never find one, at least without the use of greasepaint. But Richleigh discovered that he was the living image of that celebrated film comedian, Gene Allen. His common sense and his mathematics would tell him that things which are equal to the same thing are equal to one another. All he had to do therefore was to set about finding an actor who also resembled Gene Allen. Later came certain diabolically clever modifications so that the alibi would never be tested on people who could never make a mistake. The scene, for instance, of the test was laid in an out-of-the-way corner of France, and as Price spoke no other French than what Richleigh put into his mouth, there would be no worry about voice.

"Well, Richleigh inserted his advertisement and was lucky enough to find in Price a man who surpassed his expectations. He was keen on pleasing and most conscientious. When Richleigh got him to himself he said: 'Now, Mr. Price; this advertisement was a blind. You are really wanted by the Secret Service and you were chosen specially because you resemble a man whom the Government want to keep an eye on. But first you will have to undergo a period of training, and from now on everything you do must be secret as the grave. You say you have no relatives except a sister. If you ever want to communicate with anybody, even with her, I must be told all about it and every letter must be censored by me.'

"After that Richleigh set about Price's training. He probably said to him, 'The money is good, but you've got to earn it.

The Secret Service has eyes everywhere, though the man in the street thinks that all bunkum. If ever a single word gets out to a single soul of what you're doing you'll be dropped like a hot potato. But if you do make good, there's nothing you won't be able to ask for. Now, then; go to a certain place and do so and so. Bring a report of all that happens. And don't forget that though you can't see what's behind the apparently absurd things you'll have to do, yet there's really something definite in them which only your superiors know.'

"He kept that up for weeks. He'd even go himself sometimes on expeditions with his pupil. He made sure that Price would carry out any instructions, however, absurd, to the very last stroke of the very last letter, dressed in any clothes that were ordered and under any name. There would be heaps of flummery and bluff, and the pay would be gradually increased. Price was so trusted that he was allowed to write to his sister. Richleigh tried him out till failure was absolutely impossible. Then, wishing to show how clever he was, he wrote the 'Marius' letter.

"You will note one thing all this time. Throughout the whole of these amazing proceedings Richleigh could have drawn back at any time, even a minute before the murder, and there would have been nothing thought except that the affair was a hoax after all. If he hadn't committed the murder there would merely have been some excuse to make in order to dismiss Price after his return from France.

"But Richleigh proceeded with the scheme. He sent Price to France, probably telling him that he was about to begin the highly important and confidential mission for which he had originally been chosen. He was to assume the name of Frank Richleigh, and as the passport system was abolished last year, there was no difficulty about that. He received the most detailed instructions as to movements, but above all, on the night of the eleventh he was to be at Limoux. At about 8.00 the following night he was to be at a certain spot near Couiza, where he was to be joined by a messenger. All through the trip, and most especially on the eleventh, he was to note with faultless accuracy everything that occurred, even to the minutest detail, and record it in his diary. He was given an outfit the exact duplicate of that which Richleigh intended to wear himself.

"Then Richleigh left the hotel and went elsewhere till the night of the murder. Even when he entered the dining-room at The Grove he could still draw back. If his device of the silk stockings had failed and the maid had seen him, he could have explained it away. But once the murder was committed he had at all costs to avoid being seen. That's why he left by the window. Then he caught the train for France and, assuming some easy disguise, reached Carcassonne and took a car for Couiza, ready for his appointment with Price.

"The latter was overjoyed to find that the expected messenger was his immediate superior in the Secret Service. He told all that had happened, down to the very last detail—sore heel, coffee, Marcelle, and so on. Then Richleigh told him that the next stage was for him to carry on and that it was necessary to change clothes. Then Richleigh killed him, concealed the body, and went on to the inn at Couiza. His alibi was perfect. And once in the inn he studied the diary for the rest of the necessary details to make it bombproof."

"Thank you," said Scott. "I think that puts it very clearly. Now would you mind giving me the exact time when the train arrives at Carcassonne?"

"About 19.10. There's no local train for Couiza after that, so Richleigh would have had to take a car. It's about 46 kilometres; say 30 miles, and that would be a good hour. Say he arrived for the meeting with Price at about 8.30 p. m."

"At what time did Price leave Limoux and at what time did Richleigh arrive at Couiza?"

"I'm afraid I don't know. All I did was to verify the alibi."

"Now, then, I put it to you. Wasn't 8.30 very late for that meeting? There was the preliminary talk when they met, the changing of clothes, the murder, the concealment of the body, and other things we may not know, That would have made Richleigh's arrival at the inn very late; so late as to have called attention to it."

"If you don't mind my butting in," said Travers, "I'd like to say there's a daily service of planes from Paris to Toulouse. If Richleigh had travelled by air he'd have arrived at Carcassonne in the early afternoon."

"You quite sure about that—?" began Sir Francis and Scott together.

"Perfectly. When Mr. Franklin was away I was rather interested and looked the matter up. I wondered if he'd go by air or rail."

"That settles that," said Scott decisively. "There's one bit of luck that's come our way. Superintendent Wharton is returning from Grenoble this morning, and I'll arrange to hold him in Paris. If Mr. Franklin will take certain documents which I will hand over and cross by air from Croydon, he can see Superintendent Wharton in Paris and go over everything with him there. I won't guarantee what action Wharton will take; that's entirely up to him; but I think the offer a fair one."

"A very generous one," said Sir Francis. "It would be highly indiscreet to publish anything about the new clue?"

"Most decidedly! Richleigh must not be alarmed under any circumstances."

"This is what I was thinking. As soon as Franklin wires me a key word that the arrest of Richleigh is an actual fact, then Durangos are at liberty to publish their version of the affair. It will be a generous one; I promise you that."

Scott made a wry face. "I hate to appear ungrateful, but until Richleigh is actually arrested the public must know nothing. If anything gets out whereby he avoids arrest, even if it's in a year's time, your people will be held responsible. Afterwards you can publish what you like, subject to the laws of blasphemy and libel."

Sir Francis laughed. "Well, that's plain enough. By the way, you have every confidence in Wharton?"

Scott looked up sharply at that. "Every confidence," he replied reprovingly.

The reproof glanced off. Sir Francis gave the smile of a man who feels on remarkably good terms with himself and then took the other by the arm and led him out of the office.

(B)

Two days later Wharton and Franklin were in the train from Toulouse to Carcassonne, and in those two days a good deal had happened. At the Sûreté, where they had met, the scene had been an amusing one, what with Franklin's eagerness to discount his success and the other's perfect sportsmanship which recognised original work for what it was worth. It was rather like the traditional meeting of two ultra-courteous Frenchmen at a door.

As to the actual work done, it is the results that matter rather than the story. From the Sûreté an agent had been dispatched to keep an eye on Richleigh. A real Simon Pure Frenchman should give no cause for alarm, but in case of necessity he was to communicate *via* Carcassonne.

At the headquarters of the Aviation Company information was forthcoming that on the morning of the 12th of October there travelled to Toulouse a man who gave his name as Marinski. He had worn side whiskers, dark glasses, and had had a muffler well round his neck. He spoke French with an English accent, a rather curious thing for one of that name, since his appearance was not Jewish. The plane had arrived at 14.10 and after signing the acquittance book at the *guichet* M. Marinski had left with the other passengers. The reason why he had been noticed at all was that the police happened on that very date to be on the lookout for a defaulting cashier.

At Carcassonne Wharton presented his credentials. Thereupon the police at once began inquiries from garages and taxi drivers about a fare who, on the afternoon of the 12th of October, had asked to be driven to Limoux or Couiza. The information was forthcoming in two days, and the driver's story was a damning one.

At about 16.30, on the arrival of the afternoon train from Toulouse, there had boarded his taxi a foreigner, who had merely uttered the words, "St. Hilaire!" But the driver had seen fit to bargain and had only started when he had got what he asked. Through the town of St. Hilaire, however, the foreigner had stopped the taxi and said, "Couiza!" Once more there was bargaining, and payment on the spot.

"Didn't you think," asked Wharton, "that he was a bandit who was after your taxi?"

Not by any means, the driver assured him. The man was old and almost toothless; he wore glasses, had a limp, and was smaller than himself. At any rate, they went on through Limoux, and when within two kilometers of Couiza the foreigner stopped the taxi, got out, and actually gave the driver a fifty-franc tip. But when the driver had got only a hundred metres on the return journey he wondered what the man could possibly have got off there for, far from houses and in the middle of rocky gorges. Curiosity made him look back, and as he did so he saw emerge from behind a rock another curious person with a knapsack on his shoulders. The light at the time was none too good.

"That settles it," said Franklin.

"About the most effective and ageing disguise I know of," said Wharton, "is the removal of false teeth. What were Richleigh's like?"

"Oh, he had false teeth all right. At least, if he hadn't, those he had in his mouth were the most regular set I've ever seen. What's the next move?"

"Limoux. Now we know what we want to find we might have some luck. If that girl Marcelle is there, you tackle her and I'll see madame."

When they got to the hotel everything seemed to be ready for them. Inside the door Marcelle sat at her desk knitting and regarding the entrants with solemn black eye. Wharton slipped through into the dining-room.

"You return already, monsieur!" observed Marcelle.

"Yes, mademoiselle. It is the elusive M. Richleigh who makes all this bother. How would you feel if you had a twin sister who resembled you so much that you were always being taken for each other?"

"I would like it very much," was the unexpected reply. "M. Richleigh has then a twin?"

"Figure to yourself the trouble it makes. You remember the M. Richleigh who slept here and spilled the coffee. That was one twin. Then a day or two later his brother came with the big monsieur who has just gone to see madame. Imagine how you were deceived. You thought it was the same M. Richleigh!"

"But the heel, monsieur? The stains of the coffee?"

"Regard a little," said Franklin, limping across the room. "I have now a bad heel. If I change coats with Jerome the waiter, that does not make me Jérome."

"Monsieur makes fun of me."

"But the voice. What a difference there was!"

"But all M. Richleigh said was. '*Une chambre.*' so droll, just like that."

"But his teeth when he smiled?"

"Ah! the beautiful teeth! White as snow!"

"And he left, when?"

"Early in the morning, I think."

"Well, mademoiselle, it is indeed droll that you remarked no difference. You will laugh when you see the two together!"

"I shall laugh more, monsieur," said Marcelle slyly, "if I see three!"

Wharton's report was no better except that Richleigh had left just before 10.00 a. m.

"It looks as if Price had to lie doggo all day," said Franklin. "Some of his time he might have spent writing up the diary."

The information at the hotel at Couiza seemed to confirm that. Richleigh had arrived shortly before dinner and had gone at once to his room, apparently to attend to a sore heel.

"Did you ever have any suspicions of Richleigh?" asked Franklin as their car turned for the return journey. "Mind you, I don't see why you should."

"Well, I did and I didn't."

"The reason I asked was that you didn't seem particularly surprised when you heard my news."

"As you remarked, he was a likely suspect, but you can't get away from an alibi. There was one thing, however, that made me think a good deal, and that was the question of the paint brushes. He wrote to his brother Ernest to send him on two brushes he'd left behind. The letter set up a useful sort of alibi to start with. It shrieked out, 'You can't touch me. I'm in France.' But the brushes were *new* ones."

"Meaning?"

"Well, are you attached to *new* brushes? Old and tried ones, send for by all means. Carcassonne is an important sketching centre, and he could have got some more there. Also he exaggerated their value somewhere. I just put him down as a liar, and there was an end to it."

Wharton's plan of campaign, as he sketched it, seemed to depend on the discovery of Price's body. He proposed to call in the aid of the authorities and hunt the area near the meeting place for disturbed soil and the ravines and crevices for the body or even clues.

"Won't that be a hopeless job?" said Franklin. "Look at those slopes and the undergrowth; places where nobody could go in search of a body."

"I'll import Swiss guides or Alpini," said Wharton determinedly.

"Yes; but why did Richleigh stay so long in Quillan? Because he wanted all the time he could get to conceal the body. Except for an occasional charcoal burner, nobody ever goes into that undergrowth."

"You're right," said Wharton. "But, by God, that fellow had brains! It's funny in a way, but everything we do piles on the certainty, and yet we can get nothing definite. I'd like to hear any counsel who knew his job—Hartlett-French or any of the big guns—set about the case for the prosecution as it stands to date. He'd run amok."

Still, it was decided to begin the search in the faint hope that some clue might be brought to light. But at the police headquarters there was a further development. A telephone message from Boucher had come from Hyères.

> "Our friend intends in the very near future to take a journey. If you wish to do business it is imperative to see him at once."

"That tears it," said Wharton. "Possibly a world tour. It means watching him, for one thing, and that must give the game away sooner or later. Then he'll bolt."

Franklin had nothing to contribute beyond taking the optimistic view. "There's one thing about it," he said. "We may not be millionaires, but we do see life!"

CHAPTER XXIII

THE NIGHT OF THE 21ST OF DECEMBER

(A)

WHARTON DECIDED there was only one thing to do—to go at once to Hyères and hear Boucher's report. The police there were rung up with instructions to arrange for the agent to cross on the following day to La Tour Fondue, in time to meet the bus from the town. In the meanwhile the police at Carcassonne would continue the search for clues to the disappearance of Price.

"What I can't make out," said Wharton, "is how Richleigh knew this country so well. He told me he'd never had a holiday in France. I know guidebooks and contour maps might have told him a good deal, but they don't explain how he was able to fix the exact spot to meet Price and how he knew where to have the interview and conceal the body."

"I think he'd been here before," said Franklin, "and to Hyères too. Take a schoolmaster's long summer holiday. If he's a secretive sort of bloke like Richleigh, nobody would want to know where he'd spent the whole of it. If anybody did ask he'd say, 'Oh, just pottered round. Had a short cricket tour and then watched some matches in town.' There was a good interval between the time when he broke up and his arrival in town to watch the cricket."

"I know; but that's the very point. One can't go to Richleigh and say, 'Give me an account of how you spent your time from last July to October.' He'd say, and he'd be entitled to say, 'What's the idea? Are you trying to accuse me of a murder I didn't commit? If not, why inquire into my private business? You go to hell.'"

Franklin agreed.

"The alibi is everything," Wharton went on. "While Richleigh can prove, as he most decidedly can at the moment, that he was at Limoux on the night of the murder, he can't be touched. The question of impersonation is fantastic; it won't bear discussion as far as a jury is concerned, though you and I know better. We can prove what we like and get what evidence we like, but unless we can make the impersonation into a coherent and perfectly explicable thing, we're as far off as ever."

"The case for the Crown must be unassailable."

"Quite so. If he gets acquitted he can never be tried again, whatever the evidence that crops up."

The following afternoon, when they descended from the bus at La Tour Fondue, the sea was running strongly, and the white horses showed in the channel like the tails of frightened rabbits scurrying to their burrows at twilight. At the jetty the *Cormoran* bobbed up and down like a cork, and Franklin hoped fervently that he would not have to make the crossing. In the inn corner, farthest from the door, sat Boucher, the placid image of a bourgeois in comfortable circumstances, from the black sombrero hat to the polish of the black boots. There were the usual polite flourishes, the gripping of hands and the bowing to seats, and then over a bottle they got to work.

Boucher's story was this. He himself had come to the hotel as a native of Marseilles, where it so happened he had a brother. A severe attack of influenza was supposed to have given him a bad time, and by doctor's orders he was having a month's convalescence. In his room at the hotel he had a supply of patent medicines, and his cough still troubled him.

He had had no conversation with Richleigh, but had studiously avoided him. Twice, however, Richleigh had crossed to the mainland, and the first time Boucher had missed him. The second time he too had taken the trip. At the station at Hyères, knowing that there was no train for half an hour, he had arranged for the surveillance to be continued by a local agent, for fear that Richleigh should be disturbed. The journey had been a longer one than had been anticipated. Richleigh proceeded to Marseilles, where his first visit was to the offices of a shipping company doing passenger traffic between that port and Algiers. Whether or not he had actually taken a ticket the agent had not been able to ascertain, as it was imperative for him to follow his man on the return journey. Since then, however, Richleigh had announced his intention of leaving the hotel in a day or two.

"Why didn't *you* find out from Marseilles whether he had a ticket?" asked Wharton.

"What would you, monsieur? You say I must look after M. Richleigh. Very well, then. I go to Marseilles, and while I am there he disappears. What would you say, then, to M. Boucher?"

Wharton acknowledged the force of the argument. The fault, if there were any, lay in the peculiar nature of the case itself. But if Richleigh did go to Algeria, the point was, could he be adequately watched?

"I say, I'm awfully sorry," said Franklin, "but I've just thought of something. Richleigh is a big bug on Arabic; at least that's what they told me at the school. If he gets to Algeria anything might happen."

"That puts a different complexion on things," said Wharton. "Something's got to be done and done quick."

He looked extraordinarily serious, and the other two watched him shake his head despondently. "I daren't move. There's simply nothing to go on. Richleigh would laugh at me if I was such a fool as to tackle him with the information we've got. And he'd be alarmed, and that would mean slipping away when we didn't expect it. But it's got to be all or nothing."

They watched his face and the expressions that crossed it. It was not for them to speak. After all, Wharton was the executive power; he alone represented authority. It was a case of all or nothing, and it could not possibly be the all. The question was, what would Wharton decide to do?

"If we want to go to the island, how do we do it?" he asked suddenly.

"Try a fisherman," suggested Boucher.

"Don't like it. The wind's in the east, and we'd spend an hour or two tacking across there."

He called the patron over. "We ask your help, monsieur. Here we sat, like three imbeciles, talking of old times, and let the *Cormoran* leave without us, and now monsieur here wishes us to spend the night with him on the island. How are we to get there?"

The patron advised St. Giens. M. Fleurons of the hotel had a motor boat, not so big as the *Cormoran* but capable of holding four, and fairly fast. The way to St. Giens? Go back towards Hyères for a few hundred metres and then take the turn to the left.

The three set off. "All we're going to do," said Wharton, "is shift our headquarters to St. Giens. If we decide not to do anything we can always get back to Hyères."

Then, suddenly, as they were plodding along the rough track, Wharton made a remark. "This case means a lot to you, John?"

There was something in the tone, as well as the rare use of the name, that made Franklin aware that something was in the wind. But his answer came quickly. "Not more than to you, sir."

Wharton smiled. "Your mathematics are faulty. I can see just fifteen hundred pounds difference."

"Damn the fifteen hundred pounds! You're in charge and what you say goes."

For another five minutes Wharton said nothing. Franklin and Boucher made conversation which was as pointless as the last idle chatterings of friends who have said good-bye and still wait for the moving of the train. Then Wharton made his decision.

"You gave it as your opinion that Richleigh had a yellow streak. You prepared to gamble on that?"

"I'd gamble on the chance that he's lacking in balance. The man who wrote those letters must have a kink in him."

"And you'll absolutely leave everything to me and take what happens?"

"There'll be no squealing from me if anything goes wrong."

"Well, that's good hearing. The trouble is I can't tell you what I propose to do. If I did you might make me change my mind."

"About that fifteen hundred pounds," said Franklin. "Mr. Travers was entitled to the whole of it, as I worked things out. He refused to touch a penny. All he asked was that if things went right, enough should be set aside to buy Price's widow and her mother some little business or another. He's inquiring into their means, or was when I left. There's only one thing I want to do, sir, and that's to show my superiors they trusted the right man. If I let you down I should expect you to tell them so. That's all I've got to say. Now you carry on with the job, and I'll ask no questions."

Wharton, undemonstrative as ever, merely nodded then, "Now, what about this boat?"

In a quarter of an hour they were aboard the *Hirondelle,* with the engineer perfectly unconcerned about the choppy sea. Franklin would have liked to hear an opinion as to the seaworthiness of the boat but felt that the owner would not have risked his craft for so insignificant a sum as four hundred francs.

But the crossing was all that he feared. Boucher was ill before they reached the middle channel, and he himself lasted little longer. Wharton was not enjoying it, but he at least arrived fit for action. In just under half an hour they entered the sheltered bay by the Plage d'Argent and with engine off floated inshore. The light was failing rapidly, and the sooner they were on the road the better. The two took a stiff dose from Wharton's flask, and then, with Franklin leading, set off for the road to the village. The engine of the *Hirondelle* sounded behind them and then was lost.

In five minutes they were on the outskirts of the village, and Boucher was sent to the hotel to reconnoitre. He returned with the information that Richleigh had just gone to his room and that he was probably leaving the island the next day. His final destination he had not announced.

"How many windows to the room?" asked Wharton.

"Two. About fifteen feet up; both facing northeast and both shuttered."

"Good!" said Wharton. "You wait under those windows, M. Boucher, and if a man drops out, have him as soon as he hits the ground. You know the bedroom all right, John?"

"If he hasn't changed it. The third from the front, isn't it, Boucher?"

"That's it."

"Right!" said Wharton. "Let's move on. John, you keep immediately behind me and, whatever happens, don't say a word. Glue your eyes on Richleigh's face as if you wanted to mesmerise him. Your face is as white as a sheet, in any case. Try to scare him stiff. Stick your chin out and don't bat an eyelid. You ready, Boucher? Then let's look for that yellow streak!"

(B)

There was a whispered conversation at the hotel entrance, and then Franklin went quietly up the stairs. Wharton turned to the office in search of the manager. He was not there. Then a maid came in with an armful of clean tablecloths.

"Is M. Papini in?"

"No, monsieur. He went out a few minutes ago. Would you like to see madame?"

"Oh, no; it doesn't matter. I've come over specially to see a friend of mine—M. Richleigh—who is staying here."

"I'll go and find him," and she started off. But Wharton stopped her. "Don't disturb yourself, mademoiselle. If you will be so good as to tell me his room I'll go and find him. I'll leave my bag here."

"No. 3, monsieur. At the top of the stairs and the second to the left."

Franklin was waiting on the landing, and the two moved noiselessly along the corridor. Franklin could feel his heart racing like a mad thing, and to him Wharton seemed as cool and unmoved as if he were going to his own room and not one which held a problem of known, and it might be insuperable, difficulty. He wondered what Wharton would do and what would be his method of attack. At the best he could see nothing happening but a charge and Richleigh's sarcastic remarks and so stalemate. Then they stopped at the door. The elder man listened intently for a second or two, then rapped smartly with his knuckles. From inside a voice called cheerily, *"Entrez!"*

At a glance Wharton took in the room. On the right was the bed; in front two shuttered windows. Along the right wall, on each side of what looked like a chimney breast, was a recess; one with a washstand, the other curtained off as a wardrobe. To the left was a dressing-table with an open suitcase on the floor beside it. Almost in the middle of the room, with his back to the corridor so that the light fell on the book he was reading, was Richleigh in an easy chair. It looked as if he imagined the entrant was one of the maids, for he went on reading, unconcerned. Then something unusual struck him. He turned his body in the chair and caught sight of the two visitors. You could almost hear the catch in his breath at the recognition. His face flushed. Then he went deathly white. Then he scrambled somehow to his feet and got a grip on himself. His speech was quick and nervous, and his eyes fastened on Wharton's face.

"Yes? What is it you want?"

Wharton delayed his answer with what could only have been deliberate provocation. "Frank Richleigh, this is Detective-Inspector Franklin, late of Scotland Yard. I, as you know, am Superintendent Wharton. We are here as the result of the murder of your uncle."

Richleigh let his eyes rest for a moment on Franklin. There was a definite irony in the voice and the suspicion of a sneer in the pucker of the lips.

"The theatrical gentleman!"

Then he took out his cigarette case and with deliberation lighted a cigarette. "Do please sit down. I'm afraid there's only the bed. Which uncle did you want to see me about?"

Wharton held his ground. He did not even cast a glance at the bed. With shoulders hunched and eyes fixed exasperatingly on the other's face, he spoke as calmly as if he were remonstrating with a child.

"Why prevaricate, Richleigh? The time has gone for that sort of thing. We are here as the result of the part you played in the murder of your uncle, Thomas Richleigh, on the night of October the eleventh of this year."

"I say, please don't be absurd. You know perfectly well where I was that night!"

"That is so. We know exactly where you were. I repeat, that's why we're here."

Richleigh flashed a look at the pair of them, then his eyes fell. With his forefinger he flicked to the stone floor the ash of his cigarette. "Well, then, what is it you want to see me about?"

"What I've just told you. There is also another matter—the murder of Frederick Price!"

If anything could be seen besides the sudden stare it was the stopping of his breath, the whirl of his thoughts while they collected themselves, the summoning of his nerves to cope with a mortal attack.

"The murder of *whom?*"

"Frederick Price; the man who resembled Gene Allen."

Richleigh turned his head and petulantly regarded the ceiling. "I'm afraid you're talking in riddles. You may know the answers, but they're beyond me."

From his pocket Wharton took a sheet of paper. With eyes still on Richleigh's face he held it out. "Look at that letter and you may find the answer."

With a rare assumption of indifference Richleigh took it. Where he betrayed himself was in the sudden movement of his eyes along the lines; the speed with which he took a comprehensive survey of it. Then he read it through.

"This is nonsense as far as I'm concerned. What's it got to do with me?"

"We shall come to that," said Wharton quietly. He gave the explanation, and he took his time. He gave the impression of having the rest of his life in which to make the case clear. His voice was judicial and unruffled.

"Now you see the answer. When you allowed Price to post that letter you made a mistake. He told you he was unmarried, and he told you a lie. That letter was addressed to his wife, and it tells one of his movements."

Richleigh put the end of the cigarette in the ash tray on the dressing-table. Then he picked it up again and with it lighted another from his case. He decided to be annoyed.

"Perhaps it would save my time and yours if I repeat that as far as I'm concerned it's all nonsense. If you have nothing else to say, perhaps you'll leave my room."

"All in good time," replied Wharton imperturbably. "When we go we'll go together." Then his voice took on a new note. "Richleigh! Look at me! Look at me, I say! Not only did Price send his wife those messages; he did something else. He kept a diary! Everything he did, from the day he lined up in that queue to his arrival at Limoux, is written in it. Richleigh, we know everything!"

Then his voice quieted and once more became judicial. "Frank Charles Richleigh, I hold a warrant for your arrest on the charge of murdering your uncle, Thomas Taylor Richleigh, on the night of October eleventh of this year. I warn you that anything you say will be taken down as evidence against you."

For the first time Franklin's eyes shifted. He pulled out his notebook, unclipped his pen, and then resumed his watchings. On Richleigh's face could be seen many things. Imagine a man who thinks to pick a thorn from his foot and is suddenly struck by a rattlesnake. His anger would pass in a furious spasm, then would come fear and then panic. But the last was not yet. Though the cigarette was hardly begun, he took another from his case and lit it as before. His voice trembled slightly.

"Of course, if you will persist in being so foolish, there's no more to say. But don't blame me."

He glanced down at the pullover he was wearing. "Do you mind if I get my coat?"

The question and the movement were simultaneous, both slow and very tired. With right hand he made as if to draw back the curtain. Then there was a whisk as it flashed back, a lightning movement of his body, the slamming of the door and—Richleigh was gone!

CHAPTER XXIV

THE NIGHT OF THE 21ST OF DECEMBER (*contd.*)

SO QUICKLY HAD the others moved that they were at the curtain as the key turned in the lock. What they saw was no wardrobe but a door which the curtain had concealed. Franklin tried the handle, then hurled his body at the panels. Before he realised that he was taking charge he was sprinting for the corridor. *"Chambre communicante!* You watch the door and the passage!"

But the fourth door was locked, and it too held. He flew down the stairs to the deserted office and beneath the figure 4 found a key. Outside he collided with Papini who looked as if he had seen a ghost. Franklin scurried up the stairs and tried the key in the lock, while behind him came the voice and the pattering steps of Papini. The door opened, and he switched on the light. On the right was a bare bedstead; in the centre an easel and chair and on the floor paint-box and papers. In the far left corner was an open window!

He leaned out and listened. A few feet down was the slope of the hill into which the hotel burrowed and beyond the light of the window were the trunks of the pines, like bars in an immensity of shadow. He ran again to the corridor where Wharton and Papini were talking with violent gesticulation. He caught the *"Calmez-vous, monsieur!"* of Wharton as he dashed down the stairs.

Beneath the windows of the bedroom Boucher was waiting.

"Have you seen him?" cried Franklin.

"What is it?" asked Boucher, bewildered.

Franklin took his arm and hustled him to the corner. Then he kicked against the sharp slope and fell. Boucher regarded open-mouthed the lighted window and then stooped down to the narrow slit of light beneath their feet. “The kitchen!” he exclaimed.

Franklin took a glance too, then passed his hand over his forehead. It came away wet with perspiration. Since the time when Richleigh slipped through that door hardly a minute could have elapsed.

When they got back to the bedroom M. Papini was satisfied; at least he was listening quietly to Wharton’s explanations.

“He’s got clear away,” said Franklin.

“You know the conditions better than I,” said Wharton quickly. “What’s the best thing to do?”

“Where shall I find the captain of the *Cormoran?*” asked Franklin.

“The first house on the corner,” said Papini, throwing back the shutters. “Look, that light there!”

“I suggest, sir, that you remain here as a sort of headquarters. Boucher, you find the captain of the *Cormoran* and get him to put to sea at once and patrol the channel right along by the mainland. It’ll be fairly quiet over there once he gets over. If you see Richleigh, hold him!”

“What I’ll do,” he added to Wharton, “is see Papillot and find if Richleigh returned the motor boat.” Then he switched into Italian. “Signor Papini, will you see the *patron* and tell him what’s happened? We may want his authority to search the island and use the *Cormoran.*”

Across the road at the restaurant, M. Papillot gave the news that he was unaware of Richleigh’s impending departure. The latter had been out in the boat that morning. The two hurried down to the shore, but there was no sign of the *Dorade*. On the jetty a fisherman was found who had been there for an hour, but he had seen nothing; no motor boat, according to him, had anchored that night.

Then Franklin thought of something. Why hadn’t the boat been brought in? Had Boucher, for all his indifference, given Richleigh a suspicion? Hardly that. Nobody could have been more surprised than he at the entrance of the detectives. Then where *was* the *Dorade?* Probably out of action somewhere. If she had gone wrong, where was Richleigh likely to leave her? The Pirates' Cave or down by the Moorish Castle; that would be it.

"You will find at the hotel," he said to Papillot, "an Englishman who is with me in this affair. Explain, please, that I have gone to the Souterrain des Pirates and then on to the Château des Maures."

Franklin set off at a steady jog trot. Endurance was what was wanted; not a speed that would not last beyond its first burst. The road he had gone over once before, but the reverse way and in the dark the going was treacherous. He saved himself for the downhill finish, and then came the path to the cliffs, almost invisible in the undergrowth. From the summit he caught the lights of St. Giens and got his bearings. Far back could be heard the faint chug of the *Cormoran's* engine, though her light was not yet in sight.

From an overhanging pine he cut a slim branch and then ventured on. The crashing of the waves sounded almost beneath, and a step from the path would mean disaster. Ten minutes later he saw the drooping pines against the skyline, got to his knees, and felt for the rocky steps. Behind him the wind howled furiously, and away to the east was the steady purr of the *Cormoran*.

The last steps to the beach, cut as they were in the solid rock and descending almost sheer, were dangerous to negotiate. The hand-holds were slippery with spray and dew, and the way had to be felt for, step by step. Then, at the very bottom, with no sound of warning, something struck him. There seemed to be a dark shape and the flash of a light, and afterwards he remembered the sound of a voice in that second's consciousness before he fell.

When he opened his eyes again he knew nothing but the dull ache in his head. Then he realised that his hands and feet were bound. But there was no gag in his mouth, if that were any cause for thanks. In that small bay with its precipitous sides he might shout all night and to nothing but the echoes. Then, with arching knees and levering of elbows, he raised his head and slowly moved backwards. The first foot brought him to the steps, and he let his body sink to the newfound support.

At the same time he noticed the movement of a light, so subdued that at first he thought it was out at sea. Then he made out the white outline of a boat's hull and could discern the movement of a man. It must have been a good half hour that he lay there; now hearing the faint tapping of metal on metal and then once or twice the first coughings of an engine that spluttered feebly and then died out. Once the figure splashed through the shallow water to the shadow of the rocks and then returned. Once the engine seemed to come to life, and then it died down so suddenly that Franklin could hardly believe he had heard it.

The dark shape merged into the foreground and then seemed to be on top of him. Franklin closed his eyes until there was left the merest slit through which to peer. The figure came on. It stood above him. It stooped, and a hand felt his heart. The game must have been given away, so furiously was it racing. Then he was rolled over on his back and the bonds felt which tied his wrists.

"You can open your eyes. I see you're all right."

Franklin said nothing. He wondered how much longer he would have to live. With eyes more accustomed to the darkness he could discern the figure of Richleigh and even the slit in the trousers of the dungarees he was wearing.

"What did you say your name was?"

"Franklin."

"You're a detective?"

"I am."

"It's not the best of trades. You put up rather a good show when you were here. How did you deceive Papini?"

"I didn't. I am Italian—on my mother's side."

"That's interesting. Will you give me your word not to holler if I don't knock you out again?"

"I shan't holler," said Franklin. "If I did, nobody could hear me. And I don't feel like hollering at the moment."

"Sensible fellow! I'll have that engine going in a minute. You lie here and be thankful."

The figure merged into the darkness of the tiny bay. There was once again the sound of water splashing and the tapping on metal. Franklin's head felt as if it must burst. Everything seemed unreal, uncanny, unstable as a nightmare. There was the chill of the air, the dark, the unaccustomed spot, and that tap-tapping not seventy yards away. How long he lay there before Richleigh came again he could not judge; it might have been ten minutes or even half an hour. Only rarely the engine spluttered. Then came the splashing of water, the figure approaching, and the voice.

"I think she'll go now in a minute or two. How're you feeling?"

"Pretty fair," said Franklin. "Would you mind loosening my legs? I give you my word I won't stir."

Richleigh fumbled in his pocket and found a knife; felt for the bonds round the ankles and cut them. "I don't think you'll get far. How did you and Wharton tumble to that business of Price? His wife send you the diary?"

"Just luck," said Franklin. "Ludovic Travers saw—"

"Ludovic Travers? You mean the man who wrote the *Economics of a Spendthrift?* How did he come in?"

"He watched the queue line up for that Gene Allen advertisement of yours and wondered what it was all about. Then we found out that one of your colleagues had nicknamed you Gene Allen."

"Jenston! My God! That poisonous little swine! The filthy bastard never even washed his neck! Christ, if I'd got him here!" Franklin watched him as he looked up at the sky and raised his hands as if to strike a blow.

"Well, it's my own damn fault." He moved off towards the boat, then stopped and looked back. "Don't be such a fool as to move. I've got eyes like a cat."

"I shan't move," said Franklin.

Once again the quiet and the dark. Down in the sheltered bay was once more the tapping on metal. Out beyond, the seas crashed, and above them the wind whined in the trees. He was *feeling* better in spite of the dull ache in his head. He wondered what Richleigh would do; whether he would leave him there and would it be alive. Then for the first time the engine sounded true. It roared three or four times and was shut off. Once more Richleigh came over. Franklin watched him as he buttoned the collar of the dungaree coat round his neck.

"She's all right now. Think I'll push off."

"Richleigh, you're not going to be such a fool! Go out there in that! It's suicide!"

Richleigh was outwardly indifferent. "I don't know; I've seen worse. Wonder where you and I'll be this time to-morrow?"

Franklin watched and said nothing.

"I've got a pretty long trip to do. Guess where?"

"Algiers."

Richleigh looked at him queerly. "I'd be pretty much of a damn fool to try that. A few hundred miles of open sea! Well, cheerio; I've no particular grudge against you, but you can thank God your name's not Jenston."

Franklin made a sudden resolution. "I don't know where I shall be to-morrow—probably down with pneumonia—but I know where you'll be if you go out in that boat. Will you tell me one thing before you go? It's his wife I'm thinking about. What happened to Price?"

Richleigh waited for some seconds before he spoke and then in his voice there seemed to be an enormous regret. "I dropped a rock on his head. It was a filthy thing to do. I daren't look when I did it; I just heard it fall."

Neither spoke for a good few moments.

"He was a good chap in many ways. There'll be some money of mine at the hotel; send it to his missis. There's no need to let her know where it came from."

He felt once more the collar of the coat.

"There's something else you might like to know. I went to a specialist in town—two, as a matter of fact. Heart a bit wonky. They gave me a couple of years, perhaps three; with the last one on my back. Looks now as if it might be less."

He turned his back abruptly and before the other could put into words the questions he had half formed was almost lost in the shadows beneath the cliff. Franklin struggled to his feet, steadied himself against the steps, and then lurched forward.

"Come back, Richleigh! Don't be a damn fool!"

At the boat Richleigh turned to meet him.

"Get back or, by God, I'll make you!"

Franklin still came on. Then the other met him. Without warning his right hand thudded on Franklin's mouth. As he fell he struck again and again. Franklin sank to his knees. The blood from his nose tasted salt, and that was the last thing he knew. When he came round there was no sign of Richleigh or the boat. Out at sea there came no sound of an engine; nothing but the dash of waves on the rocks and the lapping of water in the tiny bay. His head was throbbing, and his face felt a mass of bruises. On his knees he shuffled to the shelter of the steps and tried to cut the wrist bonds against the rock. But his hands were too cold to control even that movement.

Half an hour later Wharton and Papillot found him there. Both had been alarmed at his absence and but for the violence of the sea would have nosed their way along the coast with a boat. As it was they had stopped first at the castle, as handier to the road, and that had meant delay. Two fishermen accompanied them, and with their help they got Franklin to the top of the steps. The stiff dose of brandy seemed to him to run to his feet like liquid fire.

"How is it now?" asked Wharton. "Feeling better?"

"I'm all right. What did Richleigh hit me with?"

"A spanner. Do you feel like telling what happened?"

Franklin took his time over the story; then he too wanted news. Had Richleigh been seen?

"Both M. Papillot and I thought we heard a boat's engine as we started out, then we lost it again. He'd never live in that sea."

"It was thundering good of you and Papillot; I might have got pneumonia, if nothing else."

"Feel like starting?"

"I think so. I don't know. I'm not so strong as I thought now I get on my pins."

The fishermen lent a hand, and by easy stages they made their way to the hotel. Franklin was got to bed with a scalding basin of soup, heavily laced with brandy, as a tonic. M. Papini and the patron's steward marched off with a hundred or so of men to take up stations along the north shore. Out at sea the lights of the *Cormoran* could still be discerned. Up in Richleigh's room Wharton resumed the examination of his belongings. In the bar of the deserted restaurant M. Papillot set about preparing his bill for the value of the *Dorade* and its effects, against the possible departure of the big Englishman, who was said, moreover, to represent his government. One never knew, and there was no harm in being prepared.

CHAPTER XXV
MOSTLY FOOLS

WHEN FRANKLIN WOKE at dawn Wharton was sitting in the easy chair drawn up at the bedside. His head was sunk on his chest, and he was breathing heavily. A flood of affection came over Franklin as he looked at the tired face. What a man to work with! Never a thought of personal advantage, no begrudging of another's success, but just one who saw his duty and did it.

His own head felt like splitting as he raised it on the pillow. He felt the plaster and the shaven circle and winced as he thought what might have happened if the edge of that spanner had caught him. Then Wharton opened his eyes, yawned, and stretched himself.

"Well, John, how're you feeling?"

"Pretty fair considering. A cup of coffee and I'll be all right. You were a good friend to me last night, sir."

"Drop the 'sir' and don't thank me for nothing. You'd have done more than that for me."

Franklin shook his head; then, "Is there any news?"

"The *Dorade* came ashore just after midnight, but no sign of Richleigh. Of course, he might have put the boat out to sea and then made for the woods. But that'd be pretty suicidal. He'd be bound to be taken sooner or later. Now I'll see about that coffee while you're dressing. Sure you can manage?"

When he returned, Franklin was feeling more or less himself. Just a bit tottery on the legs, perhaps, but, as he told Wharton, the virtual ending of that case was the best tonic for a man with a cut skull and a bruiser's face.

"That reminds me," said the other, and he pulled out of his pocket a sheaf of papers. "What do you think of these?"

The sheets were closely woven parchment, and each was covered with line after line of writing. The phrases were repeated, sometimes a dozen times each. Occasionally they were combined and lastly came a certain coherence.

> "Dear Sir. You are now about to see.
> "Let not him that putteth on his armour.
> "Sirius the dogstar.
> "Marry, but I shall speak.
> "He is the mysterious twenty-first.
> "Ring down the curtain!"

The writing was of the kind known as copperplate, the upstrokes delicate as if made with a tracing nib, the down ones firm and balanced. The letters stood as cold and formal as if on parade.

"He might plead all sorts of things," said Franklin "but if he's caught this will help to hang him as sure as his name's Richleigh. Where did you find them?"

"In the breast pocket of the coat he was wearing the moment before we came into the room. You see how cautious he was, even to himself. Without his typewriter he decided to compose the final 'Marius' letter and make a spectacular bow. He had to adopt and practise a colourless style of handwriting. We can see just what he was going to say, and yet he wouldn't trust himself to say it on paper. The word 'Marius' he fought particularly shy of. And yet who would have had the least suspicion of that letter, especially a foreigner?"

"His virtual confession to me would have been no good," said Franklin. "It would have been my word against his, and I should have been held prejudiced. You know that business I was telling you about last night; Richleigh's going to the specialists who gave him two or three years to live on account of his heart. I wonder if it's true?"

"Did he seem serious?"

"He spoke like a man who was going out in that sea with his eyes open. What I wondered was, if he had that little time to last, why he didn't finish at that school with a stiff upper lip?"

"Perhaps his idea was, better three years of some thousands a year than be without it and still have the drudgery. My idea is that he killed two birds with the one stone. He made his last years affluent and at the same time assured something for his brothers, as well as getting that woman Cardon out of the family."

"He was an amazing chap," said Franklin.

"He was all that. Do you know when I knew last night that we had him?"

"No."

"When he first pulled out his cigarette case. A man who's smoking with nothing on his conscience would have handed it round. Richleigh wasn't smoking among friends; he was using it as a cover to steady his thoughts."

Through the glass of the veranda they surveyed the sea. The wind had dropped, but the waves would not be calm again for many hours.

"The *Cormoran's* back, then?"

"Yes. She put in about midnight. The skipper knew no ordinary boat could live out there, so I don't blame him."

"I shall have to go over, then, this morning. You don't think I'm running away and leaving you in the lurch?"

"Heavens, no! I shall have to wait a reasonable time to see if Richleigh's body turns up and, if not, keep the coast patrolled. But your job's done in any case. I don't like your going over alone, and I've got to cross to report from Hyères."

As they stepped on the jetty at La Tour Fondue Wharton spoke to the captain. Then the conductor of the bus was approached, and the three of them entered the inn.

"M. le Capitaine here has seen my authority to open the bag," said Wharton. "You can all act as witnesses."

In it was a registered letter for Richleigh. Wharton exhibited the address and then opened it. It contained four fifty-pound notes and a brief letter from Ernest Richleigh acknowledging the receipt of some sketches and sending love from his wife and daughter.

"That's what he was waiting for," said Wharton. "I'll bet five pounds he didn't take a ticket at Marseilles."

There was a new drawing up of receipts, and the bag was sealed. An hour later Franklin was in the train for Toulon. All that he had wired to Durango House were the words—

"Commencement. Arriving six to-morrow. Franklin."

He got no news till he reached Dover, where the splash bills shrieked at him from the bookstall.

PERFECT MURDER CASE SOLVED

BRILLIANT WORK BY DURANGO DETECTIVE

SCOTLAND YARD IN AT THE DEATH

He got all the available London dailies, and all told the same story. The pictures alone on the back pages were different. That story had evidently been issued from Durango House. It began with the "Marius" letter and the crime, traced the lines upon which Franklin had worked, and ended with the promise of the presentation of the case against Frank Richleigh; the kind of presentation which might be made by eminent counsel who had for his material strange coincidences. It paid incidentally a tribute to the vast and ramificatory industry of Scotland Yard and hinted at a surprise which the Yard could never have anticipated. The story was to be complete in two further instalments. Here and there Franklin thought he could discern the hand of Ludovic Travers. Two other items were of interest. The *Record* had its headlines—

THE *RECORD* PAYS ITS £500 REWARD

and the *Wire* printed a facsimile of its £1,000 check.

He treated himself to a tea basket and then lay back in his corner, listening to the conversation of the carriage. But all the time there kept coming to his mind the death of Price: the two descending a crevasse, Price below, the sudden dropping of that rock and Richleigh's averted head. He recalled too that day when he and Richleigh had made the descent to the cave and wondered what thoughts had gone through his mind as they slowly moved down the steep steps. No wonder Richleigh had gone first!

On the platform Sir Francis and Travers were waiting, the former with a thrust-out hand and a "Well done, Franklin!" and the latter with a smile and a nod. As they went towards the entrance the sight of the bookstall reminded Travers of something.

"Have you seen the latest?"

"I've heard nothing since I left Porquerolles."

Travers handed over his evening paper and in the car Franklin read it.

RICHLEIGH'S BODY FOUND

FURTHER EVIDENCE OF GUILT

The body of Frank Richleigh came ashore this morning on the north side of the island of Porquerolles. It was terribly battered by the waves. It appears that the previous night, after a murderous attack on ex-Detective-Inspector Franklin, who had followed him, the murderer attempted to escape by motor boat but was capsized in a heavy sea. The boat itself had been washed ashore some hours before the body was found. Superintendent Wharton of Scotland Yard, who has been in charge of the case, was present, and it is understood that in the pockets of the dead man was found certain evidence that connects him definitely with the crime, irrespective of the evidence of his flight.

"A wonderful character, Wharton," said Franklin. "I probably shouldn't be here now but for him."

"You seem to have had a pretty thin time," said Sir Francis.

"It might have been worse. Richleigh could have committed a third murder if he had been so minded."

"You're sure you're feeling perfectly fit again?"

"Oh, rather. A bit sore about the head, perhaps, but nothing worth noticing."

"One must pay for romance," said Travers.

"Romance! There's not much romance in being hit over the head with a spanner!"

"Oh, I don't know I Romance, like everything else is relative. To Balham, even Tooting may be romantic."

The limousine pulled up with a jerk on the heels of a bus, and for nearly five minutes they waited in a traffic jam. Sir Francis, growing impatient, leaned from the window, and then caught sight of the lights that ran across the great stretch of the Utopia Insurance Company's new building. He drew the attention of the others.

First came a flash of scarlet and a staring

IF

then a twinkle of yellow, the full width of the tremendous building—

ANY FOOL CAN GIVE ADVICE

There followed another flash of scarlet, and by itself beneath, the one word

THEN

Franklin, who had heard of, but not seen, this monster advertisement, wondered what was coming next, and a final blaze of yellow told him.

DURANGOS ARE THE BIGGEST FOOLS
IN THE WORLD

Why Travers should think of such extraordinary things as magic and moonlight would be hard to say, but think of them he did. Perhaps, too, as he recalled those perplexed souls in the midnight wood near Athens, he saw in his mind the battered body of Richleigh, wave-soaked and icy cold, and remembered the boasts of the man who had set out to achieve a thing which should be perfect. He did not mean to speak, and yet the thought escaped in words before he was aware.

"Lord, what fools these mortals be!"

Sir Francis smiled quietly and glanced at both of them. Perhaps in his mind was the thought of Scotland Yard and the big battalions, but in his comment, too, was the charity of one who embraced in the generous scope of his gestures all mankind; fools and wise and maybe the knaves.

"Well, God give them wisdom that have it, and those that are fools, let them use their talents."

The block lifted, and the car moved on. Franklin sat thinking of two women in the tiny sitting-room of a country cottage. All around was the noise of traffic, the roar of the streets, the blare of horns. Now and again could be heard from the pavement the cry of the newspaper sellers—

PERFECT MURDER CASE! LATEST NEWS!

THE END